Between two Giants

My Grandfather's Story

Kurt Kelers

Linellen Press
265 Boomerang Road
Oldbury, Western Australia
www.linellenpress.com.au

Dedication

To my late grandfather, Karlis Kelers (senior),
whose eventful life inspired this book.

.

Contents

Acknowledgments

I would like to thank my mother, Carline Kelers, my father Karlis Kelers (junior), and my aunt Inta Albany, whose writing, and stories, kept my grandfather's legacy and life alive.

.

I

The Baron (1817)

The Baron frowned deeply and his lips thinned as he read the official letter he had just received. It had summoned him to a meeting with Emanuel von Stanecke, the haughty, ruthless Governor of the Courland Governorate, where the Baron's vast estates were situated. Von Stanecke was going to take up residence for a meeting of 'considerable importance', so the missive said, at the magnificent Rundāle Palace owned by the enormously wealthy and influential Count Pavel Andreyevich Shuvalov. The Baron had never met the Governor, but he knew Count Shuvalov well, having commanded a regiment under him in the war of 1812.

A young man with blond hair and expressive deep blue eyes, the Baron's medium height and stocky build gave him a commanding presence. Renowned for his explosive temper, but also for his warm generosity, he was well respected in the district. He scrunched up the paper he'd been reading and flung it on the ground.

"Reinis!" he roared.

His valet arrived, breathless, at the run.

"Pack me a chest, quickly. Put in my best court uniform and get me Yuris."

The Baron turned and strode into the parlour, where his stunning young wife, Amelia, was taking tea.

"I have to go to Rundāle straight away, my dear."

She looked at him expectantly.

He smiled at her fondly. "I am sorry, but it is only a business trip."

"Oh!" Amelia lowered her head; focused on her cup again.

His eyes glistened a little. "I am sure Pavel Andeyevich will have a grand ball soon. You know how he loves to entertain!"

The butler, immaculately dressed in a dark suit, appeared at the door; hesitated just outside. "Yuris is here, my lord."

"Good!"

The Baron hurried out to the porch, to where a handsome, dark-haired, tall, strong young man wearing a smart uniform with the Baron's livery, waited on the drive. When he saw the Baron, he doffed his cap.

"Get the coach and harness the white team," the Baron ordered.

Yuris bowed and hastened away as the Baron hurried to his dressing room and flung off his coat. Reinis deftly caught it and hung it, then drew out the Baron's travel coat.

"My sword!" demanded the Baron.

Reinis found the Baron's sword, the one he had worn during the 1812 campaign.

The Baron also had an immaculate dress sword, a gift from the Tsar himself, a reward for his efforts in helping liberate Courland from French occupation in the aftermath of the Battle of Borodino. The Baron's cavalry regiment had been detached from Shuvalov's division and given the task of storming the Rundāle Palace he was visiting this very day. On arrival, the Baron found that the French had already left, in a rush. He'd ordered the regiment to press on, and had surprised the French Governor and his escort of Dragoons in a thicket not far from the palace. In a short, sharp, and bloody engagement, the much-feared French Dragoons were routed by the Baron's cavalry. Jacques David Martin, the Bonapartist Governor, was captured, and the Baron sent him under escort to the Tsar and continued to mop up the sporadic resistance of bands of French soldiers.

"Rather me than the Cossacks!" the Baron had thought somewhat cynically at the time.

The feared Cossacks weren't known for taking prisoners, preferring to leave French death and destruction in their path.

The Baron and his battle-hardened regiment cleared all the French out of Courland by the end of 1812, the Baron becoming a minor celebrity as a result. The sword had been received from the hand of the Tsar himself, in a glittering ceremony at the Winter Palace in St Petersburg.

The trip to Rundāle Palace was uneventful. Yuris kept the beautiful team of white Kladrubers the Baron had imported at great expense at a steady canter.

The coach rocked and rolled across countryside of low undulating hills, skirted fields with the occasional thicket of woodland, passed the serfs' crude wooden houses scattered along the potholed road. The strips of land they labouriously farmed were an ostensibly random patchwork of colourful hues behind the houses.

The serfs were able to tend to their own strips only two days a week; the rest of the time they were expected to work on their landlord's estate. The Baron was a generous, if stern, landlord. He ensured that his serfs were well looked after, given a rudimentary education, and that they were all well fed, especially during harvest time. Up gently sloping, often tree-lined, drives, were the modest two-storey wooden houses of the local gentry.

The Baron arrived at the palace at dusk. Despite being a wealthy man and having a beautiful manor house, the magnificent yellow and white trimmed building never ceased to amaze him. He admired it now as it sat imposingly against the setting sun as his coach drove up the long driveway through the immaculate gardens. On his arrival at the grand entrance, liveried footmen ran to open the coach door.

The Baron stepped from his carriage and jogged lightly up the steps, where the bowing butler in the Shuvalov livery greeted him. "Welcome, my lord; I am sure you will wish to freshen up before supper. Count Shuvalov is expecting you. This way, please."

When the Baron was announced at the door of the vast dining hall, he was surprised at the number of people in attendance. Most of the notables of the district were there. A long table with settings for twenty ran the length of the hall, its high ceiling decorated with delicate Italian style paintings. The ceiling cornices were intricate and flamboyant, and large chandeliers lit up the room. Several Dutch and Italian masterpieces hung on the walls.

Count Shuvalov, an imposing man in an immaculate dinner suit, bustled up and greeted the Baron with a firm handshake. "Ah, Baron. Good to see you. How was your trip?"

"Good to see you too, General! The trip was uneventful."

After shaking the Count's hand, the Baron bowed to kiss the fingers of the Count's formidable wife, Catherine.

Shuvalov turned to a dapper, slim, elderly man standing near him. "Von Stanecke, have you met the Baron? He is a friend of mine; he fought with me in the 1812 war."

Von Stanecke bowed slightly. "A pleasure, Baron."

With that, Shuvalov raised his hand and liveried servants appeared at the chairs around the dining table; all the guests moved into their place and were seated. Shuvalov sat at one end, von Stanecke on his left, the Baron on his right. His wife presided over the other end of the table. All the courses were served with fine crockery and silver service cutlery, the Count sparing no expense to impress his distinguished guests. The delicate, refined food, French wine and champagne flowed freely. After the meal, the Count's wife rose and swept out of the room, and the men were served specially imported port, still rare and uniquely expensive in

Russia. The Count stood and raised his glass.

"A toast," he roared above the din. "To our great enterprise tomorrow!"

The guests stood and raised their glasses. More port was served, and all proceeded to get merrily and boisterously drunk.

Yuris, the Baron's coachman, had his meal with the other senior house serfs in the kitchen. They sat on crude benches around a rough-hewn, large table and ate from wooden platters using a knife. The food was rustic, pork and cabbage, but plentiful. They drank beer and vodka from earthenware cups and made noisy good cheer around the table. The table was presided over by the Count's coachman, as the butler who usually had that privilege, was still occupied with the guests in the main dining hall. Yuris, although a married man with two young children, tried his luck with one of the housekeepers, his drunkenness loosening his inhibitions. The pretty, sexy, young woman with wide hips, large breasts, and long red hair felt flattered by Yuris' attention and laughed at his jokes and comments.

After a while, they slipped away to Yuris' room in the stables where they kissed wildly and lustily, pulling desperately at each other's clothes. Once naked, he caressed her large breasts, felt her pink nipples harden beneath his hands. She wanted him and pulled his throbbing penis into her and rode him from the top, her lovely breasts bouncing as they vigorously made love. Her head flung back, she moaned and abandoned herself to pleasure. He thrust up into her, enjoying the smell of her body and her moistness. Afterward, they caressed each other gently. Soon she covered herself with her clothes, barely hiding her nakedness, one breast still exposed.

Before slipping out of the room, she looked at him and said quietly. "I'm Anna. Who are you?"

"Yuris," he smiled.

"Good to meet you, Yuris."

The Baron rose early. Unlike some of the other guests, he had not overindulged in the Count's hospitality. He dressed in his day garb and walked around the gardens, taking in the smells of the flowers, the dew on the lawns, and the cold, refreshing morning. The cries of a flock of birds flying overhead mingled with the crunching of his shoes on the stone pathways as he paused near an impressive artificial pond; he ran his hand through the cold water, his thoughts far away.

Von Stanecke watched the Baron from the grand entrance steps nearby, not disturbing him. He had heard about the way the Baron and Count Shuvalov treated their serfs and hoped they would be allies in the great enterprise the Tsar had entrusted to him. He had already had a quiet word with Shuvalov about the matter, but the Count had been hard to gauge; a born courtier.

The meeting was held in the White Hall, a large, airy room where the sunlight streamed in through tall windows. The high ceiling and walls had intricate cornices, with large low hanging crystal chandeliers and perfectly polished oak floors. It was a beautiful room, but relatively austere, lacking the flamboyance of some of the other rooms in the palace. The guests milled around, talking nervously, as servants dressed in their best slipped between them, dispensing tall crystal flutes of champagne. The military men, like the Baron, wore immaculate white courtiers' uniforms with golden epaulettes, colourful sashes, and black trousers with a coloured stripe down the side seam. They carried ornate dress swords at their sides and wore long leather boots – other guests dressed in trousers, long frockcoats and long, finely crafted silk shirts.

Von Stanecke, wearing a black frockcoat and trousers with a white frilled silk shirt and black leather-buckled shoes, entered with the Count. He carried a cane and, in a highly polished wooden cloth-lined box, the decree from the Tsar. He placed the box on a table and removed the document.

"Gentlemen, if you will!"

He did not have to raise his voice as a hush had fallen over the room as he entered.

He spoke sonorously in perfect French, the language of the court, his voice carrying with ease to all in the room. "This is a decree from the Tsar. He has tasked me with its implementation. I have had copies printed and everyone here should have received one. This decree forces the emancipation of all the serfs in the Governorate of Courland."

There was a collective gasp from some of the men in the room.

Von Stanecke ignored them and continued his speech. "You have until September this year to implement the provisions of the decree. Failure to do so will result in severe punishment."

Von Stanecke, pausing to let that sink in, glared at the crowd arrogantly, almost willing them to object. While some shuffled their feet sullenly, nobody did.

He continued. "However, the Tsar has generously offered to compensate you for every soul that is freed. Once again, any attempt to cheat the system will be severely dealt with."

Another haughty glare at the men in the room, and another pause.

"My staff and I, along with certain of the Tsars trusted military officers, will be randomly auditing you in the months to come. We will also help you, if we can, with the implementation of the decree. This is to ensure complete compliance with the Tsar's will. All the male serfs will retain their existing strips of land, but will still have to work on the landlords' fields for a mandated wage. All male serfs are free to leave, if they wish, but their strips will not be allowed to remain fallow. If they do not have a son or male relative to farm the land, it will be resumed to the landlord's estate. All male house serfs will have the option of receiving further strips of land for themselves or their sons at the landlord's discretion, if they choose not to continue in his service. The details of the mandated wages and compensation are outlined in the papers I have distributed."

With that, von Stanecke left the table and stalked through the crowd of aristocrats and gentry, beckoning Count Shuvalov and the Baron to follow him. The crowd parted as the three men moved between them, and when they left the room everyone started talking animatedly.

Von Stanecke took the two men aside to the portico. "Shall we walk in your magnificent garden, Pavel Andreyevich?"

He strolled down the steps to the stone drive and walked past the pond near the front entrance and down a broad path that led the length of the superbly manicured garden.

"I will need your help to implement this decree, if you are willing, Gentlemen. I know you are a busy man Pavel Andeyevich and I dare say you are keen to get back to St Petersburg and the court. But I was hoping you might be able to use your influence with the Tsar to get the resources we need to achieve this great reform."

The Count smiled and said a little self depreciatingly. "I will certainly do what I can, but I do not have the influence of my great forbears in court."

"You are far too modest, Count. If you are willing, I'm sure you will make things a lot easier for us here. Maybe you could be a sort of unofficial liaison with the court!"

Von Stanecke laughed quietly.

"I want to ask you, Baron, if you are willing – and believe me if you accept the Tsar will be grateful – to be my assistant here in this district. If you decide to take the position and the responsibility, you will be compensated and will receive a Guards Officer and small squad of soldiers to assist you. They should arrive within a fortnight or so."

The Baron thought about it as they strolled toward the end of the garden. It would be a lot of responsibility and he had his own estates to attend to. He was well aware that even though September seemed a long way off, the time would pass very quickly. Both von Stanecke and the Count waited while he mulled over his options. The three men reached the end of the garden and turned onto a narrow path that skirted its boundaries.

"I will accept your commission," the Baron said finally.

"Good," Von Stanecke nodded. "I have an official commission here from the Tsar."

He produced a paper that had the official stamp of the Tsar's minister and gave it to the Baron.

The Baron took his time on the trip back, needing time to think things through, so Yuris kept the horses at a steady trot. The coach lurched along the potholed dirt road back towards the Baron's estate.

When he arrived home, his wife, in a plain white, but fashionable dress, greeted him on the stairs. He walked towards her and she started forward before stopping herself; he smiled and bent formally over her hand and greeted her. She flushed a little, pleased to see him and eager to find out what all the fuss was about.

"Well, it has been done. The Tsar has ordered the forced emancipation of all serfs here," he said as they walked into the main reception room. She waited for him to continue.

"I have been given a commission by the Tsar and von Stanecke to help with its implementation, so I will be away a lot. I will have to leave our estates in your capable hands.

"Oh," he added almost as an afterthought, "we will be having some guests for a while: a dashing young guard's officer and a troop of soldiers."

He sat down at a table and handed her the copy of the decree, his commission and the instructions he had received from von

Stanecke. She read the documents quickly.

'This will be very hard for some," she observed.

"I'm sure the compensation provisions will be adequate," he answered.

She looked at him fondly. "Only if the government is organised enough to pay! I mean, possibly having to give the serfs land as well as having to pay them."

"Oh, it shouldn't be a problem for us. We have land at the back near Plumshē that we do not utilise adequately. The land provisions are at the landowners' discretion; they do not have to release land to the serfs if they don't wish; and no serf will actually own any land. That said, the land provisions in the edict are designed to help the serfs support themselves and their families if some landlords cannot afford to retain them. I think we should be generous. We'll still have their labour and the wage is quite modest. Also, Pavel Andreyevich will make sure the money comes through quickly!"

Amelia nodded in agreement and said somewhat cynically, "It's in his best interests. I'll draw up a list of all the souls on our estates and we will discuss if we can afford to keep all of them."

Although young, she was well educated and very astute, and did, after all, run the estates when the Baron was absent.

That night the Baron slipped into his wife's bedroom. She was wearing a sheer white silk nightgown, with nothing on underneath it, a hint of her lovely young body tantalisingly visible. She moved over to him; kissed him with passion. He picked her up and took her to the big four poster bed and they made love. Afterwards he looked at her, watching the rise and fall of her pert, small, perfect breasts as she slept. If there was one thing he regretted in his life, it was the lack of a son.

At around the same time Yuris was making love with his wife as well. Unlike the Baron's wife, she was a little worn and coarse, having had a hard life. Her beauty was fading, and her body had never recovered from giving birth to their two sons and hard work in the fields of the estate. Yuris made no mention of his escapade with Anna, and wondered if he would be able to see her again.

Yuris and his family lived in a small, wooden, rectangular one-room house on the village common on the edge of the Baron's estate. They had a stove in the centre of the house, with a chimney, which was unusual at the time. Yuris and his wife created a modicum of privacy by partitioning the rectangular house with cloth. They had a number of strips of land which, as Yuris was often away on the Baron's business, his wife tended. They had all the equipment they needed to farm the strips and, as the Baron was a fair, if stern, master, they lived quite well. While they were monetarily poor, they never went hungry and lacked for little.

Yuris had ambitions for his sons. He wanted them to have a good education and perhaps even finish primary school. His sons, one six and the other ten, were doing quite well in the estate school the Baron had set up. He wondered now what had happened that made the Baron so pensive down at Rundāle Palace.

The Baron was very busy over the next few months as he tried to visit most of the serf-holding landowners in the Zemgalieši region of Courland. He would arrive, often unannounced, with his soldiers and receive the hospitality of the landowners as he sat down and talked to them about the upcoming emancipation. He was an imposing figure mounted on his large black horse and wearing his colonel's uniform. If there were to be any problems, the sheer intimidating presence of the Baron and his well mounted, sharply dressed escort of Guards usually put it to rest before it started. The Baron was careful to make sure the estimates of the serf numbers for each estate were accurate. He warned everyone there was a good chance they would be audited before the September deadline.

All the serfs who saw this formidable man treated him like a demigod. Word had been whispered to them about what he was doing. They stopped their work in the fields, barns, and mills when he passed and fell to the ground bowing face-down to him.

One of the last stops the Baron made before he had to make the trip to Riga to report his progress to von Stanecke, the Governor of Courland and Governor-General of all the Baltic Provinces, was at his friend Manfred Burgh's estate. Burgh had recently arrived from Germany after hearing of the special privileges the Tsar allowed the German population in the Baltic provinces. He had a relatively small estate with only one hundred souls. The Baron rode up the tree-lined driveway to Burgh's modest two-storey, steep-roofed, neogothic wooden manor house, his escort clattering and jingling on their dusty, tired horses behind him. They stopped at the huge new white portico with its soaring columns and steep steps, which Burgh had recently added.

Burgh greeted the Baron cheerfully at the top of the steps and ushered him into the front room. A groom took the Baron's horse to the stable and the Guards' horses were also tended.

Once inside, Burgh looked at the Baron quizzically. "I hear you have been making quite a name for yourself all over the district on the Tsar's business. So, you are finally here to give me the bad news." A short, slim man in his late twenties with dark hair and brown eyes, Burgh spoke Russian with a thick German accent.

The Baron patted dust off his clothes and boots and sat down tiredly, accepting a drink from the butler. He answered in German. "It shouldn't be all that bad, Manfred. We are all in the same boat and will just have to adjust. The Tsar and von Stanecke are determined to see this through."

Burgh also sat and sipped his drink contemplatively. "Have you heard yet about the compensation we will be getting? I may only have one hundred serfs, but this decree could affect how many of them, especially the house serfs, I can keep on."

The Baron answered quietly. He had heard all this before, to varying degrees, on all his visits over the last few months.

"I'm going to Riga to consult with von Stanecke and Count Shuvalov, who I hope will have news from St Petersburg. Have you managed to allocate land for your house serfs?"

"Yes. I may have to let some of them go and will have to use some only on need. But, of course, I will still need all my field serfs. Anyway, Baron, we can talk about this later. Will you join me and my wife for a modest dinner?"

Burgh's dining room was small and cosy. The table was set modestly for three. Burgh's wife, a plain, quiet woman, came in and greeted the Baron deferentially in German. He bowed slightly and took her hands to his lips, and they sat down. The food was served on plain china plates by a thin, pretty German kitchen maid – German sausage, sauerkraut, and potatoes – all simple peasant food, but the Baron didn't mind; he was tired and hungry. Burgh's wife brought out a good bottle of German wine for the occasion, so the meal passed amicably. Later, the Baron and Burgh excused themselves and retired to the study where they drank good Hungarian cognac that Burgh served himself. There the Baron explained the Emancipation Decree and answered all of Burgh's questions.

A week later, the Baron received an invitation to visit Countess Catherine Shuvalov. He decided to stop by and see her on the way to Riga for his meeting with von Stanecke. The invitation included his wife, so she excitedly prepared for the trip. In the Baron's absence, Amelia had made good progress. She had drawn up a list of all their serfs and had already assigned strips for some of them in the Plumshē area on the northern edge of the main estate. She had spoken quietly to most of their house serfs to give them time to decide what to do. She was a little surprised when most of them indicated they wanted to take up the offer of land on the estate and become semi-independent peasant farmers. She was in the process of getting the deeds to the strips allocated drawn up. The Baron was pleased that his wife would be accompanying him to Rundāle Palace. It would be a good distraction for her.

As the coach trundled down the road, the Baron looked fondly at her sitting opposite him. She looked enchanting in her travel cloak, her long luscious blond hair slightly asunder, her pretty face flushed with excitement.

He smiled at her. "Don't be intimidated by the Countess, sweetheart. She is a formidable woman with a stern exterior. She, as you do, runs the Shuvalov estate here in the Count's absence, which is most of the time. She actually has a heart of gold and prefers the country life to the intrigues of court."

When they approached the palace, the wheels crunching on the gravel drive, they were greeted by the Countess herself. She sailed down the stairs and imperiously accepted their greetings: a bow from the Baron and a low curtsy from his wife.

She looked at the Baron's wife and said openly, "My, how pretty you are, my dear. You must be so happy with her, Baron!"

She took Amelia by the hand and swept back up the stairs, the Baron following along behind.

"Come along, dear, we will have to get you freshened up for dinner."

The Countess turned and looked at the Baron as she swept down the corridor, ignoring the servants as they bowed to her as she passed them. "I'm afraid it will be a simple meal, Baron, as there is only me here now."

The Baron murmured. "You are too kind and generous, Countess Catherine."

"Ha!" she snorted. "The butler will show you your suite, Baron."

To Amelia she said: "Come, my dear, I will show you the way myself."

The Baron put on his best dinner suit and appeared at the door of his wife's suite. A servant flung open the door and announced him. Amelia was already dressed for dinner. She wore a beautiful, white evening gown of the latest fashion. The dress showed the curve of her body and breasts perfectly. Her hair had been twirled up and pinned, and she had a small diamond on her neck and a gold broach on her shoulder.

She took the Baron's breath away. "You look absolutely ravishing tonight!"

She blushed shyly and smiled at him. He took her by the arm and they walked to the dining room. The countess had decided to entertain them in the formal room, the same one the Baron had dined in previously. The Baron smiled to himself at the countess's idea of a simple meal.

Yuris was excited. He had seen Anna again. He hoped she would come to him tonight. He devoured his meal and went to his room, waiting in nervous anticipation. Sure enough, there was a quiet knock on the door. He opened it and let her in. She walked into the room and straight away kissed him. Then she stepped back and let her robe drop, exposing her marvellous body to him. He kissed her again and cupped her breasts in his hands. He took her to the bed and slowly took off his clothes. Without a word, he kissed her beautiful big breasts and then kissed her slightly plump stomach. She spread her legs and moaned as he kissed her between them. She pressed his head down on her. He put his hands on her lovely round bum and pulled her up to him. He then made his way up her body again and kissed her on the lips while he penetrated her. She wrapped her legs around him, holding him tight. When she orgasmed, she cried out and he laughed, slid out of her and started to caress her breasts again. She was very sexual and wanted him again, so she gently caressed and kissed him until he became aroused. He put his hands on her beautiful big breasts as she made love with him until finally, hot and tired, they fell apart. She slept in his arms that night, slipping out early in the morning.

Yuris knew he was in trouble. He was in love with this sexy young woman. He hoped that she wouldn't get pregnant, but knew he would forget all his inhibitions if he ever saw her again. He felt guilty about his betrayal of his hard-working, honest wife and his two rapidly growing boys.

The Baron left early the next day for Riga, which was a long day's travel away. As he said his goodbyes to his wife and the Countess, he noticed that Yuris, his coachman, seemed a bit distracted. He did not think much of it, as these were momentous times in the governorate. The Baron knew that most of the serfs had heard rumours about what was to happen.

The strong white mares pulled the large coach with ease as they travelled down the road at a steady trot, the Baron in no hurry and wishing to preserve his horses' strength. On the way to Riga, not far from Rundāle Palace, they passed through the small city of Jelgava and then onto the small town of Olain. Here, the Baron took his lunch in a roadside inn. Yuris managed to get the horses watered, fed and rested.

They arrived in Riga late and clattered down the streets of the new section of the city where wealthy merchants had established their businesses and homes. The Baron had always liked the hustle and bustle of this part of the city and found the prevailing modern and practicable style of architecture interesting. They crossed the old moat, which had been redeveloped into a series of pretty parks, and entered the cobbled streets of the old city. Yuris had a hard time manoeuvring the big coach through the crowded narrow streets. They eventually reached the Baron's modest Riga residence. He did not use it much but had sent word and the servants had made it ready for him. It had been a lovely summer's day, so the Baron sat in his small yard and enjoyed the evening. He thought about his lovely wife and how they had made love the previous evening. She had been so willing and mischievous in the bedroom, almost tormenting him with her delectable body, her exquisite breasts, legs, hair and, well, everything!

The next day, he was to meet von Stanecke at his official residence in the old Riga castle, a short walk away; uncharacteristically, he walked along the cobbled streets resplendent in his colonel's dress uniform and sword, escorted only by Yuris also dressed in his smartest uniform. He strode down the bustling streets crowded with merchants on their horses or carriages, peasants with their sturdy foot carts, a few beggars, and ordinary townsfolk going about their business. Most people gave way to him and bowed deeply. A troop of soldiers marched past with their lieutenant; all saluted sharply. He approached the imposing castle, which he thought looked like a hotchpotch of architectural styles – which it was. The original castle on the site was a Livonian Order stronghold before it was destroyed in 1484 and rebuilt by 1515. Since then, it had been occupied in turn by the Poles, the Swedes, and now the Russian Empire. All had added parts to it.

The Baron approached the main gate where two sentries stood rigidly, snapping to attention and saluting when he approached. He walked into a bustling courtyard full of soldiers, some of whom were making ready to move out. Several secretaries also hurried about looking harassed. He entered the main ante-room, where an immaculately dressed Captain of the Guards sat at a desk outside an imposing door.

On seeing the Baron, he leapt to his feet, saluted and opened the door, then stood rigidly. "His Excellency is expecting you, my lord Colonel!"

The Baron walked in after being announced. It was a spacious room with high ceilings and large, bright, airy windows. Von Stanecke stood behind an imposing desk with a paper in his hand. His desk sat in front of a large picture of the Tsar, side on to one of the windows. In a leather armchair, near another window, sat Count Shuvalov. Standing in front of the desk were two other nobles, in immaculate black civilian dress suits. The Baron vaguely recognized them.

"Ah, Baron, I'm pleased that you could join us. Baron, you know Count Shuvalov, but I am pleased to introduce you to Prince Paul Orlovski and Baron Heinrich von Hessler. Gentlemen, please be seated."

Both men bowed slightly towards the Baron then sat in armchairs in front of the desk. Von Stanecke remained standing.

He looked briefly at the paper he was holding. "I have a summary of the reports you forwarded to me, gentlemen. You have all made remarkable progress and shown great diligence. I assure you, this will not go unnoticed by the Tsar. It really pleases me that everything is going so smoothly. I am in the process of sending the audit teams out now but, thanks to your hard work, there will be very little to audit! Everything will be ready on schedule by September."

He paused, smiled, and proclaimed, perhaps prophetically: "This, gentlemen, will be a model process for all of Russia someday! But Pavel Andreyevich has some excellent news!"

The Count stood up; he was, unusually, slightly flushed and excited. "I have just ridden post-haste with an escort of the Tsar's personal guards."

He waved in the air a gilt-lettered, stamped and sealed document. "This is an order from the Tsar and his ministers requiring the banks in Riga to pay the agreed compensation into the entire serf-holding landowners' accounts, in gold roubles! The funds will be released when the audits are complete and the decree is finally implemented."

Von Stanecke interrupted him. "Those that do not have accounts will have to sign for the gold in person here. In the meantime, that document is going in the Bank of Riga's strongroom. Are there any other issues that need to be discussed, gentlemen?"

A few minor issues were quickly dealt with.

When all was completed to everyone's satisfaction, von Stanecke said. "If you are willing, gentlemen, I would be honoured if you would accept my invitation to my summer residence in Jūrmala on Saturday."

With that, the group broke up. Shuvalov and the Baron walked out into the main courtyard together.

"You certainly put your time in St Petersburg to good use, General."

"I have had a busy time of it, Baron. Not only was I playing the courtier, but I also visited my estates in Russia. Unfortunately, I had to get rid of one of my stewards. He was stealing from me! The man was lucky not to end up a permanent resident of Siberia!"

"I have just visited Rundāle, General; your wife certainly runs a tight and efficient estate."

"Yes, she truly is a remarkable person."

Suddenly, the Count stopped and looked a little put out. "Where is your coach, Baron?"

"Oh, I walked. It's not far."

"How strange. I can give you a lift back to your house if you like."

"Thank you, General, but I need to stretch my legs."

Von Stanecke's house in Jūrmala was on a wide, pristine beach, clean white sand and tall old Baltic Pine trees growing at the edge of the sand. The water was shallow and pale blue with small waves and, for seawater, relatively fresh.

Von Stanecke's house was smallish, double-storeyed, and rather quaint. A tall steeple-like tower on one corner housed a telescope. His nearest neighbours were an old General from the war of 1812, and a young, very wealthy Major of the Guards – both used their cottages for the holidays. Von Stanecke had a small pavilion near the beach where his wife served them the canapés and wines herself.

The time was spent relaxing, taking long walks along the beach and taking the hot waters of the spa. Everyone was able to relax and von Stanecke and his wife were generous and attentive hosts. There were no soldiers, no secretaries, no hustle and bustle and no hassle. For the final evening, he invited his immediate neighbours to dinner. Everyone had a pleasant time eating fairly plain food and drinking good German beer and wine. As von Stanecke explained, he only had his cook and a housekeeper here and no other servants.

After the meal, feeling a little drunk and happy, the Baron took a walk along the beach in the moonlight. As he walked, leaving deep footprints in the fine sand, he reflected on what had happened in the last few months. It would all be over soon. The deadline was now only eight weeks away. Most of the work was done, but he imagined there might be a few last-minute hitches. He liked it here and he was sure Amelia would too. He decided he would sell his house in Riga and try to buy a small cottage here near the sea. He liked the isolation and relaxed lifestyle. It was not that far from his estates or Riga.

Back at Rundāle Palace, Anna waited for the familiar crunch of carriage wheels on the drive. She was anxious and upset. She also knew if anyone found out her condition, she would be ostracised, or worse. She was pregnant. Yuris was the father. After much agonising, she had decided not to tell him. She also had some upsetting news to tell him. When she heard the crunch of wheels, she pretended to be busy sweeping the steps, but her mind was elsewhere. Two carriages arrived. She recognised the large black carriage of the Count, drawn by four huge black horses. Close behind came the Baron's carriage. She caught her breath when she saw Yuris, resplendent in his uniform. He smiled down at her, quickly catching her eye.

"Anna, girl, are you not finished yet?"

Anna started and turned. It was the Countess. Anna had been so preoccupied she had not noticed her come to the head of the stairs with the beautiful young woman who had been her guest for the last few days. Anna blushed and curtsied deeply.

"Be gone with you! No loitering!" the Countess said sharply, wondering to herself: "Now, what is up with her?"

Anna was quickly forgotten as the Countess swept down the stairs, followed by the Baron's wife to greet the Count and his guest.

Anna made love with Yuris passionately that night; even a little wildly, as if it was their last night together, which it well might be. When they had finished, she stood up, naked, and looked out the small grubby window, pensive. Yuris padded over and put his arms around her waist.

"What is wrong, sweetheart?" he asked quietly.

She turned and put her arms around his neck; pressed her body against his and held him for a while.

Then she stepped back and gently took his arms off her and sat on the end of the bed. "I have something to tell you."

Then it all came out in a rush. "I'm getting married next week. My father is insisting. He has found a good man for me. I have finally decided to accept him. I have no choice really. The Countess has given the match her blessing."

She stopped, breathless and flushed.

Yuris was shocked. He had guessed it was only a matter of time before it happened. But he was still upset all the same. She looked at him timidly as he took a deep breath.

"Congratulations," he managed. It came out like a croak. "Who is he?"

"You might not know him, but he is a miller working on the

estate. He has been able to set up his own watermill and is doing all right. His name is Janis. He's an older man."

Anna looked at him, but there was nothing more to say. She sadly collected her clothes and covered herself and slipped out the door without another word. Yuris sat for a while, then rolled over and faced the wall and cried quietly, the joy of their lovemaking forgotten.

The big day had finally come. There was a buzz of excitement around the estate. All the serfs knew they were soon going to be free; free peasant farmers or paid servants and workers of a great estate.

The Baron had ordered them to all gather in front of the manor portico. They came from all of his estates. He stood on the top of the steps, feet widely spaced, hands on his hips, imposing in stature, intimidating. His wife stood to one side and just behind him. At a table at the foot of the steps, the Baron's stewards and their wives sat with a bundle of documents in front of them signed by the Baron and bearing the official stamp of the Tsar's minister. Each male serf was to receive one. It had on it the name of his wife and all his children.

When the Baron spoke, he did so loudly and clearly and the buzz of voices stopped as everyone listened.

He spoke Latvian, adequately, which was unusual for most nobility at the time. "Every patriarchal male will receive this document. It's your family's passport to freedom and it is very important. Please look after it. Once you put your mark on the paper, you are free to farm land independently on my estates, if you wish."

There was a restrained cheer at that. The Baron scowled at the cheerers and silence quickly returned.

"Baroness Amelia and I have decided to be generous with you all. There is no provision in the Emancipation Decree regarding land, but we have decided to sign the deeds of your strips over to you in a communal arrangement, and in some cases add more strips."

There was a loud cheer at that. Some threw their hats in the air, some danced a little jig, some hugged their wives and a few shed a quiet tear. The Baron allowed himself a slight smile and then raised his hand.

"Those of you who decide to remain in my service and work on my estates will be paid a modest wage. Those who decide to try their luck on their own, go with my blessing." He paused and felt Amelia's gentle hand on his arm. "I want you to come forward and put your mark on the document when you are called!"

With that, the stewards started calling names loudly. Those called came forward, bowed deeply, and put their marks on the deed. When they received them, their families gathered around them excitedly. After many hours, the people slowly dispersed back to their homes. When the senior serfs were called forward, the Baron walked down the stairs and stood behind his senior Steward.

When Yuris came forward and bowed, the Baron put his hand on the paper and exclaimed. "You have decided to leave my service and are going to be a farmer now! What sort of a name is Yuris Ķenkus for a farmer? From now on, you shall be named Yuris Kohler, a much more suitable name!"

Yuris was startled by this.

But he bowed again and said, "Thank you, my lord."

Really, there was nothing else he could say. Until he signed the deed, he was still the Baron's serf and subject to his whims.

The Baron smiled slightly at his consternation and said more quietly, "I may still need your services as a coachman Yuris Kohler. You will be paid well if you take up the work. I have also granted you two adjacent strips of land in the Plumshē area at the far end of my estate. I wish you well."

The Baron took his hand off the deed and let Yuris put his mark on it. He then turned and took Amelia by the arm and went up the stairs and into his house. It was done.

The Baron looked across at his lovely wife as they trotted down the frozen Neva River, the bells on their open sleigh jingling. The evening was cold but spectacular, the stars and moon reflecting on the ice of the river. Amelia was wrapped in an expensive, fluffy white mink coat, her cheeks flushed, her eyes sparkling at him. The sleigh turned into the Fontanki Kanal and continued towards Nevski Prospekt. They moved past the pristine expanse of white that was the Summer Garden. Opposite the garden, the palaces lining the canal were lit up. Near Nevski Prospekt was their destination, the brightly lit and festive palace of Count Pavel Andreyevich Shuvalov.

When their sleigh slid up to the door, they were greeted by footmen, who helped them alight; they were directed to a cloakroom where further servants helped the Baron remove his long dress coat and his wife her mink. The Baron wore his colonel's uniform and long leather riding boots, his dress sword strapped at his side. Amelia looked ravishing in her beautiful white, silk ball gown; the smooth white of her breasts modestly exposed. She wore a large, sparkling diamond at her neck and an exquisite eighteen carat gold, sapphire and diamond broach on her shoulder. Her luxurious long blonde hair was fashionably curled up in a silk scarf.

The Baron looked at her proudly and whispered: "You had better be careful, sweetheart, lest you show up the Countess, or even the Empress herself."

Amelia, totally out of character, giggled nervously.

He took her by the arm, and they moved towards the

magnificent doors of the ballroom. Here, they were announced and greeted by the Count and Countess themselves. "Baron, so pleased to see you. Welcome to our humble abode here in St Petersburg."

The Count bent low over the Baroness's hand. "You look truly beautiful tonight."

The Countess looked at her and tut, tutted. "Stunning, my dear, stunning!"

Amelia curtsied low to both of them.

The Baron moved with her into the large, spectacularly decorated, chandelier-lit room crowded with the highest society of St Petersburg. Uniformed waiters circulated, deftly carrying silver trays laden with tall crystal flutes of champagne. A large orchestra played quietly at one end of the room. The Baron and his wife were greeted by Emmanuel von Stanecke, who approached them with his wife and Prince Paul Orlovski.

The Baron greeted them warmly as they bowed over his wife's hand. "Good to see you again!"

"Likewise, Baron, likewise!"

Suddenly, there was a hush in the room as the Tsar and his entourage swept in. Everyone bowed deeply. The Tsar, a tall, balding blond man in his early forties, had dressed modestly in a black uniform with red trim and heavy gold epaulettes. He had a bejewelled sword at his side and wore knee-high leather boots. As he entered the room, he acknowledged the assembled nobles' bows with a slight wave of his hand. Once in the room, he strode straight towards the group the Baron stood amongst. The men bowed deeply and crisply, while the women curtsied. They all kept their stance until he released them.

The Tsar greeted von Stanecke and Orlovski, then turned to the Baron. He spoke in faultless French. "Ah, Baron, we meet again at last! Von Stanecke here has told us of your work during our recent reform. We are very pleased."

The Baron bowed again. "Thank you, sire, you are too kind!"

The Tsar waved that away.

"We wish to grant you a small reward for your endeavours. He held out his hand and an aide-de-camp put a small box into it. "We hope this modest manor, here in St Petersburg, will suit your requirements, Baron. We wish to see more of you in court."

For once the Baron was speechless. The Tsar did not appear to notice as his eyes fixed on the Baron's wife. He bowed gallantly toward her, and she blushed with pleasure.

"So lovely!" he whispered under his breath. "Baron, you must let me take your lovely wife for the first dance."

"Of course, sire, it is my pleasure indeed!"

The Tsar took Amelia by the arm and moved onto the dance floor. The Count, who had been hovering nearby, lifted his hand, and the orchestra started playing a waltz. The Tsar and the Baron's wife swept away, soon to be joined by other couples.

The Empress, a striking woman with large luminescent blue eyes and long blonde hair, wearing an exquisite flowing low cut, white and gold-laced silk gown with a jewelled neckline looked at the scene, amused. "Baron! My husband shows your lovely wife great favour."

"He does indeed, your Majesty. He does us great honour."

She leaned over toward him, her beautiful eyes laughingly considerate, and said quietly, "Take advantage of my husband's favour while you can. He is fickle, you know!"

Then she swept away, leaving the Baron, momentarily alone. He stood ruminating over his good fortune; watched the Tsar and his wife glide around the dance floor. He took a glass of champagne and sipped it.

The Tsar danced with Amelia for two waltzes before returning her to her husband.

"This is a lovely party, Pavel Andreyevich! We are pleased."

The Count bowed. "Thank you, sire."

With that, the Tsar strode away, "Please continue, Count!"

The large doors were flung open and he left the room.

The ball was a resounding success, of which Amelia was undoubtedly the star. All the young gallants in St Petersburg queued up to dance with her. The Baron smiled indulgently.

After a while, the Countess approached him. "Perhaps, Baron, you should go and rescue your wife. That young Major of the Guards seems very smitten with her!"

The Baron smiled his thanks and approached the couple and tapped the man on his shoulder. "May I, Major?"

The Major bowed and saluted crisply. "Of course, Colonel!"

The Baron led his wife onto the floor. "Are you enjoying yourself, sweetheart?"

"Yes! It's wonderful!" she said, looking at him a little contritely.

He laughed. "The Tsar has shown you great favour this evening!"

She put her hands on his chest and smiled at him, her eyes filled with love and longing. "Us, a great favour, my love! Us, a great favour!"

He smiled at her gently. "Shall we go to our modest house here in St Petersburg?"

Amelia's green eyes shone. "Yes," she whispered.

Yuris was proud of what he had achieved. He'd been hard at work for the winter, pausing only to have Christmas with his family. Now he was ready to put in his crops. He stood with his hands behind his back that warm mid-morning spring day and looked over the Plumshē strips of land the Baron had granted him. They were in a prime area and had fertile, deep, brown loamy soil. The only problem was they were a good hour's ride in his small creaky wooden cart from his house at the newly formed peasant's commune on the edge of the Baron's estate. To rectify that, with his wife's permission, he'd taken some spare rough-hewed wooden planks and built a rudimentary barn structure with a small room attached for himself.

In the barn were his plough, a small stall for his horse, and his precious stock of seed. His room was just that, a room with a bed and a small stove, with a shuttered window and a door leading outside. He had brought a few spare pots and pans from his house. It was not much, but it was a break from the commune. He hoped to be able to sell his crops here independently.

He looked at the land and scooped up a handful of soil and let it sift through his fingers. He was confident he could plant a crop here, then return and, with the help of his wife, plant one of his strips back at his home to feed his family. The other he would leave fallow, as had been decided by the village elders. He felt it in his bones; they were going to have a good year. It was going to be hard work, but he was not afraid of that. He was uncertain what to crop though; had contemplated rye or wheat and had procured cheap seed for both. Perhaps he would plant both.

As he moved back to his room, he noticed a small cart approaching.

"Yuris, Yuris!" a familiar voice rang out.

He looked up and could not believe his eyes. The person in the cart was Anna, driving herself.

"Anna?" He was dumbfounded.

He had not expected to see her again. On seeing her long red hair blowing in the breeze, her wide hips and large breasts, he felt a familiar stirring.

She stopped the cart and flung herself off it and into his arms. "I cannot believe I am seeing you again! I have missed you so much!"

She started to kiss him hungrily. He stiffened at first and then relaxed as he felt the longing and lust for her flooding back. He picked her up and took her into his rudimentary room, where he ripped her top off and hungrily kissed her lovely big breasts. Before he knew it, she was naked and on his bed with her legs spread as he passionately kissed her between them. She arched her back and received him there, moaning. He kissed the rest of her body, up over her hardened nipples until she eagerly pulled him into her. They vigorously made love until she orgasmed and they fell apart, hot and sweaty.

Afterward, he gently caressed her between her legs.

She smiled at him. "I still love you, Yuris. My husband is a good man, but he is not you!"

"What are we going to do? Being without you is torture. Now it is going to be even worse."

She snuggled up to him. "I hope to be over here quite regularly. I work for my husband, sourcing grain for his mill. We sold our mill at Rundāle to the Countess and are building a new larger one in Dobele. So we need wheat from independent farmers like you. I came here to offer to buy your harvest!"

"I love your negotiating technique!" he said as he ran his hands up from between her legs to her lovely breast, her nipple still hard. "I was thinking of planting wheat, and definitely will now!"

She let him caress her, enjoying his gentle touch and said tentatively, "Did you know, Yuris, I have a little boy. He is with his father for the day. I have only been away a few hours and miss him a lot and cannot wait to get back to him!"

Yuris had not known.

He was startled but strangely pleased for her. "Congratulations! No, no, I'm really happy for you!"

She glowed happily and rolled on her side and kissed him on the lips hard and passionately. He became erect, and she eagerly pulled him into her, moaning when he was inside her as they made love again, more quietly now, but still passionately.

Afterward, she held him for a while before gently pushing him away. "I had better get going. I have other visits to make, and I really do need to get home tonight."

She rose and, from a pot of water on the cool stove, washed. He watched her as she did, admiring her plump stomach, her surprisingly smooth skin, her alluring wide hips and round bum and, of course, her fabulous big breasts that moved erotically as she bathed. When she finished, she pulled on her clothes and came back and leaned over him to kiss his lips gently before disappearing out of the room.

It was if she were an apparition. As though their passionate lovemaking had not happened at all. Yuris rose and dressed. He laughed for the sheer joy of life and went out to water and feed his horse. He stroked its head as it nuzzled him.

"What are you looking at?" he asked it.

An exciting new part of his life was about to start. He hitched up his plough to the horse and prepared to plant his first crop of wheat on Plumshē land.

II

The Farmer (1911)

Heinrich Kohler's brow creased and his hands trembled. He had just heard a rumour that the man who had done the most for his family since the Baron long ago had helped to set up his great-great-grandfather as an independent peasant farmer, had been assassinated. Prime Minister Pyotr Stolypin, who had pushed through the Duma in Russia, the crucial agricultural reforms that enabled Heinrich to break away from the commune, was now dead. Stolypin had also, in Heinrich's opinion, saved the empire, including Courland, from the terrible revolutionary turmoil of 1905 to 1906. And now, the firm hand of Stolypin was gone. Heinrich feared for the future. He feared the empire would just drift without Stolypin in the government; he was afraid that the four years of relative peace, freedom, and prosperity would soon come to an end.

He looked, with some pride, at what he'd achieved over the last four years as he walked along the edge of his wheat field. He ran his hands through the immature grain. The fine seed spilled into his hand. The head of wheat looked good. The whole crop was good. It should be a good yield this year. He looked over his fields with pleasure; continued walking along his fence line, the dust of this fine summer's day stirred up by his footsteps. In the next field, his crop of rye looked just as promising. Once again, he lovingly ran his hands over the grain. It was good. He smiled again. All his hard work would pay off this year.

On the way back to his house, he walked past the field he had deliberately left fallow. He bent down, scooped the soil into his hands, and let the rich brown loam run through his fingers. It was good soil. He was lucky. His farm was in one of the best areas in the empire for wheat, rye and dairy cattle; all of which he farmed.

Back at his home he paused at the gate. His house was a rustic, wooden, three-roomed with a steep shingle roof and several shuttered windows. He could not afford to put glass in the windows, yet. The main room, where all the family activities took place, had a stove in it. The other two rooms were bedrooms for himself and his young wife and for their three young sons. There was a rudimentary, enclosed washroom and privy out the back on the verandah. He had built it himself four years ago, using useable timber from the old ruined place that was already there and lumber he'd labouriously carted the nine versts from the commune. He had a barn out the back and his wife and sons tended the vegetable patch, the young fruit trees and the chickens. In a good year, they were self-sufficient if they were frugal, meaning all his crops and most of his milk could be sold to the mill and dairy in Dobele. He had even been able to save some money. Heinrich was determined to give his three young sons a university education if they wanted – it was something he never had.

He flung open the gate; closed it behind him, and walked between the fruit trees to the front door. His attractive young wife, Wilhelmina, looked up as he entered and smiled, revealing beautiful white teeth. She was short and plump, with pretty large dark eyes and short brown hair, and was surprisingly well educated; she shared his determination that their boys get a better education. Heinrich was ten years her senior, and only a little taller than her, being a small man, with blond hair and a large moustache. He had a strong, wiry frame, and large calloused hands from hard work on the farm.

"Where are the boys?" he asked, already guessing the answer.

"Oh, out the back getting up to mischief, I dare say!" she smiled fondly.

"It's time for them to come in and do their chores." He went to the back door and yelled. "Boys! Get in here! It is time to come in and do your chores!"

"Aw, Dad, it's still early," the eldest answered back.

Heinrich glowered. "I will only ask you once!"

"Yes sir!" was the response as they scurried off to the yard where the chickens had to be tended and the barn cleaned out.

Wilhelmina laid her tiny hand, which was surprisingly smooth and white, affectionately on his arm. "They're only boys, love, don't be so hard on them."

Heinrich walked back to the table and smiled at her. "They still have to know their place and be able to work and be self-sufficient. Remember the hard times."

She looked at him quietly and spoke softly as he sat down at the table. "I do. I do. But I hope they do not."

The hard times Heinrich referred to were the turbulent revolutionary years from 1905 to 1906. Back then, he had still been a peasant farmer living in the commune. He had been better off than most as he had some fields outside in Plumshē bequeathed to him, making him semi-independent.

During the summer of 1905, there had been rumours around the area of shootings in Riga. In this atmosphere, his cousin Janis Feldmanis, a teacher at a local school, came to him flushed and excited. "There is a big meeting in Dobele, in protest against the shootings in Riga! Come, we should find out what's going on!"

Heinrich was reluctant but decided to go along.

He grabbed his hat and said to Wilhelmina. "I am going into Dobele with Janis to attend a rally. Keep the boys inside and keep the door shut until I get back."

She looked worried but nodded.

He ran to Janis, who was already starting down the road in his cart.

They drove into Dobele, along with a lot of other people, the atmosphere almost festive.

The meeting was held in the main square, where an excited crowd of peasants had already gathered, many armed with sticks and other dangerous-looking farm implements. A man wearing a red scarf pushed to the fore and leapt onto a cart.

"Comrades!" he roared, silencing the crowd briefly. "It's time we took matters into our own hands. The Tsar is finished. His soldiers are shooting sturdy workers and peasants! People like us – our people! We must form our own Parish Council to resist this blood-soaked criminal autocrat! Who is with me?"

There was a roar of excitement.

"I nominate Martins Putnis to be president of any council!" another man bellowed above the hubbub.

Yells of approval came from all around. The man on the cart waved his scarf excitedly.

One man in a smart uniform, obviously a high Tsarist official, stood at the back of the crowd; he spoke out in an act of great bravery and bravado. "That's treason! Why should you be the leader of this so-called council, Martins Putnis?"

The man's audacity silenced the crowd for a moment. Then they started to shout him down.

"At least I'm a peasant and from Courland, unlike you, you German exploiter!" Putnis spat out angrily, glaring down at the man from the cart.

The crowd bellowed its approval and started moving as a mob towards the man, menacing, their sticks and other implements waving.

Though agitated, the man stood his ground and thundered: "I'm a Latvian, like you, Putnis! My forebears might have been German, but the family has lived here for several decades now!"

Heinrich vaguely knew the man: he owned a large property near the commune. Heinrich had nothing against him and was appalled the crowd threatened him with violence.

Inspired, he yelled, with Janis echoing him. "Putnis for council! Putnis for council!"

The crowd took up the chant and the well-dressed man was forgotten.

"To the town hall! To the town hall!" Putnis screamed, trying to retake control of the crowd. He leapt off the wagon and led the way. Janis, excited, joined the mob.

Heinrich followed the crowd more slowly, fascinated and afraid about what was going to happen next. He watched as the crowd, Janis in amongst them, stormed the town hall, sweeping aside the unarmed policeman outside the gate. He decided it was time to leave when he heard smashing from within the building as the crowd looted it. His friend, Janis, had disappeared, caught up in the moment.

Heinrich hurried away from the town hall across the main square, expecting the army or, even worse the Cossacks, at any time. As he passed the square, he noticed the brave, if foolish, man sitting on a bench under a tree, his smart uniform rumpled.

Heinrich went up to him and said roughly. "You're not wanted here, Bergs. You should go home and stay away!"

On hearing the voice, Bergs startled. He looked at the man standing over him, still in shock at his narrow escape. "You are Heinrich Kohler!"

Heinrich nodded curtly, wanting to move on quickly.

"There's going to be trouble, Kohler. The Tsar will not allow that rabble to take over!"

"True. I suggest that you leave Courland or barricade yourself in your home!"

"I'm not leaving, Kohler. We have lived in this place for generations. But you are right! I shall go home."

With that, Bergs mounted his horse and rode off quickly, leaving Heinrich standing in a cloud of dust. Heinrich glared after him and set off on the long walk back to his home.

"Where in the hell is Janis?" he muttered to himself.

He hoped his cousin was not foolish enough to become involved in any so-called parish council. He couldn't see any good coming from such an arbitrary, despotic organisation – it seemed as bad as the Tsar's government, if not worse!

Heinrich spent the next few days and weeks keeping to himself and hoarding what food he had, having decided to keep to himself and stay out of trouble. To his great regret, he had temporarily abandoned his strips in Plumshē. In these troubled times, it was too difficult and dangerous to farm them, as they were a long way from the commune. He would still try to bring in his crop here though, with help from other peasants in the commune, and was quite pleased the council of elders had agreed on the strategy he had proposed to try to stay out of the troubles.

Two weeks after the rally in Dobele, Heinrich was coming home from his strips, where his crop of wheat was just about ready to harvest when he noticed an unruly bunch of peasants on the road. He hurried home and only just got in when his door crashed open. Four of peasants he had seen from the road rushed inside. Heinrich hurried Wilhelmina and his sons into the other room.

"What can I do for you, comrades?" he asked politely.

Their leader answered rudely: "We are from the Dobele Parish Council. We are tired and expect your hospitality, comrade."

He arrogantly sat at the table and flung his dirty, tattered boots on it as he leant back on Heinrich's chair, the only one in the house. His men crowded into the room.

"As you can see, comrade, I am only a poor peasant, but what I have is yours! I and the elders of the commune will be of service to you, if we can."

He turned and yelled out to the other room. "Woman, come

and serve these fine men!"

Wilhelmina came out and glared at him. He was in trouble, he knew it, but he hoped she would hold fire for now. Thankfully, she put some platters of rye bread and butter on the table and, rustling about in the cupboard, found some sauerkraut she had recently made and a bottle of vodka. Heinrich found some cups and poured liberal shots of vodka for the men. They ate and drank noisily and uncouthly.

When they had finished and were a little more relaxed, Heinrich asked, "What news of Dobele, comrades?"

Their leader answered proudly, "We are in charge now. There has been fighting in the streets with those German landowner scum, but we will sort them out in time. When is your crop due, comrade?"

"We'll start to harvest in a week."

"Good, I hope you'll see fit to support the Dobele Council." He said that with malice, glaring at Heinrich and leering at Wilhelmina, who audaciously glared back with unhidden hostility. The man seemed to enjoy her resentment, and lurched to his feet, his leering smile widening as the chair crashed onto the floor; he stalked out, his men following him, without a word of thanks.

Heinrich picked up his chair and slumped into it.

He raised his hand to Wilhelmina. "I know, I know, sweetheart."

Just then, one of his sons started to cry. Wilhelmina glared at him again and rushed into the other room to tend to her children. When she had settled them, she came out a little timidly and sat on his knee and kissed him.

He kissed her back and then murmured, "Not now, sweetheart, I just don't feel in the mood after what just happened."

She whispered, "I know, just kiss me."

They took the crop in: it was a very bad crop.

As Heinrich and the other peasants walked back from the fields with their sickles over their shoulders, he said to one of the elders: "There should be barely enough for us this year. What are we going to do about the Dobele Council?"

"We'll hoard all our grain," the man answered. "I'm not going to let my children go hungry because of some rebel council. You were wise to suggest we try to stay out of it, Heinrich. It is only a matter of time before the army, or worse, the Cossacks, arrive. Mark my words!"

"You may be right. Still, I will go to Dobele and try to talk to the council and see if they will relent on their demands."

"Go with my blessing, brother," the elder answered.

Heinrich decided to walk into Dobele, so he left at sun-up, taking a lump of rye bread and some water. He had told Wilhelmina to keep the children indoors and start threshing the grain for storage. He would be back as soon as he could.

He was walking out the door when she flung herself into his arms and kissed him passionately. "Please take care."

As he walked past the recently harvested fields in the morning chill, he reflected on his previous trip to Dobele with Janis. Now, it was eerily quiet. The country seemed deserted. He wondered what had happened to Janis that day. He had not heard from him since. He strode quickly down the road, his feet stirring up the dust. It was still so dry, and he really hoped the autumn rains would come soon.

Nearing Dobele, he was walking around a curve through a small thicket when he heard the clip-clop of horses and the jingle of harnesses. Without thinking, he plunged headlong into a ditch. As the horses approached, he hid behind a tree and warily looked out, realised it was as he feared – the Cossacks! He watched hidden from view as they rode slowly past on their small, but muscular, dark horses with white feet. They were tough, determined-looking men, wearing long greatcoats and fur hats in the early morning chill. Their sabres and rifles were loose in the holsters. There was a company of them, Heinrich estimated, and they were scarily impressive.

As soon as the last Cossack rode past him, Heinrich bolted into the thicket. He ran into Dobele through a side street; warily approached the main square. Peering around a building, he saw the Cossacks lined up on their horses, their sabres loose in their hands. A crowd stood sullenly in the square. The officer edged his horse forward and said in a loud voice: "You will disperse in the name of the Tsar. We are here to arrest the ringleaders of the so-called council and urge you to disperse immediately or suffer the consequences!"

An eerie quiet fell for what seemed an eternity; then a shot rang out from the town hall. The officer raised his pistol, and the Cossacks charged the crowd. Pandemonium broke out, and more shots rang out from the town hall. People screamed and fled; some were trampled under horses' hooves. One of the Cossacks fell, his throat gushing blood. The officer forced his horse up the steps of the town hall and rode into the building, firing his pistol. His Cossacks followed, crashing their horses through windows and doors, slashing with their sabres. Another flurry of shots rang out, then silence. It was all over in a minute.

Heinrich stared at the scene in fascinated horror. He saw the Cossack soldiers drag a man out of the ruins of the once pretty and distinctive town hall. It was Martins Putnis. He struggled and wept, suddenly finding God, but to no avail. The soldiers unceremoniously flung a rope over a tree and hung him then and there. They left him kicking on the branch. More people were dragged out of the building and taken away, the place left a shattered ruin.

After the last Cossack left, Heinrich, terrified, but morbidly curious, crept out of his hiding place and walked into the square. It was quiet and blood splattered. None of the people in the square had been killed. The Cossacks had removed the body of their comrade. He crossed himself and shakily prayed to God. Some injured people were being treated on the street, and others were taken away by their families. He walked gingerly into the now deserted, smashed building that had been the town hall, grimly looked past Putnis's body. Armed police had taken up positions around the building, but they ignored him. He was just another lost soul searching for loved ones in the destruction. He stepped past the front door into a large hall that was now a complete shambles. Broken glass was everywhere. The furniture was smashed and the walls bullet-ridden. A picture of the Tsar hung precariously, strangely untouched by the carnage. The grand staircase leading up to the second floor had many of its carved balustrades smashed.

Suddenly, he choked, turned and fled, stumbling down the stairs in his desperation to get away. He had just looked into the open, staring eyes of his friend Janis, dead near the foot of the staircase, with a great gash from a sabre in his head.

He ran blindly out onto the square and collided with a man. They both fell over then leapt up again. It was Bergs, blood-stained and bruised. He was tired and carrying a rifle loosely in his hand. Heinrich stared at him blankly, not recognising him, and fled across the square.

Bergs sighed. He had been shocked by the violence of the Cossack assault. He'd been involved in the fighting in the town, holed up in friends' houses who were trying to defend themselves against the fanatics of the Parish Council. They had been largely unsuccessful. Many of the German manor houses in the district had been burned to the ground by the mob. One of the first things the Parish Council did was take over the mill and evict the owner, a man who Bergs thought looked remarkably like Heinrich Kohler.

The mill owner complained: "Comrades, I'm a peasant. My ancestors were serfs. I'm from Courland, and my family have lived here forever!"

In response, Martins Putnis had screamed. "I don't care who you say you are. You are capitalist swine and the mill is going to be taken over for the people by the council. Get out of the way!"

He had then shoved the man aside and led the mob in. The mill had been largely looted and then left, the mob moving on to other things. The owner had come back to a ruin.

Despite everything, Bergs had never dreamed that the government would send in the dreaded Cossacks. He knew the government had finally secured the town, but at what cost? He shouldered his rifle. He was going home and staying home, staying out of it like poor Heinrich Kohler. He knew it was not all over yet. But he was finished. Whatever happened, he was finished. He had to look after his own property and family.

Heinrich ran for a long time. Finally, he slumped under a tree by the side of the road and rested. He remembered that he had some food, so he forced the bread into his mouth and drank some water. He was hungry and thirsty but felt too sick at heart to eat much.

Eventually, he rose and walked home. When he arrived, he put on a cheery face for his children's sake, and when they were put to bed, he walked outside and told Wilhelmina what had happened. Shocked, she put her arms around him; they held each other for a long time.

She said quietly, "Poor Janis. Poor, poor Janis. Poor Anda and their children."

Heinrich held her tightly and choked back his genuine tears of grief for a cousin and friend. He knew he had to visit Anda with the bad news and do whatever he could to ensure Janis received a decent burial. But that could wait for a little while.

Over the next week, Heinrich helped collect Janis' body and made arrangements for his friend's funeral. He flung himself into the work of threshing the harvest but was uncharacteristically grumpy and surly; he worked hard, with little time for his small children. His sons sensed something was wrong and left him alone, their natural cockiness gone for a time. Wilhelmina understood and was quietly supportive. They stored all they had for the coming winter; would not take any to market this year.

Soon after the threshing was completed and the winter was upon them, they received a visitor in the New Year. He rode up on a fine horse and tied it to the fence outside the house. It was Bergs. Heinrich was surprised to see him, invited him in, and gave him his seat next to the fire. Bergs stooped and entered the small house, somewhat distastefully. He took off his coat and fur hat and sat down. Wilhelmina offered their guest tea while their sons looked on from the other room.

Heinrich sat on a stool at the table. "For what do I owe for the honour, Mr Bergs?"

Bergs accepted the tea and drank it contemplatively.

When he saw the children, he smiled. "I have a daughter about the same age as your youngest, Kohler. How old is he, about three?"

Heinrich nodded. Bergs smiled again as the little boy peaked into the room shyly.

Heinrich smiled. "Come on, Karlis, come out and say hello to Mr Bergs."

The little boy, a strong, healthy child, ran out, choked out a word then ran back to his mother's skirts.

Bergs smiled indulgently. "I have come to warn you, Kohler. I hope you were not involved in the nasty Parish Council business last year. The Tsar has a new Interior Minister. A man called Pyotr Stolypin. You can be sure this Stolypin will crush the rebellion ruthlessly. I have heard that he was a provincial governor. When everything was in chaos elsewhere, he kept an iron grip on his province. I expect he will do the same for the Empire now."

Heinrich sat and looked into his tea while he contemplated this news. "I have always been a supporter of the Tsar. I never supported the Parish Council and tried to keep out of it all, as did all the other members of our commune."

Bergs looked at him approvingly. He actually quite liked the man.

"Good, then you have nothing to worry about. I just hope this Stolypin fellow can restore order and peace."

He finished his tea, stood up and bowed ever so slightly towards Wilhelmina, who flushed a little at his attention. "I will take my leave. I thank you for your hospitality."

He hesitated at the door as he put his coat and hat on. "Did you hear that the mill in Dobele will not be able to take grain this harvest? I heard you had a bad harvest this year and you were unable to farm your Plumshē strips, so that might not affect you. Will you be alright this winter?"

Heinrich smiled. "We'll be fine, Mr Bergs. We'll be fine," he lied.

It was a tough winter. Heinrich and Wilhelmina often had to go hungry so their children had enough food. After much debate, they decided not to break into their hard-earned savings, mostly from the sale of grain from the Plumshē strips, unless absolutely necessary. They were both glad they had hoarded as much as they could during the summer, so managed to scrape by without using their savings. Heinrich made sure he put aside enough seed for next season's harvest.

Despite the deprivations, they were snug and warm in their little house. They spent their time around the stove. Heinrich fixed his tools and Wilhelmina darned their socks and fixed their clothes.

When they had a small amount of privacy, which was rare in a small house with three little boys, he made love with his pretty wife, marvelling at how unaffected she seemed by their hard lives. Her skin, even on her hands, was still soft, white and flawless. Her breasts, despite giving birth to three boys, were still pert and perfect. She had a cute, plump bum, and was still keen to have sex with him, when they could. Afterward, he loved to hold her while he watched her sleep and see the gentle rise and fall of her breasts and hear her breathing.

The boys, unaware of the turbulence and bloodshed in the countryside, as Stolypin brutally got to work, were happy. So was Heinrich. As there was not that much to do around the commune because of the frost and snow, he indulged the boys a bit with tobogganing and snowball fights. They built a big snowman outside their house. He even risked taking his eldest, who was nine, ice fishing. They actually caught some good fish which was a welcome supplement to their meagre diet. It was almost peaceful, though Heinrich always tried to find out what was going on elsewhere. Surprisingly, if he could get hold of an old newspaper, the violence was openly reported. It seemed that since the formation of the Duma and a quasi-constitutional government in 1905, censorship had been relaxed. The little community was unaffected by the troubles that winter.

When spring came, at last, the fact that the Tsar's government was still in serious trouble, but fighting back under the ruthless guidance of Stolypin, came home to them with a vengeance. As the ice and snow thawed, Heinrich and the others in his commune prepared to sow their crops. But they had heard that, after the winter, the troubles had flared up again. Once again, Heinrich decided it was too risky to sow his Plumshē strips. As soon as he could though, he walked out to inspect them. There was still a chill in the air, and as he walked through the icy slush of the thaw, he stamped his feet and rubbed his hands. His strips looked forlorn and unkempt. He knew he had to do something with them, so he visited Schillings, a friend of his who lived near the land and arranged to have him graze his cattle on the strips in the summer, or they would become overgrown.

"For payment, you understand. Very little, whatever you can afford."

Schillings understood. This way Kohler would retain his ownership rights on the strips in these troubled times. He was well aware that the strips had been owned by the Kohler family for nearly a hundred years.

He thought for a while. "You know it was a very tough winter. I don't have much to offer you and, as we didn't go to the market last season, I have no money."

Heinrich spread his hands.

He understood well the dilemma Schillings faced. "I heard you had a good peach harvest last fall. How about some jars of your wife's famous preserve for my boys?"

"Done! Don't worry; I'll look after the land. Come in, do you want tea, or something stronger?"

Heinrich went into his friend's two-room house, very similar to his own, and sat near the fire. Schillings brought out a bottle of vodka and poured him a generous shot. "To the Tsar! I hope these troubled times will soon be behind us!"

Heinrich raised his glass and gulped the strong spirit. It warmed his stomach and made him feel good. Schillings' wife, a large, big-breasted lady, with long dark hair, and faded beauty, brought in the jars of preserves. Heinrich finished his drink and shook hands with his friend and left with four jars in his bag. It would be a nice treat for the family.

As Heinrich walked back towards his village, he was saddened by the state of his strips at Plumshē. He really hoped the troubles would end so he could get back to farming them. He was wandering through a village halfway home, distracted by these thoughts when he noticed the village seemed very quiet. As he walked down the dusty track past the common, he was shocked and horrified to see two bodies swinging in the breeze on roughly hewn gallows. He stood stunned, not knowing what to do.

I had better get home! was his first thought.

He was hurrying past a house when an old man peered timidly

out the door.

"What happened here?" Heinrich managed to gasp.

The old man looked down the street and growled. "The Military Commissioners have been here. Those two were self-elected leaders of the local Parish Council, in defiance of the Tsar. I had better cut them down. I don't care who they are. They deserve to be buried with some dignity.

"It seems that the army has been at work with Stolypin's necktie!" he added with morbid humour.

As they talked, people started coming quietly out of their houses. The bodies were quickly cut down. Heinrich thanked the old man and hurried away, still dazed by what he'd seen.

When he returned to his village, he saw the soldiers on the common, bayonets fixed, their rifles on their hips pointing above the cowering villagers. A young army Captain stood arrogantly on a platform haranguing the people. Two other officers stood calmly behind him. Heinrich saw a young man hiding in a house as he hurried past.

He hissed at the man. "You know Mr Bergs?"

The young man nodded.

"Get him quickly, quickly!"

The young man quietly ran off.

Heinrich hurried onto the common.

The Captain screamed, his eyes wild and spittle spraying out of his mouth as his soldiers stood grimly. "You are all rebel scum! You defied our beloved Tsar! You cannot expect me to believe that you were not supporters of that swine in Dobele!"

Heinrich, somehow, found the courage to answer. "We're all loyal supporters of the Tsar, Captain, sir."

The Captain glared at him and raved. "Who are you, insolent shit? Are you daring to defy me?"

Heinrich quaked but stood his ground. "Please, Captain, sir, come and see!"

He slowly backed away and opened the door of the nearby communal meeting house, a small wooden building. Hanging on the wall was a faded and tatty picture of the Tsar. One of the soldiers saw the picture and whispered to the Captain. He was mollified somewhat, but still stood on the platform, hands on his hips, glaring at the crowd menacingly.

One of the other officers, a Colonel, stepped forward and said quietly, but with real authority. "Enough, Captain. Tell your men to stand easy."

The Captain snapped to attention, saluted, and passed on the order. His men immediately relaxed and grounded their rifles. The officer stepped off the platform and walked quietly into the meeting hall. He stood for a while and looked carefully at the picture of the Tsar.

"That has been hanging here a long time, unlikely in a nest of revolutionaries!" he mused.

Just then, Bergs arrived at a gallop, his horse in a lather.

He leapt off it and bowed towards the officer. "I can vouch for these people, Colonel. They are good people and loyal to the Tsar."

The Colonel smiled, nodded his recognition, and said grimly, "I believe so, Bergs."

He then looked at the surrounding villagers and calmly, but sternly said: "We are here to restore law and order. I have special authority under the martial law decree and on direct orders of Minister Stolypin, to severely punish all rebels against the Tsar. If you go about your business peaceably, you have nothing to fear. But those who do not will be dealt with. Those who harbour rebels will be dealt with."

With that, he turned and nodded to the Captain, mounted his horse, and left. The Captain saluted, stood hands on hips, and glared balefully at the crowd then, mounting his horse, rapped out orders to his soldiers, who formed up and marched out, heading towards Dobele. The villagers had, in the meantime, gathered around Bergs and thanked him effusively for his support. He was somewhat abashed by the fuss and waved at them casually before mounting his horse and leaving as well.

Heinrich breathed a sigh of relief. He hurried back to his house and flung open the door. There he found his whole family inside. Wilhelmina, as a practical wife, had kept his children indoors as soon as she heard of the soldiers' arrival. He hugged them all and kissed his wife. Later that night, he told her what he had seen in the neighbouring village.

Luckily for Heinrich and his family, their commune was an island of calm in a still turbulent environment as the military commissions Stolypin had put in place carried out summary punishment of all rebels. Heinrich heard about more hangings and people being exiled. He found out about what was happening in the country because, incredibly, the news was reported freely in the newspapers, which he occasionally got hold of. He tried to ignore it and get on with the harvest and his life, not letting on to his children what was going on in the outside world and, as a consequence, their lives were happy and peaceful.

By the winter of 1906, the revolution in Courland was over. The newly appointed Prime Minister Stolypin had ruthlessly put it down in the name of the Tsar, and was crushing dissent elsewhere in the Empire, most likely saving the Imperial government in the process. When peace finally returned, Heinrich and his family were doing quite alright as the 1906 harvest, for them, was a good one. He only regretted that he had not been able to farm his strips in Plumshē, as he heard that even though the mill in Dobele was not fully restored, the owner was willing to pay for the grain of his long-time suppliers.

Heinrich was one of the peasants that had taken advantage of the great agrarian reforms that Prime Minister Stolypin had pushed through the Duma in November 1906. Once the ukase (*decree*) had been signed by the Tsar, it meant that all the land the peasants held in the commune became freehold. Now, they could buy and sell their land and consolidate their disparate strips into one farm. The ukase also provided for affordable credit. This was a godsend for Heinrich, who had for a long time wanted to use his strips in Plumshē to break away from the commune. He was now able to do so.

Over that winter, he had acted quickly. It had been hard on his family, but he had traded his strips in the commune for three contiguous with his land at Plumshē. He had then cobbled together a shack there, while he moved everything from the commune. Later, he built a three-room house and barn.

He also transferred his cows over from the commune in a small cattle drive that was quite amusing. The whole family walked the cows down the road, the beasts always wanting to wander off to find scarce feed. They kept the boys busy, and a great time was had by all. It was very cold and clear that day, with snow on the fields and icicles on the trees, making the countryside picturesque. They managed to get the cows safely into the new barn at the end of a long day, just as the low and feeble sun set.

By the end of the winter, in time for the next harvest, all was set up. Heinrich worked hard and planted wheat and rye on his land. Luckily for him, the mill in Dobele had been partially repaired after the troubles and the owner offered to buy his grain.

Heinrich used all the profits from his first harvest at Plumshē, plus all his hard-earned savings, to get a line of credit and purchase more land adjacent to his new farm. By the summer of 1909, he had put together a good-sized farm. It consisted of fifty hectares of prime cropping land. He was also totally broke. He was lucky, though, having made his own luck by his vision and hard work. The next harvest was a good one, so they had survived. But it had been tough. Once again, Heinrich and Wilhelmina had to sacrifice themselves for their children.

Heinrich sat on his chair at the table and looked at his pretty wife as she bustled about the room cooking and boiling water. "Have you heard that Stolypin has been shot?"

She nodded grimly: the terrible rumour had spread like wildfire around the area.

He continued quietly: "I'm afraid with Stolypin gone the government in St Petersburg will just drift. It will drift into war. Germany is getting more and more aggressive. Can we survive a war with a weak government?" he asked her rhetorically.

Wilhelmina looked at him contemplatively with her beautiful, large, dark brown eyes, and answered softly: "Hush. We can only hope and pray it will not come to that."

"I hope so too. I'm worried that Stolypin's reforms have not had enough time yet to strengthen the rural areas. They are still backward and conservative in Russia, I've heard."

She was slightly preoccupied by his gloomy words, but she managed to answer brightly. "Yes, but I also read the other day, in that old newspaper you got hold of, that the peasants who have taken up land in Siberia are doing very well."

"True. We can only pray for time; time for others to take advantage of the reforms."

Now there was peace and prosperity in the Empire. The Tsar's authoritarian rule had been moderated, somewhat, with the formation of the Duma, and the Empire had a free press and judiciary, even by European standards of the time. Heinrich could sit at his table and talk to Wilhelmina without fear. He was happy that all the hard work of the past few years had been worth it. He was an independent farmer now and doing well. But, the terrible possibility of war worried him.

His wife looked affectionately at his ruggedly handsome face. "Cheer up, sweetheart, we are doing well. Our boys will have a good future, whatever happens. We should not forget our plan and continue along with it and enjoy these times of peace, prosperity and freedom. There is no point worrying about a war that may not even happen!"

He smiled at her pretty face and her quiet determination.

She yelled out the door. "Boys! Come and get your dinner. I hope all those chores are done!"

The three boys trooped noisily in and sat at the table. Heinrich looked at them proudly. Yes, whatever happens, they would have a good future. He would do everything he could to ensure that.

III

The Three Brothers (1914–1917)

The summer of 1914 was a time full of foreboding. It seemed all of Heinrich Kohler's predictions, made in the summer of 1911, were about to come true. The Russian government had drifted without the strong hand of Stolypin to guide it, and it seemed that war with Germany was inevitable. The Russian army had mobilised, and for a while now, troops and supplies had been moving through the Dobele area to the frontier with Prussia in Lithuania. As the army marched through, the Baltic-German nobility and landowners in Courland declared their support for the Tsar in the event of war with Germany. Many of them left their houses and properties and joined the Russian army.

Heinrich Kohler was determined to support the army in any way he could. He had offered his harvest to the army, when it was collected, thus avoiding the mandatory requisition that he believed would happen. Once again, Heinrich was right. When the army came in early July 1914, he had already pledged his crop to them at a reasonable price and had a signed document from the army supply commissariat.

He was out in the front of his house, helping Wilhelmina tend to the fruit trees they had planted in the summer of 1907. A number of the apple and peach trees, though still young, had started bearing fruit. He was pruning the trees, enjoying working with his wife in the warm summer sunshine, when a khaki-uniformed officer on a horse approached the gate. He had a sword at his side and a holstered pistol in his belt.

"Are you Kohler?" he asked.

Heinrich answered. "Yes, what can I do for you?"

The officer paused on his horse and took in the fruit trees and the fields of young grain just over the fence. He looked at the rustic rough-hewn wooden and steep shingle-roofed house, noting that two rooms had recently been added, and the glass in the windows; the shutters flung open in the summer sun. He heard the laughter of Heinrich's sons behind the house. It was a peaceful scene and the harvest looked good.

Wilhelmina stopped her work and came forward also. "Come in for a cup of tea, officer."

He smiled, disarmed by her, but said: "No, thank you, I am here on duty. When will your crop be in, Kohler? As you may know, we are mobilising in the event of war with Germany. The army will be compulsorily requisitioning all crops in this area to supply the troops."

"The harvest is not due for another month. But I have already pledged most of the crop to the army."

The officer looked pleased. "That's good, Kohler. There has been lot of support from everyone in this district, for the army and the Tsar. It's very pleasing to see the patriotism toward the Empire and Mother Russia here."

Heinrich plucked his courage and asked: "You are certain there will be war then?"

The officer looked grim. "It's only a matter of time. That mad Serb who shot an Austrian Archduke has set everything in motion. The Tsar will have to support our orthodox brothers in Serbia."

War came on 28 July 1914. Russia declared war on Germany and launched an invasion of eastern Prussia. Heinrich was lucky. He was too old to be conscripted into the army, and his sons were too young. They had all grown into tall, strong boys and were a great help on the farm. Arturs, his eldest, was seventeen and was doing well in school. Unfortunately, Heinrich's dreams of him being able to continue his education at a university seemed impossible due to the war. His other sons were Adolfs, fourteen, and the youngest Karlis, twelve.

At first, the war did not affect them. Heinrich and his family all worked hard and harvested the crop by the end of August 1914. It was a good crop and he was able to provide what he had pledged to the army, and also put aside some for his family. Heinrich and Arturs loaded the sacks of grain into their large four-wheeled cart, harnessed their plough horses to it and drove into Dobele to the local army commissariat depot at the train station. As they plodded along the road, they noticed a flurry of activity further ahead. Imperial Courtiers dashed past.

When they arrived at the depot, there was chaos. A train laden with grain supplies and troops was leaving for Jelgava, and despatch to the front.

A harassed officer came up to them. "Unload the grain on the platform over there. It is going straight to the front in Germany. Here, sign this."

He thrust a document at Heinrich. "When you have unloaded the grain, go to the office and get the agreed payment."

Heinrich and Arturs took the cart to the platform and unloaded it. The sacks of grain were weighed then immediately loaded onto a train that was belching steam and smoke at the siding. Another officer signed confirming the weight of each sack and handed over a receipt to take to the office.

Heinrich stood on the platform surrounded by frenetic activity, wanting to know what was going on. He went to the office and asked the harassed clerk.

"Oh, you wouldn't have heard," he answered impatiently. "The Russian Army has been defeated in Germany at a place called Tannenburg. They are in retreat but are going to try to stabilise the line at a place called Masurian Lakes. Here, ten, twenty, thirty, forty and fifty roubles as agreed. Sign here."

As they plodded along the dusty road back to their farm, Heinrich slowly digested the news. It was not good. If the army could not stabilise the front, there was every chance Courland would be invaded by the German Imperial Army. He kept the news to himself, not wanting to frighten his son, but when he reached home, he had to talk to his wife. They found her in the front yard tending her fruit trees.

Heinrich sent Arturs around to the barn to unhitch the horses and to feed and stable them. "Get your brothers to help, then get on with your chores."

Wilhelmina looked up. There was something in his tone. She looked at him curiously. "What's wrong, Heinrich?"

He told her. She was disturbed but, having a sunny disposition, put her hands on his chest. "I'm sure it will not come to that!"

"We had better prepare all the same, Wilhelmina. Lucky, I have this money, plus the little we have saved."

Then he said, exasperated, "Can you believe that it is only seven years after the revolution and we are at war again? Seven good years of peace and now it is all over! This war will change everything, I'm sure!"

She hushed him.

But he continued pensively. "I have said it before, but I'm not sure the Empire can survive a long war."

She smiled at him lovingly and kissed him. "We will get through, just like we did last time."

Still he was pensive. "Our sons are older this time. I'm afraid we will not be able to shield them from any troubles now."

"We will worry about that when it happens. You must be tired. I'll make you a cup of tea and then put dinner on."

The troubles came to them more quickly than either of them

hoped. The Russian army suffered another defeat at Masurian Lakes in September 1914 and was driven out of Germany. It was only because the Germans had to divert troops to the Polish sector and the onset of winter that they were not able to follow up and invade Lithuania. A proclamation was published in all the newspapers and posted on all the church noticeboards in the winter of 1914. All children were to be evacuated to Russia in the thaw. They could take only one suitcase each.

Early in March 1915, Heinrich quietly and sadly helped his sons pack their bags. He pressed into Arturs' hands most of their remaining roubles. They loaded up the cart and trundled into Dobele. There was a stream of people on the road. Many laden carts creaked down the icy, muddy road, lurching in potholes as the horses strained at the harnesses. Some people were walking. Everyone had rugged up against the cold and moved grimly down the road with their battered suitcases.

Heinrich unloaded the cart near the train station. He waited as his sons gently kissed Wilhelmina's tear-stained face. She was frantic and flung her arms around all of them.

"Why can't you come with us? The Germans are on the way! What will you do?" the younger boys cried urgently.

"We'll be alright. You know we can't leave the farm. And besides, the evacuation is only for children and essential war effort factory workers. Arturs, I have arranged for you and your brothers to stay at the Jenkis place in Riga. Keep the money I gave you hidden. Don't give it to Jenkis, as you may need it later. You remember him?"

"Yes, Father, the tall, thin, dark-haired man. His place is not that far from the railway station."

Heinrich smiled at his eldest, now almost a man.

He put his hand on his shoulder and said earnestly, "Look after your brothers. Please stay out of trouble and keep away from the recruiters. I do not want you getting involved in this war; you're still only seventeen … much too young."

Arturs nodded grimly but said nothing.

A young officer hurried up to them, the crowd parting as he strode forward. "Move on! Move on! This way. So, you and your wife are staying, Kohler?"

"Yes, sir."

"The German army is on the move. We don't know when the front will be stabilised. But hopefully this is only temporary. Your horses, man, the army needs horses. I'm afraid I'll have to requisition one of them."

Heinrich was saddened and distressed. "You can have the grey mare, sir. It's young and strong. But how am I to get a harvest in with only one horse?"

"That's not my concern. Your generous gesture, Kohler, is much appreciated. I will make sure you get some compensation."

"Thank you. Please make sure she is looked after."

"I can't promise anything, Kohler. It is war, and horses, unfortunately, do die. It looks like a good horse. I'm sure it will be used for moving supplies behind the lines."

Heinrich pushed his family through the thronging crowd. There was chaos on the platform as large numbers of panicked people struggled to get into the carriages. The guards and soldiers struggled to control them. A train moved out from the platform, screeching as the wheels tried to gain traction on the icy tracks. It was fully loaded; people hung out of the windows crying and waving to loved ones as it moved. Slowly it gathered pace towards Jelgava.

Heinrich and Wilhelmina hugged and kissed all of their boys one last time. They clung to one another, not wanting to let go, as people streamed around them.

Finally, a rail guard came up. "Get aboard. The train leaves in a minute!"

Heinrich helped his family onto the train. He swung their

suitcases up into the carriage and put his arm around his pretty, plump wife. His sons, caught up in the excitement, were already scrambling up the steep steps into the carriage and to a seat near the window. People pushed and shoved as they all frenetically tried to get on board. Once aboard, they all rushed to a window and waved vigorously. The train lurched forward. Wilhelmina strained all her sinews to have one last glance of her sons, tears streaming unabashedly down her face as the crowded train gathered pace. She waved frantically; ran along the platform, her blind impetus brushing aside people until the train pulled away. Wilhelmina's last glimpse of her three beloved sons was of them hanging forlornly out of the carriage windows, waving. She didn't know it at the time, but she wasn't to see any of them again for over three long years.

The crowded train eased into Riga train station with a screech of wheels on icy tracks and a huge release of steam and soot. The platform was strangely quiet, with just a few soldiers standing desultory guard in the grey evening. When the train finally stopped, the carriage doors sprang open, and people clutching their battered suitcases streamed off onto the dirty, unkempt platform.

Arturs shouldered his suitcase and hustled his brothers out of the carriage and onto the platform. "Adolfs, Karlis, hurry up! We have to find Mr Jenkis. Stay together!"

They pushed their way through the crowd and onto the icy, dirty street, the ice turning to mud as they sloshed through it. A gaunt middle-aged man was waiting with a small taxi cart across the road.

Arturs recognised him and jostled his brothers across the busy street. "Mr Jenkis?"

The man nodded and tersely indicated for them to load their bags onto the taxi cart. The boys scrambled aboard and sat, their feet dangling off the back, as Jenkis rather haughtily sat at the front beside the driver. It was not a long ride as Jenkis had a modest, two-storeyed timber and slate house between the railway line and the Daugava River on Šaurā Iela. When they got there, Jenkis paid the driver and stalked away as the boys hurriedly grabbed their suitcases and followed him around the house to a shed.

He said rudely before he left, "You'll stay here. Dinner is at six. You've missed it and I will not have you disturbing Mrs Jenkis and my daughters now."

The shed, where they were to stay, was cold and dark, with a high, steep shingle roof. Three rusty iron beds stretched between the dusty workbenches, each with a lumpy mattress and thin blankets. One dirty window looked into the yard towards the house and a kerosene lamp lit the interior.

The next morning the boys were woken from their slumber by a loud banging as Jenkis hammered at the door. Groaning, they stumbled out of the creaky, uncomfortable beds and threw on their clothes.

Jenkis stood outside the shed, hands on hips, looking stern and imposing. "If you are to stay here you will obey my rules. You will eat in the kitchen at six after we have had dinner. I expect you all to go to the local boarding school as day students. You will work for your board here. Karlis, I expect you to help in the kitchen, washing dishes and cleaning. You will also clean out the privy. Adolfs, you will help keep the garden in shape and clean the outhouse. Arturs, I expect you to help me with my job on the weekends. You will not come into the house unless specifically invited by myself or Mrs Jenkis, and you will keep your room clean and tidy. Understand?"

"Yes, sir," they all yelled, shocked by this brusque treatment.

"Right, you can wash in the outhouse. Get to school."

With that, he turned on his heel and stalked back into the house.

Life was tough for the Kohler brothers at the Jenkis household.

Jenkis was at best distant, and at worst harsh. The school they were sent to was austere, with strict discipline and the lunch provided was usually dry black bread and cabbage soup. Jenkis, as he promised, made them work and they were only allowed to eat in the kitchen. It soon became apparent their meal was the leftovers from the Jenkis family table, and they often went to bed hungry.

Riga, at that time, was in a state of nervous turmoil. People fleeing from the advancing Germans streamed into the city and trains loaded with troops rushed out to the front, which was remorselessly drawing closer. When the wind blew in the right direction, the thump of artillery could be heard in the distance. The government continued the evacuation of the essential armaments, industry workers and their equipment. After a tense month, good news finally came when posted notices proclaimed the front had finally been stabilised at the Daugava River. Riga was safe, for the moment. Despite this momentous event, while relieved, Arturs worried. His parents were stuck on the other side of the front, leaving him responsible for his younger brothers. He tried to get Jenkis to lessen the work he required, especially for Karlis. He also complained about the poor food they received, all to no avail.

Karlis and Adolfs got on with their lives as best they could. As summer approached, the days became longer and warmer. The two boys, when they could get away from the Jenkis house and the school, would spend time with friends down at the Daugava River and at the railway yards nearby. The Daugava in Riga was a wide, grey, sluggish river with plenty of activity as boats scurried across and down it. Karlis could just see on the other side Russian army activity as the front was only a few miles away. He would occasionally hear a stray shell thump into the ground nearby, causing him to dive nervously into a ditch or behind a tree. He would watch the rickety observer aircraft take off from the nearby aerodrome for the short flight to the trenches. It was all surprisingly peaceful, as there was only desultory activity on this part of the front.

Karlis was fascinated by the Jenkis sisters. He was not allowed to talk to them or, for that matter, be seen anywhere near them. But he did see them inside the house and when they were home-schooled by their mother. He thought them very pretty with their slim bodies and long brown hair, wearing their white petticoats and black leather boots which, compared to his tatty clothes and worn boots, looked beautiful.

Sometimes he would sneak a look through the window at the stylish dining room, to see the family eating good rations of bread, cuts of meat, potatoes and sauerkraut. His mouth would water at the smell of the roasting meat when he worked in the kitchen. Sometimes he would risk Jenkis' wrath by stealing a hunk of bread to share with his brothers. If he was caught, he knew he would be beaten, but he was hungry.

Despite the spring weather brightening and the flowers starting to bloom, the conditions in the Jenkis household for the Kohler brothers were getting worse. The rations received by the Jenkis family were reduced, so the amount of food the boys received decreased. Jenkis became more and more unwelcoming and constantly complained about how much of a problem and burden the boys were. For Arturs, it became humiliating and intolerable to have those silly sisters constantly giggling behind their hands at him and his brothers. He was also worried about Karlis' fascination with those girls. Only trouble could come from it.

Deciding that he had to do something, Arturs put a plan into action. Early in May he slipped out of school, after telling the headmaster what he planned to do, and went to the recruitment office in the old part of Riga. An elderly sergeant in a khaki uniform at the reception desk looked at him in his scruffy clothing and worn boots and sighed in despair.

"Name?" he barked in Russian.

"Arturs Kohler, sir!"

"Don't call me sir, boy. How old are you?"

"Eighteen sir … er … sergeant!" he lied.

The sergeant was not fooled for a minute. "OK, sit there and fill out this form. The officer will see you in a while."

Arturs took the papers and sat on a wooden bench near a number of other young men waiting.

After an hour Arturs' name was called by the desk sergeant who, with a wave, indicated a door. At a desk near a window in a surprisingly light and airy room sat an elderly Russian major in a perfect deep-grey dress uniform. His medals glittered in the light. As Arturs entered, he looked up from reading the paper.

He stared with hard, knowing eyes at the young man standing before him; took in his fine physique and shabby clothes. "Kohler, you wish to serve your motherland in this war?"

"Yes sir!"

The officer shuffled the papers and frowned. "You are a fine-looking young man. I see you are from Courland and are well educated. That is good. The Tsar is recruiting a Latvian Rifle regiment and will need soldiers."

The major looked up at Arturs standing stiffly before his table, looked down at his papers and then made a decision. "I am going to recommend that you apply for a position in the Officer's Academy here in Riga, Kohler. You will require a medical and to sit the entrance examination. The desk sergeant will give you a pass to the hospital. I expect you to be there at nine tomorrow morning. If you pass the medical and entrance examinations you will report to the academy for the summer intake on 1 June."

Arturs hurried out of the office onto the cobbled streets of the old town, feeling both elated and scared by what he'd done. He rushed around the corner to the post office and mailed a number of letters before heading back towards Jenkis' house, carefully approaching the house from the direction of the school. When he burst into the shed where they lived, he noticed that his brothers were already there. They both looked up as he entered.

"Where have you been? I didn't see you at school … better not let old Jenkis catch you wagging!" Adolfs said cheekily.

Arturs slumped onto his bed. "I've made a decision about something I have been thinking about for a long time. I've decided to enlist and have been down at the recruiting office."

His brothers gawked at him.

Adolfs gasped. "Are you mad? Part of the reason father sent us here was to get you away from all that! There is a war on, or did you forget that?"

"Course I didn't forget it. I'm trying for the Officer's Academy. There's every chance the war will be over before I get out and, anyway, we have to get away from here before old Jenkis works or starves us to death."

"Great … so you propose to go out and get yourself killed by some German shell or bullet instead! You really are mad …" Adolfs said tetchily.

Arturs glared at him. "The decision's been made. I'm your guardian here in father's absence and you will do as I say."

"What about us? Where do we go if we're not staying here?" Karlis asked.

It came out like a wail, and Arturs' flushed and angry face softened. "Karlis, I've made arrangements for you to go and stay with your godfather, Jonas, in Estonia, and you, Adolfs, will stay with Klavins," he answered quietly.

"Klavins? Isn't he taking his family to Siberia or somewhere?"

"Murmansk, I believe."

"You are mad … completely barking mad. But I suppose it couldn't be worse than having to live with old Jenkis. Murmansk might be quite an adventure."

Arturs smiled at his brother. "That's the spirit, Adolfs. Keep this quiet. I have a lot of work to do if I am to pass the academy entrance exam."

"But we'll all be separated!" Karlis cried.

His brothers looked at him soberly. There was nothing much they could say.

Once the decision had been made, Arturs felt relieved. He did not go to school the next day, sure he would receive a good hearing from the patriotic headmaster, and instead showed up at the Riga hospital as requested. He was shown into a white, grim, sterile room and a doctor in a white coat prodded and poked him, checked his reflexes, poked a finger into his mouth, checked his blood pressure and asked a whole lot of questions; finally declaring him to be fit.

"Take this to your recruiter and he will arrange for the academy to receive you for the examination. Next!"

After that it was just a matter of studying, which Arturs did by the light of the kerosene lantern in the shed every night. He passed the entrance examination with ease.

The day after passing the entrance examination and becoming a cadet, Arturs spent some of the roubles his father had given him and bought himself two cadet uniforms. He spent some money getting Karlis a train ticket to Yuryev in Estonia and put some money aside for his brothers to give to their godfather and Klavins respectively. That done, everything was ready.

"We move tomorrow. Pack your bags tonight," he told his brothers.

The next morning Arturs carefully dressed in his smart new cadet's uniform and walked straight into the house and into the dining room where the Jenkis family were having breakfast. Jenkis leapt to his feet, glowering. "What are you doing here, boy? Get out, before I whip you!"

His pretty daughters tittered, blushing, as they looked at the handsome young man resplendent in his smart new uniform.

Arturs stood his ground and answered rudely. "We're leaving, Jenkis. I'm enlisting … If you had any brains you would recognise a cadet's uniform. I've been admitted to the military academy and I'm taking my brothers away from here!"

He turned, bowed to Mrs Jenkis and her daughters, who blushed, eyes agog, as he marched out of the room, leaving Jenkis fuming impotently.

As Arturs walked out into the yard and back to the shed, he felt pleased. Satisfied he had done the right thing, he yelled at his brothers. "Get your stuff. We're leaving!"

His brothers grabbed their suitcases and followed him out onto the street. As he walked hurriedly towards the train station, he spoke rapidly to his brothers who struggled to keep up. "Karlis, I have a train ticket for your trip to Yuryev. I have written to your godfather and he is aware you are coming. Adolfs, I will drop you off with the Klavins family. They will be leaving for Murmansk soon. I suggest once you get there you try to get a job to help them with your upkeep."

Arturs looked earnestly at his brothers before continuing, breathless and emotional. "I hope this is all only temporary until this awful war is over and we can go home to our parents. Here is your share of the roubles that father gave me. Keep them hidden and spend them well. There is no more money after that is used up."

Arturs flagged down a taxi cab and told the driver to go to the train station. Once there, they sat and had tea while they waited for the train. Nobody said much – they were all a bit dumbstruck by what was happening. Arturs and Adolfs went with their brother onto the crowded platform and with heartfelt hugs watched as Karlis shoved his suitcase up the steep stairs and climbed up himself. As the train lurched forward, the steel wheels screeching on the slippery track as they struggled to get traction, Karlis hung out the window and waved until he could no longer see them. Suddenly he felt very alone. Alone and rushing away from his family. The three brothers would be separated for the rest of the war.

When he arrived in Yuryev in Estonia, Karlis received a warm welcome from his godparents and their son Alexander, in stark contrast to the cold reception by Jenkis in Riga. His godparents lived in the poorer part of the city, not far from the Emajõgi River.

"It is a small, pleasant city," Alexander told him as they travelled through to their home in Supilinn. "The Emajõgi River passes through it and joins Lake Võrtsjärv to Lake Peipus on the Russian border. We live not far from the river."

His godfather, noticing Karlis's gaze casting up over the buildings, continued. "With the Treaty of Nystad in 1721, the city became part of the Tsar's Empire and was initially known as Derpt," he told the boy. "Fires in the eighteenth century however destroyed much of the medieval architecture and the city was rebuilt in late baroque and neoclassical styles, like this." He pointed to a particular building. "We have a very good university here too, which was founded under Swedish occupation in 1632."

Eventually they arrived at a slightly rundown wood and tin single storey abode with a steep-roofed attic. The front door opened up straight onto the muddy street and there was no yard; but the house was cosy and warm in the wintertime and the family were happy there.

Karlis settled into life with his godparents and soon had a number of good friends from the neighbourhood. During the summer of 1915, it was almost possible to forget there was a war on as Karlis relished the freedom his kindly godparents gave him. He ranged far and wide with his new-found friends, and received regular letters from his brothers, as the Imperial Postal Service still worked efficiently. Arturs was doing very well at the Academy and Adolfs, now in Murmansk, had a job working in the forest. Karlis felt slightly envious of his middle brother, who seemed to be having quite an adventure with the Klavins family, though his letters were full of complaints about swarms of mosquitoes. There was still no word from his parents stuck on the other side of the front.

Soon after arriving in Yuryev, Karlis found a rusty, broken bicycle in a back room of the house. He asked his godparents if he could use it if he fixed it. They were agreeable, so he spent a week fixing it up as best as he could. He was soon wobbling down the street on the decrepit old machine, but at least it worked. He was lucky two of his friends also had bikes so it gave them a great deal of freedom to explore the countryside around the city.

They ventured, that summer, as far as the lakes; cycling down dusty tracks, past vast fields of rye and wheat and through small forests of conifers. They struggled up the gentle hills before hurtling down the other side, the reward being a refreshing swim at the end. Sometimes they would take a rudimentary fishing line of a stick, string and a bent nail as a hook and attempt to catch lunch, with little success. Karlis often arrived back late, dirty and sweaty, much to the consternation of his godparents.

The biggest adventure for Karlis and his friends was an epic camping trip down the beautiful Ahja River. He packed a bag with some black bread, cheese, a thin blanket, a coil of rope and some matches. His friends provided some potatoes, more bread and a small axe. Thus encumbered, they rode out in to the small, pristine river not far from the town.

After abandoning their bikes, they cobbled together a raft of sorts and launched the contraption into the river. By some miracle it did not sink immediately and they were able to drift down the clear waters of the forested river, occasionally passing low limestone cliffs. It was an idyllic way to spend an afternoon.

Unfortunately for the boys, their raft became stuck in a small rapid and started to disintegrate. They abandoned it and managed to scramble to the bank and luckily found a small clearing near the river below one of the low cliffs. It was a beautiful place. Here they lit a fire, ate the bread, cheese and roasted the potatoes in the coals, finally sleeping in the gentle warmth of the summer night in their blankets under the stars.

Karlis arrived back at his godparent's house late in the evening the next day; dirty, dishevelled and elated. It had been a great adventure. His godfather was not impressed and promptly grounded him. He was lucky. He knew his father would have been a lot more severe if he had tried such an escapade back at the farm.

The idyllic summer did not last. As the leaves in the trees turned to the yellows, browns and reds of the fall, the rains came; the beautiful light of the summer started to fade and the streets became muddy: it was time to go back to school. Back to a day boarding school, similar to the one he went to in Riga; back to the drudgery and discipline of the Tsar's education system.

Karlis was a good student and mostly stayed at the school, but he was bright and the lessons bored him. Sometimes he would 'go missing' and spend his time on the banks of the Emajõgi on the outskirts of the city, skimming rocks off the clear blue surface and attempting to fish.

Before too long the fall became winter and the beautiful colours of the leaves disappeared and were replaced by stark grey trunks and branches. The mud on the streets was replaced by ice and the ice by snow, which then became ice again. Things became harder as coal, bread and other foodstuffs became scarcer. The family was comfortable and warm in its little house and for Christmas they managed to get hold of a goose with what was left of the money Karlis had bought with him. It was a good Christmas: Karlis heard from his brothers, though was saddened by the long silence of his parents on the other side of the front.

The winter was surreal as the war seemed to grind to a halt. The appalling casualty rates seemed to slow but they received very little news while the vast Eastern Front seemed to stabilise. Everyone knew it was just a lull for the winter, but there was renewed optimism in the city. People ice skated on the river, tobogganed down the small hills and made snowmen. Karlis and his friends held regular and somewhat chaotic snowball fights.

Interestingly enough, they were much more successful at ice fishing in the Emajõgi River that winter than they ever were during the summer. The boys would rug up and take their fishing poles out to the river and cut a hole through the thick ice. They would join many other people who would brave the cold and fish to supplement their rations.

The carefree days of the summer of 1915 were replaced in the summer of 1916 by work and deprivation. The money Karlis had brought with him was mostly gone, and it became increasingly harder for the family to make ends meet. His godparents expected Karlis to help contribute by going out to collect wood from the countryside for the winter, which they anticipated would be a hard one. The countryside that summer, in contrast to the lush greenness and thriving crops of the previous summer, was sparse and brown in the unremitting heat.

His godfather grimly predicted famine. "It'll be a bad crop here this summer. If this situation is repeated across Russia, we could be in trouble next winter. Mark my words."

His godfather scanned the newspapers for whatever information he could find. That summer they were full of news about the massive Brusilov offensive the Russian army had launched somewhere in the Ukraine against the Austrians. The headlines were triumphal, as General Aleksei Brusilov used unique tactics to smash holes through the Austrian lines. There were also reports of the taking of hundreds of thousands of Austrian prisoners. The Russian army advanced rapidly into Galicia. But that caused problems, as the lines were extended and the grain in storage was diverted to the front. Also, reports trickled through about the appalling Russian casualties. In amongst all the war headlines, there were some reports of crop failures across the Empire and of dysfunctional government as the Tsarina became more and more in the thrall of a monk called Rasputin.

Karlis' godfather grumbled presciently. "The crop is poor, but all the stocks are being sent to the front. There will be famine this winter. Mark my words."

He then started to hoard what he could. Most of the fish they managed to catch was dried or pickled for the winter.

By September 1916, Brusilov's great offensive had ground to a halt, having advanced over fifty miles and smashing the Austrian army, which was not a significant fighting force for the remainder of the war.

The cost to Russia, however, was considerable as the appalling casualties were finally revealed and disaffection in the army reared its head. While Brusilov himself was revered by his soldiers, the incompetence of the other generals and continued dysfunction of the Tsar's government let them down and caused mass desertions, especially as the soldiers heard from agitators of the hardships back home. For the people of Yuryev most of this did not affect them, but the increasingly stringent rations did. It was simply becoming harder and harder to eat well.

By the winter of 1916 all of his godfather's predictions had come true. Karlis was taken out of school to stand for hours at a time in the breadlines. He would stand in his threadbare coat, stamping his worn boots and blowing onto his hands to keep warm as the line inched forward through the snow. Everything was grey and grim as the snow fell, icing up the streets. On the whole, everyone appeared to accept their lot and patiently waited in the queue, mostly keeping their thoughts to themselves. When he finally got to the end of the queue, he would hide his dark, hard loaf in his coat and scurry as quickly as he could down the grim streets, back to the warmth of his house. The family were able to eat and keep warm that winter because of his godfather's precautions, but it was difficult.

Whenever they could, the family read the newspapers and proclamations. There was news of desertions from the army that winter, along with food riots in St Petersburg and Moscow. While it was quiet in Yuryev, the news elsewhere was disturbing.

Worse for Karlis, months had passed since he had heard anything from either of his brothers. He did not even know where Adolfs was, or how Arturs was going. Was he still safe in the Academy, or had he already been sent off to the front? Karlis did not hear from his brothers again until the end of the war. The three brothers were totally out of contact. Karlis was alone in a troubled world.

IV

The Revolution (1917–1918)

A bitter wind blew, and a light sleet fell, making the icy, grey streets even more grim and depressing. Karlis stamped his feet on the slick pavement and blew on his hands before thrusting them into his pockets. The line seemed endless as the thickly coated, muffled people shuffled slowly forward. Nobody said much. Talking took too much effort, so they grimly kept to themselves.

Karlis noticed a number of men shuffling along the streets in threadbare grey-brown military greatcoats, stained and travel worn.

"Sir! Sir! Where are you heading?" he called out softly to a man who shuffled by him.

"What is it to you, boy?" the man growled quietly and continued on.

Karlis said to his friend in the line. "Keep my space. I'll be back in a minute."

He caught up to the man.

"Where are you from? You look hungry … here …" He held out a small piece of salted meat he'd been keeping for his lunch. The soldier grabbed it thankfully and ate hungrily.

"I am going home. To near Tallinn. I have to help my family. They are really suffering from the famine," he said between bites, looking for the first time at the boy who walked beside him. Karlis looked around and said quietly. "You're a deserter?"

He quickly added as the man glowered at him. "No. No. I understand. Your family must come first. It is very hard at the moment, as you can see. Was it very bad at the front?"

"Terrible. So many dead. Mud and trenches. Constant shelling. Terrible and senseless attacks. Bad food and water, little ammunition. Useless officers. There were not even enough rifles. We had to grab one from our dead comrades after going over!"

The man shuddered, hesitated, bowed his head, his face creasing with emotions, before saying sharply: "Leave me alone, boy. Leave me alone." He walked down the street more quickly, glancing fearfully over his shoulders.

Karlis let him go and ran back to the breadline. It had hardly moved in his absence.

When he finally reached head of the queue, an hour and a half later, he thrust the small, hard, black loaf into his coat pocket and hurried home. When he burst into the house from the street, it was cold inside as only a small fire was lit in the stove. They had run out of coal and were burning the last of the previous summer's wood that had been collected.

His godmother looked around when he entered and said to him quietly. "Come here, Karlis. I have to talk to you."

She stood wearily at the fire.

Taking the loaf from him, she continued. "There has been very bad news. Our beloved Tsar has been forced to abdicate because of the food riots, the strikes and protests in St Petersburg. There is a new government now. The so-called Provisional Government. I'm sure things will only get worse."

She looked at her godson sadly and continued gently. "I'm sorry, Karlis, but it is becoming too difficult for us to keep you. There is no money and very little food. I have arranged for you to go to stay with Lomanis. Do you know him?"

"No," the boy answered, looking sadly at his godmother. "Who is he?"

"He's a good man; a trader and quite well off for these troubled times. He has two sons and is happy to have you stay with him. He lives in a place called Vyshny Volochyok on the railway line between St Petersburg and Moscow. Your godfather is getting you a train ticket with the last of the money your father gave us. You will be leaving next week."

There was nothing more she could say and she turned back to the miserable fire that the pot of gruel for dinner bubbled away on.

Though upset by this turn of events, Karlis tried hard to hide it from his godparents. The week went past quickly. His godmother fixed up his tattered coat as best she could; his godfather found some glue and sole tacks and fixed up his boots. As he packed his suitcase the day before he was to catch the train, his godmother gave him some gloves and socks she had knitted.

She smiled sadly at him as she pushed them into the top of his suitcase. "Hopefully, you will not need these until later, but you never know, especially near Moscow!"

The next day, Karlis and his godfather trudged down the icy, muddy streets. The ice turned to mud during the day, before snap-freezing in the night to form an uneven, treacherous surface. Karlis carried his heavy suitcase through the streets, while his godfather walked somewhat absent-mindedly beside him. As they neared the train station, the streets became more crowded and chaotic as carts and vehicles competed for limited space. When they reached the station, his godfather handed over the train tickets and thrust a small loaf of black bread into his hands.

"It's all we have to give you," the man mumbled miserably. "Here are the tickets – one to St Petersburg, or Petrograd as they call it these days, and the other onto Vyshny Volochyok. You will arrive at the Baltiysky Station and have to make your way to the Nicholaevsky Station or whatever they call it now. Perhaps you should call it the Moscow Station? There should be plenty of time. But be careful and stay out of trouble. Petrograd is quiet now, so we have heard …"

His voice trailed away sadly. He hugged the boy roughly and left quickly, without another word. Karlis was left alone standing on another train station to catch another train. He quickly found his carriage and scrambled aboard, dragging his suitcase with him; he showed his ticket to the harassed ticket inspector, who hardly glanced at it before waving him on.

The train arrived in Petrograd, strangely enough, on time. Karlis grabbed his bag and joined the rush out onto the eerily quiet, grey streets. He noticed people, heads down, shuffling along the icy streets in grey coats. Everyone looked grim and preoccupied, the city atmosphere tense and full of foreboding. Armed men with red armbands guarding the station and on street corners were watched over, nervously, by khaki-clad soldiers. The men from both groups fidgeted apprehensively with their loaded weapons.

Karlis hurried out of what once had been an impressive train station, its two storeys of arched windows and towers flanking a large glass arch and clock now grimy, its pale-yellow paint peeling, and riddled with bullet holes from recent riots. He stopped and stood on the street outside the station, uncertain, as battered trams clanged past.

One of the armed Red Guards approached him. His gun looked huge, menacing. "Boy! Where're you going?" the man growled in accented Russian.

"To Vyshny Volochyok, sir," Karlis gasped excitedly.

When he heard the boy's accent, the man's face softened and he spoke quietly in Latvian. "Where? You'll need the Moscow line. You're a long way from home, boy. Here, this truck is going to the Nicholaevsky Station."

The man grimaced when he said the word. He waved a battered truck over and spoke sharply to the driver, who tersely indicated for Karlis to get on the back.

As the truck, fumes belching from its overused and undermaintained engine, rattled down the potholed, muddy streets, Karlis shivered from the cold and pulled his coat around him; braced against the lurch of the vehicle. He noticed more loitering soldiers and recent damage from the riots. People still queued patiently for bread, stamping nervously in the cold, watched over by groups of soldiers. The streets were edgy as the opposing groups faced off. The truck soon ground to a stop on Nevsky Prospekt outside the imposing two-storeyed train station. Karlis jumped off and thanked the driver and looked up a little overawed at the edifice. The building once again showed signs of the recent rioting and general deprivation of the war. The clock in its high central tower, however, still regularly chimed the hour.

Karlis gathered his wits and walked across the wide cobbled street, dodging the trams and other mostly horse-drawn carriages before passing through a large arched doorway into a high vaulted hallway and onto the platforms. He sat down; leant up against the wall in the cold to wait for the train, and ate some of the chunk of bread he carried. It was hard and stale, but he was ravenous and ate hungrily.

After a long, uncomfortable and tiresome journey in a rundown, crowded third-class carriage, Karlis finally arrived in Vyshny Volochyok, a pretty little trading town halfway to Moscow, on the Vyshnevolotskoye Reservoir. A canal ran through it, connecting the reservoir to the Msta River, a north-flowing river that terminated in Lake Ilmen. Though the town had a number of sawmills and a large textile factory on its outskirts, Karlis thought Vyshny Volochyok had seen better days. Even so, a number of pretty churches had their doors open and the stylish shopping arcades were busy; he noted the town seemed largely untouched by the war and troubles in the rest of Russia.

He was greeted warmly at the train station by Lomanis and his two sons. Lomanis, an energetic, short, slightly plump man with dark hair, travelled extensively throughout Russia – sometimes as far away as Siberia – selling lemonade. His sons, Jancka and Nikoaijs, who were slightly older than Karlis, were already taller than their father.

Lomanis and his family lived in a modest but comfortable two-storeyed house near the centre of the town, not far from the railway station. Mrs Lomanis, a tall, pretty, but listless, wan woman – a stark contrast to the exuberance of Lomanis and their sons – gave Karlis a room to himself.

Soon after Karlis arrived, Lomanis left for Moscow and Vladivostok on a business trip, telling the boys to look after their mother before he left. He also arranged for them all to be employed gathering and stacking wood at one of the local sawmills.

"You are all strapping lads and can contribute to your upkeep in these hard times. A bit of hard work will not hurt you," was all he said.

Karlis and the two brothers were soon best of friends and, with Lomanis away, had the run of the place.

Life was hard but good that summer. The war and the troubles in Petrograd and Moscow were largely forgotten and the boys worked during the week stacking the wood they gathered. Jancka soon figured out they could stack less wood and make the pile look impressive by leaving large holes in the stacks.

They also recovered logs that had been floated down the river by the millers. It was a great job to have in the heat of the summer as it involved walking out into the cool waters of the reservoir and pulling and shoving the logs onto land before rolling them up the embankment to the yard.

The mosquitoes were terrible, and the only peace from them to cover up as much as possible. Karlis soon discovered the best thing he could do was wrap his face and head up in a scarf, just leaving his eyes visible, even if he did look like a bandit.

Away from the wood stacking, the boys formed a gang of like-minded youth and ranged far and wide. Jancka and Nikoaijs stowed away on goods trains that went past the town and showed Karlis how to do it. "Come, we'll show you. Stand here. See the train? We try to get on before it picks up too much speed."

As the train approached, they sprinted alongside the track.

"Come on! Come on!" they yelled at him as Jancka, who was slightly older and stronger, scrambled onto the carriage. The other two were still running alongside when Jancka reached down and heaved up his brother.

"Grab my hand! Grab my hand!" they screamed, hanging on and leaning down off the carriage.

Karlis, with one last gasp, leapt at the now fast-moving carriage, grasping desperately at their outstretched hands. At the last moment they swung him up and all three collapsed in a pile onto the hard boards of the carriage floor.

Karlis lay on the boards for a number of minutes recovering his breath. After a while, he sat up and enjoyed the wind in his hair and the rattle and clanking of the wheels on the tracks. "Where are we going?"

"The train crosses the Tvertsa, a tributary of the Volga not far away. We'll get off there. Do you swim?"

"Sure do!" Karlis grinned. "How do we get off?"

Jancka and Nikoaijs laughed. "You'll see!"

The boys lay back and enjoyed the view as the train passed through low hills, small rustic villages with their farmland, forests of birch and conifer trees and small fast-flowing streams. After a couple of hours, the train, in a screech of wheels and steam, started to slow as it approached a large river. Jancka and Nikoaijs stood up.

"Quick, there is not much time. We'll get off as the train slows to cross the river," Jancka grinned rakishly.

Karlis gasped. "You're mad!"

Jancka's grin grew wider.

He grabbed hold of Karlis and his brother by the hands. "Come on! One, two three, *go!*"

With a sudden jump, he leapt into the unknown, taking the other two boys with him. They plunged into the wide, deep, sluggish river. When he hit the water, Karlis gasped as the cold took his breath away. He surfaced in a rush. The other two boys' heads bobbed up nearby. Karlis swam ashore and lay on the bank in the sun, breathing deeply to regain his breath, the other two soon joining him.

"Woo hoo!" they whooped exuberantly, the adrenalin still coursing through their veins.

A relatively short one-hour walk along the railway line was Tver, the city at which the Tsertsa and Volga rivers converged. As they wandered the streets, hungry and tired, Karlis noticed it too was largely unaffected by the war; the imposing neoclassical buildings still in good condition. Near the edge of the city they found a small house with plum trees in the front yard and helped themselves to the sweet fruit before being chased away by the irate owner.

Then time ran short and Jancka declared, "We should head home. The trains here leave regularly … we'll get on one!"

Once again, as the large goods train laboriously approached, they scrambled aboard. Karlis stretched out on the boards of the empty carriage and fell asleep to the click clack, click clack of the wheels on the track.

His dream was broken by a rough shaking and he woke with a start.

"Wake up! Wake up! We're here. We have to get off!" Jancka urged.

The sun was setting over the fields as the train slowed at a bend in the track near the approach to Vyshny Volochyok.

"Come on. We have to go. When we jump, you have to hit the ground running. Take a running jump. Once again one, two, three, GO!"

The three of them ran off the carriage and leapt onto the ground as the train rumbled by, scrambling to maintain their balance as they careered down the railway embankment and onto the flat of a field near the town. Somehow, they managed to pull up without hurting themselves.

Mrs Lomanis was too tired to comment when three dirty, dishevelled boys slipped in the back door.

It was a long, warm, and mostly fine, summer. Sometimes, warm rain fell gently, exhilarating and cooling sweaty bodies as they worked.

The boys often visited a local river on the weekends where they would swim, boat and pick mushrooms. One time, they noticed a number of pretty young women swimming not far away. These girls looked risqué and alluring, their wetness and long costumes, cut above the knee, accentuating their slim, pretty physiques. Intrigued, the boys approached them. Jancka whistled uproariously, and the girls blushed, laughed, ran out of the water and covered up with towels.

Karlis boldly went up to them. "Who are you? I'm Karlis. The loud one is Jancka and this is Nikoaijs."

The girls tittered.

The boldest of them answered brightly, "I'm Lebegiv. Nice to meet you, Karlis!" Karlis was certain her lovely smile was directed straight at him.

She had long dark hair, large, bright hazel eyes and a slim shapely figure – Karlis instantly became smitten with her; tried to spend as much time as he could with her. They developed a strong friendship and, much to his other friends' amusement, he started going for long walks along the river with her.

Jancka and Nikoaijs ribbed him mercilessly about it. "Karlis is in *loorrve!*"

He ignored them.

After a while, Karlis decided to boldly show Lebegiv how he felt about her, and stole some lilacs from a garden; gallantly presented them to her. She laughed and accepted the flowers, burying her pretty nose in them as she inhaled the scent. "They're lovely, Karlis! Thank you so much."

Then she kissed him, directly on the lips, before slipping away from him. He chased after her, catching her, breathless and excited.

Suddenly, he heard a yell. "Boy! Where did you get those flowers?"

Karlis stuttered, looking woebegone and the moment was lost.

Lebegiv laughed at his expression, before taking his hand and running down the road with him, away from the enraged woman. "Did you steal these?"

"Yes, only for you."

She laughed again. "She was a grumpy old biddy anyway!"

The famine was over, but the food shortages were starting to bite and once again they heard about agitation in Petrograd and Moscow as the Provisional Government struggled to retain control. The war ground on and at times they heard about casualties and desertions. Despite this, it was strangely peaceful in Vyshny Volochyok. Between working in the mill yard and ranging far and wide on the railway network, the boys helped supplement their meagre rations by stealing eggs, potatoes and fruit from their neighbours. Most of the time they got away with it.

After eight weeks, Lomanis returned from his business trip on the Trans-Siberian. He was full of stories of his travels and the hardships he encountered.

"The Reds will take over," he predicted dismally. "The Provisional Government is losing its grip. They managed to crack down in Petrograd a week ago, but I'm sure that is only a temporary reprieve. The Red Guards are everywhere and are getting stronger. They regularly confront Provisional Government troops these days in Moscow. Everywhere the people are tired of this accursed war. The Reds are promising to stop it and are getting a lot of support, especially in Moscow it seems. I really do not think things are going to get better for Mother Russia, for a long time after!

"Oh well, what can we do …?" he concluded somewhat fatalistically.

"We should support ending the war, Father," Jancka piped up.

His father glared at him. "I'm afraid of civil war … Let's hope not …"

Lomanis' voice trailed off and he sat miserably near the open window and stared outside at the peaceful scene on the street. He didn't say another word for quite a while.

Life went on. Lomanis went on another brief trading trip and the boys once again regained the freedom they had lost when he came home.

Some of the turmoil in the larger cities encroached into Vyshny Volochyok for the first time: late in the summer, a strike in the timber mills and textile factory occurred, and workers from the local sawmills and factories, along with other agitators, marched the streets waving red flags and shouting slogans. "Peace, bread, land and all power to the Soviets."

They dispersed peacefully when the local mayor and police commandant went out and spoke to them.

Jancka was caught up in the moment and rushed out and joined the newly formed city Red Guards unit. He was soon sauntering around the house proudly sporting a red armband – much to Lomanis' disgust – and immediately lost his job at the sawmill because of it. The other two boys continued to work stacking wood.

After the strikes, an air of general tension and excitement fell over the city, this also reflected in the Lomanis household. Lomanis himself tried to stay neutral, while Nikoaijs was not that interested in Red Guards and slogans – he just wanted the old times to return. Mrs Lomanis was too ill and listless to take part in any of these discussions, and father and sons all agreed to disagree, out of respect for her.

In late September, Lomanis, having recently returned from Moscow, called Karlis into his study.

He looked at the tall, muscular, good-looking boy in front of him and said quietly: "I'm afraid there's bad news, Karlis. The Russian army has virtually collapsed. The Germans are on the move again and have taken Riga. An attempted coup against the Provisional Government by General Kornilov has been a disaster and greatly strengthened the Bolsheviks. It's only a matter of time before they take over. I'm afraid if you stay here you will be caught up in all of this, so I'm going to send you back to your godparents. At least you will be closer to home if the government does collapse. God help us all if that happens. There is a train going to Petrograd in two days. You'll be on it."

He considered at the boy fondly and smiled. "I believe Jancka and Nikoaijs have taught you how to catch trains!"

Karlis nodded slightly abashed, but expecting something like this would happen, answered. "I shall pack at once, sir."

Karlis only had a short time to say goodbye to all the people he had met that summer. It was really hard, especially with Lebegiv. When he last saw her, he hugged her and kissed her. They clung together desperately before Lebegiv gently pushed him away, looking sadly at him.

She still managed to smile, before saying rather forlornly. "Maybe I'll see you again."

"Yes, I really hope so. I'll never forget you."

She smiled again but said nothing.

A few days later, Karlis clutched his battered suitcase. He stood by the railway line with Jancka and Nikoaijs. Both boys pressed some bread and fruit they had acquired into his hands and hugged him as a laden goods train approached slowly from the station.

He quickly shoved the food in the top of his suitcase and smiled, trying to keep up his good cheer. "Here I go again; one more time!"

The other two nodded grimly.

Jancka grabbed his suitcase as the train chugged labouriously towards them. "Come on, quickly now!"

The train drew increasingly closer, stream and smoke from the engine billowing over them as they both started to run as it slowly passed and gathered speed. Karlis jumped up, grasped hold of the side of a carriage and hauled himself up. He then leaned out to get his case from Jancka who was sprinting alongside.

"Quickly, quickly, Jancka!" he bellowed.

With a last lurch, Jancka heaved the suitcase up and Karlis deftly caught it, tumbling back onto the floor of the carriage.

"Good luck!" Jancka screamed as the train gathered pace, and the distance between them increased.

Karlis picked himself up and waved as the other boys disappeared around a bend.

He would never see Jancka or Nikoaijs again. Much later, he heard they had been separated during the ensuing civil war in Russia. In a terrible family tragedy, Jancka found his brother's dead body outside Petrograd. Both brothers had taken part, on opposing sides, in the battle for Petrograd, a major assault on the city by a White army under General Yudenich in October 1919.

The carriage squeaked and groaned as the train clattered down the track. The wind had changed, so the smoke billowing from the straining engine blew straight over the carriages. Even though the day was warm, the wind had started getting chilly. Karlis shivered and, burrowing in his suitcase, found his coat. He wrapped it around himself and sat back against the sides of the carriage and ate the plums Jancka and Nikoaijs had given him. The train flashed past the fields, lakes, rivers and forests of north-western Russia as it approached the capital. On occasion other trains rumbled past in a gust of noise, wind and smoke.

After what seemed a long time, the train finally moved through the outskirts of Petrograd, past grim, ugly looking factories belching fumes from large smokestacks. The armament factory compounds, many with red flags and banners along the walls and fences, were closely guarded by jumpy soldiers of the Provisional Government. The few workers visible looked scruffy, surly and resentful, the atmosphere in this factory district oppressive.

Karlis decided he should get off as the train slowly passed an open patch of dirt near one of the factories. Grasping his suitcase tightly, he jumped from the carriage; landed hard on the ground and careered down the rail embankment. He lost his footing and rolled down with a crash, becoming separated from his suitcase in the process. Landing in a heap, he lay there, gasping for breath. Eventually, when his lungs had refilled, he gingerly picked himself up and brushed the dirt and grass from his clothes. He was in one piece. He found his suitcase, which was even more battered and scratched but amazingly enough, it too had survived the fall.

Picking up his case, Karlis walked onto a road and flagged down a peasant with a horse and cart. The man, rugged up in his greatcoat, tersely indicated with his thumb that Karlis could climb up on the back. They clip-clopped down the dirt street, past desolate looking apartment buildings attached to the factories, into the better part of the city near the centre. Here, the Red Guards seemed to have taken over and strutted around arrogantly. The few solders of the Provisional Government, guarding essential government buildings, nervously kept their distance.

Karlis got off at Nevsky Prospekt, which he recognised from his previous visit, and walked towards the Baltiysky Station where he hoped to get a train to Yuryev. The capital was in a state of extreme tension. People walked the streets warily, not looking anyone in the eye. Trucks full of Red Guards rumbled by. They seemed to be going in the same direction he was, so Karlis managed to scramble onto the back of one and clung precariously to the tailgate, his suitcase swinging in the breeze. The Bolshevik soldiers on the back laughed at this audacious boy, but let him stay. Once at the station, Karlis got off with the soldiers and tried to blend in.

He approached one and asked carefully. "Where are you going, comrade?"

The man, with a passing glance answered curtly. "Estonia, tomorrow morning. What are you doing here?"

"Trying to get back to my relatives in Estonia, comrade."

The man shrugged indifferently.

He had seen many lost waifs in the last few months. "Good luck."

The soldiers, on arrival at the station, bivouacked for the night in the spacious arrival and departure hall. Karlis found a small bit of floor and sat to eat a little of his bread. He then wrapped himself up in his coat and tried to sleep on the hard, cold floor. Though hungry and exhausted, he slept surprisingly well.

The next morning Karlis woke with a start. The station had exploded into activity as a train shunted into one of the platforms and the Red Guards started to board it. Karlis was caught up in the moment and heard orders being shouted in Latvian. Quickly eating his last bit of stale black bread, he ran towards the noise. Once again, he was lucky as he managed to stow away on the train without anyone noticing, just before it slowly left the station. He perched between the passenger carriages, clinging precariously to the coupling, while wedging his suitcase near the carriage rear door.

The morning was cold and clear, the ice just starting to appear along with the colours of autumn. As the train gathered momentum and steamed into the countryside outside Petrograd, the cold wind buffeted him. The air gushed around his coat and his hands felt chilled despite his gloves. Nevertheless, it was manageably uncomfortable in the clear fresh air and sun. As the train rattled down the track nobody noticed the boy hanging on dangerously to the rear of the carriage. He sometimes stood on the coupling and stretched his legs, stamping his feet against the cold wind, or sat on the thin ledge against the door wrapped in his coat, desperately trying to keep warm. The tracks rushed below him and the carriages swayed in unison. Inside, he heard boisterous singing as the unruly soldiers indulged in too much vodka.

As the train rushed down the line towards Estonia, Karlis started to feel the cold. Stranded between the carriages for hours, he was cold, hungry and tired to the point of exhaustion. As the afternoon wore into evening, a cold rain started to fall and his discomfort increased. Now he started to shiver violently and it took all his concentration to hang grimly onto the train and not succumb to exhaustion. He knew if he fell asleep it would be all over.

Just when he was at the point of losing his will and succumbing to the cold, the door between the carriages flung open. Startled, Karlis nearly plunged into the darkness rushing below him. He was slipping off, still clinging with a vice like grip with his frozen hands to his suitcase, when a strong arm grabbed him and hauled him into the carriage.

A voice boomed in his ears as he collapsed. "Fucking hell, boy! How long have you been out there?"

Karlis babbled incoherently in Latvian.

The man who rescued him was big, with a large moustache, and wearing the khaki uniform of one of the Latvian Red Rifle Regiments. "Ivan!" he roared to one of his Russian comrades. "A blanket and some tea for the boy!"

He spoke kindly in Latvian to the urchin he had rescued. "You are a bold one! Are you trying to get home?"

Karlis shivered violently and gratefully wrapped himself in the blanket. His hands shook uncontrollably as he tried to sip the hot tea, the tremors reducing as he slowly recovered and warmed up.

"Yes, comrade, to Estonia to stay with my godparents before trying to get back to Riga," he managed to slur, slowly and hesitantly.

"Not much chance of that. Riga has been taken by the Huns. We are moving to the front to protect Petrograd. What's your name, boy?"

No answer came as the tea fell out of Karlis' hand with a crash as he slipped into an fitful, exhausted sleep.

The tough Latvian soldiers developed a soft spot for the boy who had stowed away on their train. He became like a company mascot and they looked after him as he gradually recovered from his ordeal. They told him they were being rushed to the Estonian border as the Bolsheviks took control of the country, nominally in the name of the Provisional Government. Yet they dropped Karlis off at Yuryev.

Nobody greeted him at the station, so he wearily walked the short distance to Supilinn, down the cobbled streets in the centre of the town, past the impressive buildings. Everywhere flew banners of the Bolsheviks, and Red Guards loitered on street corners. There was no sign of government troops. To all intents and purposes the Bolsheviks had taken over the town. He was glad when he passed into the poorer surrounds of Supilinn, down the familiar dirt streets and dilapidated wooden buildings. This part of town seemed much the same as before, and Karlis guessed the people here would be the natural supporters of the Bolsheviks and would be left alone by the Red Guards.

He walked up to his godparents' house and nervously knocked on the door. It was opened by his godmother.

She looked at the thin, dirty, dishevelled boy and cried out in delight and shock. "Karlis!" Then she flung her arms around him before bursting into tears. "Come in! Come in! You must be thirsty and hungry. I'll make some tea and heat up some water for a bath. Take those dirty clothes off. You can wear some of your godfather's old clothes for now."

Things had grown worse in Yuryev since Karlis had left. The Bolsheviks had effectively taken over the city, but ruled chaotically. There was little food and no coal. His godfather had, once again, taken the precaution of hoarding as much food as he could for the winter, and sent Karlis out to collect wood. Karlis was enrolled as a day student in the boarding school but rarely attended class. When he did, the classes were cold and bleak and there was no food for lunches any more so he went hungry.

Soldiers still loyal to the Provisional Government and the Red Guards had stabilised the front just north of Riga, but nobody was able to stop the German army invading the islands off the coast of Estonia in October 1917. The people of Yuryev prepared as well as they could for a hard winter. Some thought it was only a matter of time before the Germans took over the rest of Baltic States, and maybe even the capital as well.

While civil disorder increased and even the schools were struggling, the one place the chaotic government managed to keep running well was the hospital in the city. The patients in this institution received far better rations than people out on the streets. Karlis took to faking various ailments so he could be admitted to the hospital and receive a decent meal.

In early November 1917 the inevitable happened. The Provisional Government collapsed and Lenin's Bolsheviks took power in Petrograd, though this had little effect on the citizens of Yuryev – they were too engrossed in eking out an existence. Some celebratory trouble occurred as the local garrison boisterously looted the liquor stores and shot their rifles into the air. For a couple of days, in the aftermath of what became known as the October Revolution, things were precarious in the city. The remnants of the army that had remained loyal to Kerensky melted away, leaving a power vacuum. Karlis and his godparents stayed indoors.

Order was finally restored by the tough, disciplined Latvian Riflemen, who were diverted into the city before being rushed back to Petrograd to support the precarious new regime. And a semblance of normality returned.

Karlis and his godparents carried on with life as best they could that bleak, depressing winter. The streets were dark and icy, the skies grey, and sleet and snow fell on stark, leafless trees. Their house, which was relatively warm and light, was a small oasis of comfort. While food was scarce, they had at least one hot meal a day. After the Latvian Riflemen left, the chaotic Bolshevik government in Yuryev managed to keep control. Rumours circulated around the city about civil war in Russia, despite the steady stream of positive, patriotic propaganda the local authorities disseminated. Karlis' godfather managed to find out what was really going on outside the city, and lamented the situation deeply.

"The front is still stable. There seems to be enough soldiers there to at least watch the Germans, though I fear a serious offensive will smash through the front. We're only safe because it's winter! There are terrible rumours of civil war in Russia. I hope that is not the case. I hear there is a new military leader, a man called Trotsky, who is reorganising the Bolshevik soldiers. Hopefully he will be able to stop the Germans. We should pray for the future."

As winter continued, Karlis was in and out of the hospital, for both genuine and faked ailments. His constitution suffered from the deprivations and hunger that affected everyone in the city. The hospital was still the only place people could get a decent hot meal, so he determined to take advantage of that as much as he could. His schooling was abandoned, and he was occupied for hours at a time standing in the cold, grim bread queues and using up his strength to collect wood for the fire. On rare occasions, he was able to get away and supplement their rations by doing some ice fishing in the Emajõgi River.

One day, when spring was slowly making its presence felt, and a weak pale sun managed to shine through the grey skies and slowly melt the ice during the day – though it froze up again at night – there was terrible news.

Karlis' godfather burst into the house waving a proclamation. "The Germans are coming. The Germans are coming. We've been betrayed. We've been abandoned!" He was white and shaking; almost hysterical.

Karlis grabbed the bit of paper and read it quickly, the brief, terse communiqué announcing peace with the German Empire and ordering the remaining Red Guards units to retreat towards Petrograd.

"Surely peace will be good, Godfather?"

"But why the war? Why all the bloodshed and hardship to defend the Empire only to abandon it? Maybe we should have saved millions of lives and just let the Germans march in," the distraught man almost wailed.

Then he stopped, embarrassed, and his face lit up a bit. "You're right, Karlis. If the Germans take over, you'll be able to go home! Your parents will not be on the other side of the front anymore!"

Suddenly, they both laughed, the man and the boy who were so different, but so close. They laughed, for the first time since the start of that awful winter.

Things happened rapidly. The Red Guards left in a hurry, but not before looting anything that was not bolted down. Soon after the stern faced, grey uniformed German army took over the city. They disembarked from a train in a clash of arms and harsh guttural commands and marched to the local hall, where they were being accommodated. Karlis snuck into the station to watch. He was struck by how well disciplined and equipped the troops were, in stark contrast to the unruly, underequipped Red Guards. With their steel helmets, the soldiers seemed to exude menace; but they were only men. It soon became apparent that all the horror stories that had been disseminated about German atrocities were largely untrue. The garrison solders, at least in Yuryev, stayed in their quarters.

After the shock of being occupied by an enemy army, the people of Yuryev continued with their lives. As stories filtered through about the bloodshed of the civil war in Russia, they were grateful the Germans at least brought with them peace and security, though the rations did not increase and life was still hard. Something else started to happen in the city: People began to talk quietly about an independent Estonia now that the Bolsheviks had left. But that seemed to be a distant dream as the all-conquering German army seemed in complete control and entrenched for the long term. At least the people dared to dream.

In June 1918, Karlis mustered the courage to approach the local German commandant's office to get a pass to go home; back to Latvia to hopefully see his parents for the first time in over three years. Nervously, he approached the impressive town hall where the Germans had set up their headquarters. He was able to walk past the sentries into the building where he joined a queue to see the receptionist. Once he reached the head of the queue, he was passed onto a German sergeant who issued the document with an indifferent shrug. And that was that. Karlis was impressed with the German efficiency.

Excitedly, he danced out of the office and onto the street, clutching his precious pass. He rushed down to the telegraph office and spent what little money had on a telegram to his parents then scampered to the train station and purchased a ticket. After that he had spent all the money they had. His godparents did not begrudge him the money; it was not in their nature.

In a bitter-sweet moment, Karlis finally went with his

godparents and Alexander to the station for the last time. He was both excited to be going home and sad to be leaving such loving people who had treated him like a son and brother. He hugged and kissed his godmother, shook his godfather's hand and quickly hugged him and Alexander before he climbed up into the carriage. The train left exactly on time – German precision. Karlis hung out the window and waved at his godparents for as long as he could see them before settling back in his seat.

The train finally arrived at the train station in Dobele.

Karlis climbed down the steep steps of the carriage and onto the platform with nervous anticipation. And there they were: his parents and Adolfs. He dropped his suitcase and ran towards them, laughing and crying as he hugged them all, they so excited and pleased to see him after such a long time they all spoke at the same time, competing for his attention in their exuberance. "Welcome, welcome. You're safe! It's so good to see you. We were so worried."

Karlis looked around.

"Where's Arturs?" he asked breathlessly.

Their faces fell and their smiles faded.

Finally, Heinrich answered quietly, a worried look on his face, "Shhhh … he's at the farm. It's not safe for him. He has to keep his head down, as there is a German garrison here. Being a former cadet and subaltern in the Russian army, he would be interned if they found him."

"Your father was furious when he heard about that Academy escapade," Wilhelmina chimed in.

Heinrich smiled wryly at his wife. "What's done is done. Come on, son. You must be hungry and tired. We have a lot to talk about but we can do that at home."

He put his arm around his son's shoulders and they walked out of the train station, past the German sentry, and onto the street where the cart was waiting. In the harness was the same horse, looking thin, worn and old, its hair patchy and sparce, that Heinrich had saved from the Russian army in what seemed like a lifetime ago.

V

The Soldier (1919)

The hulking cruiser lay at anchor just outside the Latvian port of Liepāja in the steel grey Baltic Sea. Low waves lapped against its hull causing a gentle rocking motion. Its forward guns, elevated for extreme range, were trained silently and menacingly over the city. An ensign of the Royal Navy hung limply from one of its masts in the desultory wind.

Arturs Kohler was strangely comforted by its presence. He lay in the snow, in a small stark thicket on a hillock outside the port, his rifle on the ground in front of him. After a while, he turned his attention away from the cruiser and trained his field binoculars towards the soldiers in front of him. They were dug in, just out of the range of the cruiser's guns, in a stark white field, a small thicket of oaks on their left. There was no movement. It looked like the Red Army's advance into Latvia had finally stopped, and Arturs was glad of that. He was tired of the continual retreat that had dogged the fledgling Latvian Army, which he had joined as soon as he could at the end of the German occupation, despite his father's protestations.

A young lieutenant slid carefully up beside him. "The boss wants to see you, Arturs. I'm here to relieve you. Is there anything happening?"

"No, it's all quiet. Take care, though, Harijs. There's a sniper in the thicket over to the left."

Arturs backed quietly away on his stomach, pulling his rifle along in front of him, before he stood up and moved quickly back towards the city behind him.

Colonel Oskars Kalpaks looked out the window of his office at the cruiser in the distance. He was a handsome young man, with hard brown eyes and a finely manicured moustache of which he was inordinately proud. There was a knock at the door.

He turned back and stood behind his desk and barked. "Come in!"

The door opened and a young man in a dirty, crumpled uniform marched into the office and stood to attention in front of the desk; snapped a sharp salute. "Lieutenant Arturs Kohler reporting as requested, sir."

"Ah, Kohler, stand at ease," Kalpaks stared thoughtfully at the man in front of him and looked at a paper on his desk. "You are fluent in German, Kohler?"

"Yes, sir."

"Good, I have an important assignment for you. I want you to be our liaison with the Freikorps Iron Division. You will report to General von der Goltz immediately, though I suggest you put on a clean uniform first. For your information only, Kohler, I have been forced to subordinate our forces to the Germans for the big push against the Reds in March. Your job will be to keep me informed of all their plans. Is that clear? I'm giving you a field promotion to brevit Major for the appointment. Here are your orders. That will be all!"

When the young officer left, Kalpaks turned and stared out the window at the silhouette of the cruiser. He hated what he had to do. He had only recently been fighting against the Germans in the Imperial Russian Army. Now he was being forced to fight with them against the Reds, who were fellow Latvians.

Arturs felt excited and nervous about the appointment and about his temporary promotion. It was quite a responsibility. He put on his smartest uniform and his new shoulder insignia and went to the headquarters of General Rüdiger von der Goltz, the formidable commander of the German Freikorps in Latvia. He walked up the stairs and received the salute of the sentry and proceeded to an ante-room, where an immaculately dressed captain sat at a desk. The captain, noting his uniform and insignia, insolently stood and lazily saluted. Arturs ignored the slight and handed over his papers.

Speaking fluent German, he said. "I'm here to report to the General, Hauptmann, please announce me."

The captain looked at the papers, and went into a room.

He soon returned. "The Generalmajor will see you now, Herr Major."

Arturs went into the room and, snapping to attention, saluted the man standing near the window. Von der Goltz was a tall handsome man in his mid-fifties, though he looked younger, with a thin moustache and cold, grey eyes. He had Arturs' papers in his hand.

He looked sternly at the young man standing rigidly in front of him, noticing the new insignia on his smart uniform. "So, you are to be Kalpaks' spy on my staff, Kohler?"

Arturs said nothing and continued to stand at attention, not so much as batting an eyelid.

Von der Goltz laughed, ironically. "So be it. Report to my Chief of Staff; Oberst von Hessler."

He dismissed Arturs with a wave of his hand.

Arturs saluted again and, turning sharply on his heel, left the room.

For the next month, Arturs was busy. Kalpaks and von der Goltz were building up their forces with British naval and materiel support. Arturs' position was sensitive and he had to be careful and diplomatic. Tension existed between the headstrong German General and Kalpaks. Von der Goltz seemed, as far as Arturs was concerned, to be determined to undermine the formation and training of Latvian national units and also appeared to be trying to drive a wedge between the Latvians and the British. In part due to Arturs' insights and Kalpaks' patience, the forces were able to cooperate. By the end of February, the preparations for an offensive against the Bolsheviks were complete. Von der Goltz called a final briefing at his headquarters.

The meeting was held in a large room overlooking the harbour. Arturs stood unobtrusively at the back with a young British naval lieutenant. They were there to quietly translate, as required. At the briefing were Kalpaks, Major Alfred Fletcher, commander of the Baltische Landeswehr, Rear Admiral Walter Cowan, commander of the British naval squadron in the Baltic, and Oberst von Hessler. They stood around a table on which sat a large map of the region.

Von der Goltz called everyone to order. "Gentlemen, first of all, as there has been some unavoidable tension between us recently, I wish to assure you that the Freikorps has one aim. That is the defeat of the Bolsheviks in the Baltic region!"

"Here, here," Walter Cowan muttered.

Von der Goltz continued. "With that in mind, we will launch our offensive against the Red Army on 3 March. The Iron Division will attack eastwards towards Saldus. Fletcher, you will, with support from Admiral Cowan, attack northwards and take the port of Ventspils. Once these objectives are achieved the Iron Division and the Baltische Landeswehr will march on Riga in a pincer movement via Jelgava, Ugāle and Jūrmala."

He pointed at the towns on the map with his finger as he spoke and paused for effect. "That way, God willing, we will clear the Reds out of Kurzeme un Zemgale forever!"

Kalpaks nodded appreciatively at this deliberate use of the Latvian names for the region. Von der Goltz stared around at the group. "Are there any questions?" There were none so he said, "Good, you have your orders. Good luck!"

Von der Goltz began his assault on the Red Army lines with a short intense artillery barrage, supported by the grim and menacing cruiser, which pounded their positions with its guns as well. He then followed up by a shock assault on the lines, similar to the method developed by Brusilov in 1916. It worked. The poorly led, trained and disciplined Bolshevik troops were broken and swept aside by the assault.

A few days later Arturs was involved in an unfortunate incident that soured relations between the Freikorps and the Latvian government. He had been on horseback with a small escort of mounted Latvian soldiers, approaching Kalpaks' lines that were to the north of the road to Saldus, when he heard a German machine gun open fire on his right. Thinking it might have been a surprise Bolshevik attack, he had spurred his horse toward the gunfire, urging his escort forward. They approached the gunfire over a small hill, behind the German soldiers. From there, Arturs was horrified to see that the Germans had opened fire on the Latvian contingent.

Galloping up to them with his escort, he screamed at the Germans. "Cease fire! Cease fire!"

The gun stuttered to a halt quickly when the crew noticed the furious Latvian officer. Arturs dismounted, as did his soldiers. They angrily trained their rifles on the Germans.

Arturs roared at the German soldiers. "You imbeciles! Those are Colonel Kalpaks' soldiers! Generalmajor von der Goltz will hear about this."

He turned to his escort. "Corporal, arrest these fools and take them back to the Generalmajor at once! Take this."

He quickly wrote a missive to the General and handed it to the corporal. "I shall go and find the Colonel."

He quickly mounted his horse and cautiously rode towards the Latvian lines. He found the Latvian soldiers in uproar. There had been one casualty in the incident: Oskars Kalpaks.

Arturs found Jānis Balodis, who had been Kalpaks' deputy,

astride a black mare. He was barking orders to the officers under his command as he restored order and discipline amongst the Latvian ranks. Arturs rode up and reported what he had done.

Balodis nodded and said tersely, "Good work, Kohler. I want you to escort me back to von der Goltz immediately."

Arturs spurred his horse and galloped back towards the road where he'd last seen the General. They raced past the marching German troops and rapidly approached the General, who had parked his staff car beside the road and was watching the soldiers march past. Reining in their dusty, sweaty horses, Arturs and Balodis leapt off, approached the General and saluted. Von der Goltz' face looked like thunder as he stood with the missive in his hands, the Latvian soldiers and the cowering German machine gun crew in front of him. A young officer stood rigidly, ashen-faced, nearby.

Von der Goltz nodded tersely to Balodis, whom he knew. "You can be rest assured, Colonel, that these men will be dealt with under German military law. I will show no mercy."

"I should hope so, Generalmajor. The fools killed Oskars Kalpaks. This shall have to be reported to the Latvian Provisional Government and I shall expect retribution for this outrage. It was lucky Kohler here managed to stop them quickly, or the incident could have spiralled out of control."

Von der Goltz nodded and said quietly, but with real menace. "Take them!"

German soldiers roughly grabbed the offenders and hustled them away.

"Report back to your units, Colonel. We march on Saldus and you must protect my flank."

Balodus glared, about to retort, but held his tongue.

He took Arturs aside. "Continue your assignment, Kohler, we need as much information as possible about this Generalmajor von der Goltz' intentions."

Arturs marched with von der Goltz and his headquarters' staff. He was present when the town of Saldus was liberated and formally placed under the Latvian government control four days later.

At Saldus, the Iron Division paused to ensure their supply lines and waited for news of the Baltische Landeswehr campaign to the north. By mid-March they were ready to launch an assault on Jelgeva. News came that the Baltische Landeswehr had taken Ventspils and were preparing to march on Ugāle. The pincer movement had the Bolsheviks on the run. After the initial breakout they never recovered. They retreated and prepared to make a stand at Riga. By mid-April 1919 the Freikorps and Latvian troops had liberated the whole of Kurzeme un Zemgale after the Iron Division took Jelgava and the Baltische Landeswehr Jūrmala.

Everywhere, they were treated like liberators, people cheering and bands playing. The Latvian people were tired of the chaotic, incompetent, ruthless Bolshevik administration they had endured for the last six months. Von der Goltz kept iron discipline amongst his soldiers and there were no incidents. Once his initial objectives had been achieved, von der Goltz halted his advance and set up his temporary headquarters in Jelgava. Here he prepared for his planned assault on Riga.

Having heard about the victories of the German and Latvian soldiers against the despised Latvian Bolsheviks, Karlis felt excited. He knew his brother, Arturs, had been involved in the victorious campaign, and Arturs had now sent word that he had some leave and was coming home! Walking into Dobele to wait for his brother, Karlis felt elated. The local Bolshevik commissars had already left in a hurry as they heard about the approach of the all-conquering Iron Division. Karlis hoped to see the Freikorps, and was not disappointed. He was soon watching the stern-looking German troops march through the town, dust rising from their boots. Along with the people of Dobele lining the streets, Karlis waved and cheered as they marched past.

Then came the German staff cars motoring down in the road. In the back of one Karlis noticed a cold eyed, hard faced German officer, who disdainfully took no notice of the cheering crowds. *Could he be the infamous General Rüdiger von der Goltz?*

Suddenly, Karlis saw Arturs mounted on a fine-looking horse.

Karlis yelled and laughed. "Arturs! Arturs! You're here at last! It's so good to see you!"

Arturs hurriedly dismounted and ran up to his brother and hugged him. "It's so good to see you as well, Karlis! I've really missed the family and farm over the last few months. I've been worried as well, you being under Bolshevik rule and all."

"It's been okay, Arturs. I'm sure father will have a lot to say about it! Come, brother, let's go home to the farm. I hope you have a bit of time. Father and mother are really looking forward to seeing you. There must be so much you can tell us," Karlis babbled in his excitement.

He calmed down to ask. "Who was that haughty officer in the staff car?"

Arturs smiled at his brother's enthusiasm. "That was Generalmajor von der Goltz. Come on, Karlis, climb up. My horse can take both of us."

It was a pleasant ride down the dusty roads, past the flat fields the local farmers were preparing for planting. In the distance Arturs could see the farmers strain against the plough as they urged their horses forward. It was much the same as it had always been. He knew his father and mother would be busy in the fields as well; hoped they could afford some help, as it was a lot of work. He noticed his brother's chaffed hands and guessed that he'd been hard at it as well. Life had gone on here, despite the warfare and turbulence in the country. He was glad of that.

Delighted to see their son, Heinrich and Wilhelmina ushered him into the farmhouse and laid out food and drink for him. They put freshly baked rye bread, sauerkraut, potatoes, eggs, fruit and a roasted chicken on the table, most of the produce from their garden. It was an entertaining meal as everyone caught up on news and gossip, the food washed down by beer and vodka.

Heinrich, after the meal, made a special pot of coffee and sat down with his sons to talk further.

"Tell us everything, Arturs. Are we on the verge of becoming an independent country?" he asked excitedly.

"We have to get rid of the Bolsheviks first, Father. They are closely linked with the Reds in Russia and I fear they will just swallow us up if they can. So far, the Freikorps have been a great help in getting rid of the Reds in Kurzeme un Zemgale, though I have suspicions that von der Goltz is trying to pursue his own agenda. But there is still a long way to go. The Latvian Bolsheviks still hold Riga, the north and Latgale."

"How much time do you have with us?"

"Only one week, then I have to rejoin the army in Jelgava. That is where we will prepare for the push on Riga. How is it going here?"

"Well, we have kept to ourselves since the Bolsheviks took over. They were starting to collectivise and used force and terror against those who were not willing to give up their land. We were lucky here, as the commissars did not get here before the Iron Division arrived. So, life here has not changed much."

Arturs nodded and smiled. "We were treated like liberators at every town. The Bolsheviks certainly made themselves unpopular."

Heinrich's eyes twinkled. "As you can see, we are preparing for harvest. Any help you can give us will be welcome."

Arturs smiled at his father. "Where's Adolfs?"

"Adolfs is at university in Riga, studying forestry. I hope he'll be alright if there is any fighting there."

"He'll have to keep his head down but, so far, von der Goltz has shown no tolerance at all for any breaches of discipline. On the whole, the Germans have not been involved in any unnecessary destruction of property and have paid for everything. I'm sure the Latvian Provisional Government will claim Riga as soon as it is liberated."

Arturs spent a pleasant week with his family on the farm. He helped out a bit with the preparations for planting and spent some time revisiting old friends in the district. Everyone peppered him with questions about the war and the prospects of Latvian independence from the Russians and Germans. He had to be careful about what he said, but he was quietly confident about their prospects. All too soon though, he had to go back.

When Arturs rode quietly back into Jelgava, the first thing he noticed was the tension in the air: the Latvian soldiers he saw clutched their rifles nervously. Sensing something was wrong he hurried to report to Jānis Balodis.

Arturs found him in a small borrowed office, at a desk covered in papers, with clerks and soldiers constantly coming and going. He looked stressed and harassed. Balodis waved Arturs over; spoke quietly, but Arturs could see he was very angry. "Kohler, bad news I'm afraid. A bunch of German traitors have conducted a coup against the Provisional Government and set up an alternative government in Liepāja. It seems the Provisional Government is holed up in some ship under the protection of a British cruiser's guns. We are loyal to that government, not this farcical new German bunch of pretenders. I have had it out with von der Goltz, who swears that he had nothing to do with it, claiming it is an internal Latvian problem."

Balodis laughed harshly and humourlessly before continuing.

"The offensive against Riga is to go ahead at the beginning of

May, simultaneously with a large-scale Estonian offensive in the north. I want you back at von der Goltz' headquarters. You will report directly to me everything you can about his intentions. At the moment it's in his best interests to drive the Reds out of Riga. But who knows what he'll do after that."

He paused, as if to gather his thoughts. "You must report everything you see and hear, Kohler, no matter how trivial. Do you understand? I will give you a number of motorcycle couriers and will expect a brief report daily. Here are your orders."

He dismissed Arturs as another officer rushed into his office.

As Arturs was leaving, he heard Balodis say to the other man. "I want your troops in Riga immediately after the Germans take it. I have arranged for Admiral Cowan to provide naval cover. It is essential that we secure Riga in the name of the Provisional Government."

Arturs left feeling confused and despondent. He also knew that this new assignment would be fraught, as he doubted von der Goltz would include him in his inner council, but he resolved to do the best he could. He had some friends in the General's staff and would try to quietly talk to them. He rode to the Freikorps headquarters not far away and secured an appointment with von der Goltz. The General received him briefly. He glanced at the credentials Arturs proffered, before staring at the young man standing rigidly in front of him. His cold, hard eyes seemed to bore straight through Arturs, but he made no comment and waved him away.

As he left, Arturs noticed Alfred Fletcher in the ante-room. The man nodded tersely at him, before being ushered in to see the General. Arturs nodded back and left. He called over one of his couriers and gave him quick handwritten note: *Baltische Landeswehr to lead assault on Riga.* He gave strict instructions to take it directly to Balodis.

It was a busy month for Arturs. He was involved in a web of

intrigue and deceit as Balodis and von der Goltz danced at shadows with each other. Despite that, they somehow managed to work together well enough to coordinate their plans. Arturs reported his observations, as ordered, to Balodis but as yet had not worked out what the Freikorps intended to do after the assault on Riga.

That operation went perfectly. The Iron Division moved northeast from Jelgava in order to try and cut off the Reds and threaten their flank, while the Baltische Landeswehr assaulted them from Jūrmala with support from one of Cowan's cruisers. At the same time the Estonian and Latvian forces smashed into them in the north of the country. After a week of fighting in Riga it was all over. The Latvian Bolshevik government and most of their soldiers abandoned the city and made a hard-pressed forced retreat to the east. Balodis poured his troops along the coast into the city and, after heavy fighting on the beaches with remnants of the Latvian Bolshevik army, hoisted the flag of the Latvian Provisional Government over the castle in the old town. Riga was liberated. It was 23 May 1919.

Soon afterwards Arturs met up with his brother, Adolfs, who had been studying forestry at the University of Riga. When the assault on Riga began, the university had been shut down. Adolfs had hidden in his quarters and was uncertain when it would start up again. He decided to go back to the farm; would try again next year. "Just give us our country back so we can all start normal lives again," he advised his brother.

Arturs laughed. "I'll see what I can do."

"But seriously, Arturs, please stay safe."

"Oh, it's okay. I'm in the staff at the moment. I rarely see any action!"

On that warm, cloudy summer's day, Arturs walked the cobbled streets up to Riga Castle. He liked the old part of the city, with its colourful old buildings and narrow streets, and sadly noted the damage to various buildings from the recent fighting in the city. The damage was worse the closer he drew to the castle. Once inside the courtyard, he walked into the office Balodis had commandeered for himself. He found the Colonel in a rage and quaked as he was shown in. Out of a window he could see the reassuring grey silhouette of a cruiser anchored in the Daugava River.

"The fool!" Balodis roared at his aide-de-camp. "He just let the Reds escape!"

Seeing Arturs, he snapped. "Kohler, you will accompany me to see von der Goltz, now!"

Balodis stormed out of the building, Arturs hurrying to catch up with him. In a staff car they rattled down the streets to the former German consulate where von der Goltz had his headquarters. Balodis leapt out of the vehicle and rushed into the building, brushing aside the German sentries. He stormed into an ante-room, ignoring the aide-de-camp at his desk and flung open the door to von der Goltz' office. Von der Goltz, working at his desk, looked up, his annoyance at this interruption obvious.

"What is it, Colonel?" he growled with quiet menace.

"Why have you stopped, Generalmajor? We have the Reds on the run. You must keep up the pressure and push east into Latgale!" Balodis answered with barely restrained fury.

Von der Goltz glared at Balodis, his steel grey eyes hard and uncompromising. "It is not up to you to dictate tactics to me, Colonel. The Reds are weak and are not a threat at the moment, he said icily.

"They'll regroup and receive support from Russia."

"Russia is a mess. That tyrant Lenin and his lackey Trotsky are fighting for their lives. There will be no support from them."

"So, you will not march east?"

"No, Colonel, I will not."

Von der Goltz turned haughtily away.

As he left Balodis said quietly to Arturs, "Stay here and find out what he's up to!"

After Balodis had gone, von der Goltz flung open the door and roared at his aide-de-camp. "Get Fletcher at once!"

The man left at a run.

Arturs, lurking unseen, wondered what was to happen. He waited and, soon enough, Alfred Fletcher walked in and disappeared into the office, shutting the door behind him. Soon after, Fletcher hurried out of the office and through the room.

Not seeing Arturs, he blurted out as he passed the aide-de-camp, "We move against the Estonians! Get Oberst von Hessler immediately!"

Arturs' jaw dropped open. Obviously, von der Goltz was showing where his true loyalties lay. Not to the Latvian Provisional Government and Latvian independence! After a time, he sauntered out of his hiding place, coolly, as though he should have been there all the time. Casually, responding to the salute of the aide-de-camp who was talking on the telephone, he strolled out the door. Once out of the building he hurriedly made his way back to the Riga Castle.

Balodis stood stunned. "Are you sure, Kohler?"

"Yes sir. I was hidden in the ante-room and heard it from Fletcher himself."

"It seems von der Goltz regards the Estonians as more of a threat to the Germans than the Bolsheviks! Are they trying to set up a German state here?" Balodis mused.

Then he said decisively, "We have to warn Jorģis Zemitāns, our commander in the north and General Põdder, commander of the Estonian Third Division, straight away."

He went to his desk and quickly wrote a note, which he signed and sealed in an envelope. "I want you to get this to Zemitāns.

Take my staff car, a driver and a soldier as escort. The Baltische Landeswehr will take the direct route north, via Cēsis. They'll move quickly, especially if Fletcher has a rocket up his arse from von der Goltz. I suggest you take the coast road before cutting inland to Valmiera, where the Third was last reported. You must avoid any of Fletcher's scouts at all costs. I will try to radio as well. Get a move on!"

Arturs took the letter, saluted and ran out the door. He bellowed for Balodis' driver and ordered him to get fuel and be ready in half an hour. He ordered the captain of the headquarters guards to provide him with a soldier. He then ran to his quarters and got his greatcoat, rifle, pistol and a bag with a spare set of clothes. When he returned, the driver had the big Crossly 20/25 ready, the engine running. A soldier armed with a British Lewis machine gun sat in the front next to him. Arturs climbed in the back.

"Let's go. Drive north out of the city, along the coast road to Tūja."

The vehicle rattled down the road. Arturs felt uncomfortable and a little cold in the open car, but they made good progress. The dirt road was slippery from recent rains, and potholed, but the driver knew what he was doing. They drove beside the grey sea, through birches and pines that grew right up to the water. At Tūja, Arturs told the driver to turn east. The road markedly deteriorated as they moved away from the coast. Worse, it started to rain and the road became even more muddy and slippery. As they climbed the low hills on the road inland, the car slipped and lurched through the deep mud and holes. Arturs, vigilant in the back, was soaked and tired, as were his soldiers, but they pushed on into the evening. Luckily, they didn't see many people and no German troops.

As the sun settled slowly behind the hills, they drove into the small city of Valmiera. They were stopped by Estonian soldiers at the outskirts of the town. Arturs wearily demanded that he see Jorģis Zemitāns or General Põdder. The soldiers, seeing the British staff car and the dishevelled officer in the back, escorted them to a small house near the river. Arturs climbed out of the car.

"Stay here," he ordered his escort then ran up the stairs into the house. An Estonian captain tried to stop him at the door as he forced his way into a small hallway.

"I have a message from Colonel Balodis. I must see General Põdder, immediately!" he barked in Russian.

A door opened at the end of the hall, letting out the light and warmth of an open fire. A tall, young man with a large walrus moustache and spectacles stalked into the hall.

"What's all the racket?" he demanded.

Another man walked into the room behind him. Both of them stared at the wet, mud splattered, dishevelled man in front of them.

"Who are you?" the second man asked.

Obviously, they had not received any message on the radio.

"Major Arturs Kohler, sir. I've just come from Riga with an urgent message from Colonel Balodis for General Põdder and Colonel Zemitāns."

The man with the spectacles grumbled. "I'm Põdder. This had better be important, Major."

He took the letter and opened it.

When he read the note, his face darkened. "Damn, that slimy, treacherous dog! Are you sure of this, Kohler?"

"Yes sir. The Baltische Landeswehr is driving against you. We expect them to be in Cēsis soon!"

"Damn him to hell! Not much we can do about it now. We'll have a council tomorrow at 7am, Jorģis. Captain! Get my chief of staff, also house and feed the Major and his men!"

Arturs was glad to have a hot meal, a bath and to sleep in a soft warm bed. He slept well, pleased that he had done his duty.

He arose early, washed, put on a new set of clothes, ate a quick breakfast of tea and bread and attended the meeting General Põdder had called. When he hurried into the meeting room in the small house by the river, the others were already there.

Põdder looked up from the table, when Arturs was announced.

He came to the point straight away. "Ah, Kohler, you're just on time. Please brief us about the situation and spare no details."

Arturs looked around at the surrounding officers, none of whom were familiar to him, except Põdder and Jorǵis Zemitāns. He walked over to a large map on the wall.

He tapped the map as he spoke. "Very good, sir. Riga, as you know, was taken by the Baltische Landeswehr on 23 May. Soon after that, it was secured for the Provisional Government by Colonel Balodis' Independent Latvian Brigade. There is also a British cruiser anchored in the Daugava River, so it would seem unlikely that von der Goltz will try to retake Riga. In my opinion, he would most likely march the Iron Division to support the Baltische Landeswehr as they advance on Cēsis. The Iron Division is, at present, positioned to the south-east of Riga near the town of Ogre. According to Colonel Balodis' intelligence, the Reds have retreated into Latgale and are little threat, at present, to either his forces or the Germans."

Zemitāns interrupted. "What of the Provisional Government?"

"When I left, sir, they were safe. They are still holed up in some ship under the protection of British guns, but safe."

"Continue, Kohler. How long do you think the Baltische Landeswehr will take to get here?"

"I'm not sure, sir, but they can move quickly. I guess they will reach Cēsis in the next few days."

Põdder frowned. "So, it seems that von der Goltz does not regard the Reds as being a threat to him, at least in the short term. What do you think he is trying to achieve, Kohler?"

"Sorry sir, but I'm not privy to that. I can say, though, that Colonel Balodis believes he might be supporting the traitors in

Liepāja and trying to set up a German dominated state here.”

Silence reigned as the men around the table contemplated that scenario.

Finally, Põdder grumbled tersely, “We cannot allow that. I will send an urgent message to my government’s high command. In the meantime, we will extend our patrols towards Cēsis and the town of Limbaži to the west. I will send troops to take control of Gulbene and the railway there. We will use our armoured trains to flank the Baltische Landeswehr and to keep an eye on any Bolshevik movements in Latgale.”

He then sighed, took off his spectacles and wiped his face. “Very well, you will all receive your orders today and I want you to implement them immediately. Kohler, you will return immediately to Balodis, with his car, taking a despatch regarding our plans. You should be able to outrun any patrols, but the paper cannot fall into German hands.”

He then dismissed everyone with a wave of his hand.

The sun shone between the white fluffy clouds when the big staff car moved quietly out of Valmeira. Arturs, in the back, wrapped his greatcoat around himself against the cool morning air and patted the despatch for the third time. It was secure in his pocket. They drove down the low hills and through the fields and small creeks along the same road they had taken previously. It was cool and dry, as the big car lurched through the ruts on the road. They passed one of the Estonian patrols on the side of the road, who appeared silently out of a thicket of oaks and stood aside and watched the vehicle lurch by. Arturs urged the driver to move along as quickly as possible.

They passed the town of Limbaži without incident and continued down towards the coast. Outside the coastal town of Tūja, Arturs ordered the car to stop on a small hill and stood up with his field glasses. It was a fine clear day and the coast road snaked in front of him beside the pale blue of the Baltic. Seeing nothing, he ordered that they cautiously enter the town. Once through, they accelerated into the open fields and along the road, beside the sea.

All was going well; the big car motored rapidly down the road, dust swirling round its wheels. Suddenly, they rounded a corner and raced straight at a German patrol, who were walking along the road in loose formation. The soldiers, taken completely by surprise, scattered as the big car roared past them. Recovering, they opened fire with their rifles. Bullets whizzed past the car.

Arturs roared angrily. "What the hell are they doing here? The Lewis gun, soldier. Quickly!"

Taking the machine gun from the man in the front, he cocked it and, steadying it precariously on the back of the bouncing vehicle, opened fire with a short, withering burst. The Germans dived for cover. Arturs was sure he hit nothing, but that did not matter: they had survived the incident without any damage or injuries. The rest of the trip was uneventful and they rattled into the courtyard of the Riga Castle at midday.

Arturs immediately went to deliver his despatch to Balodis. Entering the office, he found the Colonel speaking on the phone. Balodis hung up and waved Arturs in.

"I have a despatch from General Põdder, sir."

Balodis took the despatch.

"Good!" he muttered after he read it. "Is there anything else?"

"We encountered a German patrol on the coast road south of Tūja, sir. They opened fire on us and we had to run for it."

"Baltische Landeswehr?"

"No, sir – they looked like Iron Division."

"Mmm, our intelligence has reported that the Iron Division is advancing towards Cēsis. That patrol was a long way from the main force. Perhaps von der Goltz is planning to advance towards Limbaži from Cēsis?"

He sighed and muttered grimly. "It's up to the Estonians to

stop them now."

Before dismissing Arturs, Balodis looked at him and said, "Your appointment to von der Goltz' staff has been terminated due to circumstances. Unfortunately, Kohler, your promotion to Major was temporary and associated with that appointment. However, in recognition of your achievements, I am promoting you to Captain. You will report to the Third Battalion that is being formed now."

He stood up and offered his hand. "Congratulations!"

Arturs shook his hand. "Thank you, sir."

Balodis looked away and said quietly to himself. "We'll need all the soldiers we can get if we are to fight the Bolsheviks *and* the Freikorps!"

Arturs nodded, saluted and walked from the room, leaving Balodis to his reflections.

Lying in the icy mud just outside Jelgava, Arturs looked through his field glasses – he could see the hastily constructed defences the Freikorps had thrown up just to the east of the city. Tiredly, he trained his glasses north – it looked clear there. He hoped it was.

As he lay there, he reflected bitterly on recent events: the Latvian army, strongly supported by General Põdder's Estonian Third Division and the British Cruiser Squadron, was finally overcoming the German occupation forces, as Arturs cynically referred to them. He remembered how the people of Latvia had treated the Freikorps as liberators only seven months previously. So much had changed. Now they were a hated scourge that had to be defeated and driven out of the country. But there was still work to do.

When General Põdder had defeated the Iron Division and Baltische Landeswehr outside Cēsis, von der Goltz was recalled to

Germany. With the formidable general gone, the German soldiers lost all discipline; they had retreated and joined with a bunch of desperate White Russians, led by a so-called Duke Pavel Bermont, to attack Riga. So, not only did the fledging Latvian nationalist army have to fight the Freikorps and Latvian Bolsheviks, but the White Russians as well. The war was as chaotic and variable as the mess in Russia.

After a month of heavy fighting around Riga, the unholy and cynical alliance of Germans and Russians were finally driven out of the capital. Arturs' battalion had been involved in the defence of Riga and had recently lost their commander. Arturs, ironically, was once again an acting Major and commanded the battalion.

His reverie was now interrupted as a young captain slid up beside him. "All is ready, Arturs."

Arturs nodded.

He looked once again at the German lines. "Very well, Mentis. Get back to your position and open up covering fire with your machine guns in ten minutes. Make sure the Second Company attacks their northern flank."

Arturs slithered backwards and crawled into a small thicket. There, hidden behind the trees, as close to the German lines as they could get, was their precious armoured car. He said to the driver and machine gunner in his turret, "We move in ten minutes. I want you to drive straight at the weakest part of the line over there."

Arturs pointed at a spot in the defences he had identified.

"The First Company will follow you in. I want you to lay down as much fire as you can and move as quickly as you can. Surprise is of the essence."

Exactly on time the stutter of the machine guns sounded on Arturs' right. He raised his hand and, with a roar, the armoured car lumbered towards the German lines, its turret machine gun blazing. Arturs ran after it, urging his soldiers forward, using the armoured vehicle as protection. The German soldiers opened fire with machine guns and rifles. Bullets clanged into the iron machine and whizzed past Arturs as he sprinted forward. Two of his men fell near him. One minute later the armoured car crashed through the defences. Arturs and his soldiers followed. Arturs shot at a German at close quarters and missed. The soldier next to him bayoneted him, before reeling from a shot to the shoulder. Arturs shot at the man who had fired. Then his rifle jammed. Cursing he threw it away and, drawing his pistol, shot at another German.

It was all over in five minutes. Surprised by the ferocity of the frontal assault as well as being flanked, many Germans abandoned the city and retreated to the south.

Soon afterwards, Arturs met up with the commander of the Second Company who had swept into the city from the north, encountering minimal resistance. The combined companies moved carefully through the city, fighting house to house, clearing out any remaining German soldiers. The abandoned German's either died at their post or tried to run. No prisoners were taken.

When the fighting died down, the people timidly looked out of shuttered houses. When they saw who it was that had taken the city, they ventured carefully outside and onto the street. Soon Arturs and his battle-hardened, victorious soldiers were surrounded by cheering people. They were hugged and showered with flowers. Arturs walked to the town hall. He found the armoured car already there, its turret turned towards the retreating Germans, the gun silent. There he found the Mayor, who was almost weeping with relief.

"Have they gone?" he blubbered.

"Yes."

"We have had a terrible time of it here. Terrible, terrible. There has been a lot of shooting and looting."

Arturs was appalled. He had heard that the Germans had lost discipline in retreat. "Show me!"

He turned to Aldis Clavins, the Commander of the Second, who stood beside him. Writing quickly, he wrote a despatch to Balodis.

Jelgava is taken with minimal casualties. The Freikorps is retreating south. The battalion will not pursue them today. The Mayor here reports that the Freikorps has indulged in looting and shootings. I will investigate.

"Get a motorcycle courier and send this to Colonel Balodis at once. Tell Captain Yurevis to bring his machine gun company and set up a defensive position to the south of the city. The armoured car can go there as well, and send a patrol to follow the Germans. No heroics, I just want to know that they're not coming back."

The man nodded and ran off, shouting orders to his lieutenants.

Arturs followed the Mayor who led him down the street. Items left by the Germans during their hurried retreat lay strewn all over it. Arturs looked sadly at a broken grandfather clock in a gutter.

He spoke over his shoulder at one of his men. "Sergeant, find Captain Clavins. Get him to assign a squad to assist in cleaning up here. Also, tell him to find a warehouse and take all the loot there and place it under guard. We'll try to get it back to the owners."

A number of bodies lay, arms flung out in grotesque poses, in the gutters, left where they had been shot days before. The stench of rotting flesh pervaded the street. Flies buzzed around them and rats crawled out of their orifices.

The Mayor blanched and put a cloth over his nose. "These people were indiscriminately shot by the Germans."

"How many did they shoot?"

"I'm not sure. At least one hundred."

"Find the families and give them a decent burial. I will get our battalion chaplain to say a few words."

As they walked down the narrow street, Arturs noticed that a number of houses were burnt. "What happened here?"

"These houses were burnt by the Whites. Apparently, the occupants were Bolshevik sympathisers. They were shot. There is a mass grave in a field outside the city. They even started a fire when they tried to loot Rundāle Palace!”

Arturs shook with fury, but he spoke calmly and quietly. “Very well. We’ll stay here until I receive further orders. Can you find accommodation for my officers and soldiers? Also, can you find me an office with a telephone?”

The Mayor smiled, for the first time. “I will arrange it straight away.”

Two hours later, Arturs sat in the office the Mayor had provided. In front of him sat his two captains; weary and dirty from the hard work of cleaning up the city and burying bodies.

“Is our southern flank secured, Mentis?”

“Yes, we have positioned the armoured car and four machine gun crews in position on the road to the south and every fifty metres east and west of that. All the guns can cover each other.”

“Good. Are the rest of your men accommodated?”

“Yes. The Mayor has been very helpful.”

“Make sure everyone gets a good bed and a hot meal. Have you heard from our patrol yet?” he asked Clavins.

“Yes, Arturs, they sent back a man on a motorcycle. The Germans are still moving south. It looks like they may be running for the border.”

“OK, let’s hope that’s the case. Tomorrow at dawn, I want you to take the First and Second companies along with the armoured car and advance to the border. Make sure the swine don’t come back! The machine gun company can stay here. I’ll ring Colonel Balodis and get further orders. Okay, go and get a meal and some sleep.”

Arturs rang Balodis.

The Colonel answered. “Balodis!”

“Kohler here, sir. Good news, I hope. We have secured Jelgava and are starting to clean up the mess the Germans left behind. They have moved south. I sent a patrol to follow them and they have reported that it looks like they are going to retreat across the border into Lithuania. Tomorrow, unless you order otherwise, I will send the First and Second companies to track them and make sure they do not try to come back."

"Very good, Kohler, carry on as you are. Hopefully the Lithuanians will finish them off! Don't your family live nearby? Why don't you take a bit of leave to visit them to make sure everything is all right? Make your arrangements and take a week."

Arturs was glad to leave Jelgava. He found the desecration of the city by the Germans depressing and disturbing. He rode his horse slowly westward, towards Dobele, along the icy road. The fields had their first sheen of icy snow on them and the trees were stark and bereft of leaves. It was cool, with a grey sky that extended to the horizon. People looked out of their houses at the dishevelled officer in his worn, dirty uniform and waved at him. Somehow, everyone knew that the Germans had finally been chased out of the district.

When Arturs reached Dobele the town was quiet and he was pleased to see it had escaped the depredations that the remnants of the once proud Iron Division had inflicted on Jelgava. It was not far to the farm now. Suddenly, he felt a strong longing for peace. He was tired. The war against the Freikorps and their awful Russian allies had been long, hard and bitter. But it seemed to be nearly over. Now, all they had to do was to get rid of the Bolsheviks in Latgale and Latvian independence would be secured.

Arturs rode over a small hill and saw the familiar farmhouse in the near distance. Smoke poured from the chimney, a smoke that promised warmth and a good meal. It had been a long time, but finally he would be seeing his parents and brothers again. They would have a lot to talk about. He hoped they would all finally be able to get on with their lives again, free of bloodshed and desperation of this terrible war. It was something he was looking forward to with an aching longing.

My grandmother Lydia's father, Ferdinand Bergs (circa 1910).

My grandfather Karlis Kohler (circa 1923).

My great grandfather Heinrich Kohler with Karlis (circa 1923).

The three Kohler brothers (left to right)
Adolfs, Arturs, and my grandfather Karlis (circa 1923).
The brothers changed their names to Keleris (Adolfs) and Kelers
(Arturs and Karlis) in around 1927.
Arturs is wearing his Lāčplēsis Military Order medal,
received for valour during the Latvian civil war (1919).

Hay harvest at Plumshē Farm (circa 1922),
at around the time Karlis took over the property.

*My Grandmother Lydia Kelers (nee Bergs)
and her mother outside Kambaris (circa 1934).*

Wedding of my grandparents Karlis and Lydia Kelers (circa 1936).

*My grandparents, Karlis and Lydia Kelers, with the tractor,
in front of the house at Kambaris (circa 1936).*

Harvest time at Kambaris (circa 1942)
*Standing top right corner, the Kelers family, Karlis (holding my father
Karlis Junior), Lydia and the Nanny, with my aunt Inta, in front of them.*

Kelers family at the Schleswig Castle
Displaced Persons Camp (circa 1948).

VI

The Latvians Part 1 (1920–1926)

On a cold day with a fine sleet billowing in the air and icy snow coating the cobbled streets of the old town of Riga, the Kohler family, rugged up in their best clothing, trudged up the gentle slope to Riga Castle. They noted as they walked the still evident signs of the fighting in the city the previous year. They were let into a cloakroom, just inside the doors of a grand reception room, before being ushered inside and shown to their seats. The room was decorated with flowers and streamers. At the front, above a podium positioned on a stage, draped the blood red and white flag and coat of arms of the free Latvian Republic.

Standing on the podium was Kārlis Ullmanis, the Prime Minister of the fledgling republic. He was a large, thickset man in his forties, with thick fair hair, who was immaculately dressed in a black suit. Ullmanis was presenting medals to the heroes of the bitter and brutal Latvian War of Independence. The Latvian Nationalists had finally emerged victorious, with the recent defeat of the Bolsheviks in Latgale.

The announcer called out a name. The Kohler family stirred excitedly as Arturs marched onto the stage from a door to the left. He wore the dress uniform of a Major of the Latvian Army, complete with a sword at his side. He snapped to attention before saluting Ullmanis. The great man took a white enamelled cross with crossed swords and a red and white ribbon from a smartly dressed aide-de-camp and pinned it on Arturs' chest. Rapturous applause rose from the crowd, especially from Arturs' family, as the young man received the medal of the Lāčplēsis Military Order. Ullmanis shook Arturs' hand.

Arturs stepped back and saluted again before turning on his heel and marching out of the room.

Later that evening Heinrich hosted a party for his family in one of the few restaurants open in the old town of Riga. The building, in a small courtyard, was largely empty, with only one other group at a table in the corner. The Kohlers had a lot to celebrate: Arturs getting his medal; the end of the war; and the opportunity to get on with their lives.

Heinrich stood up and raised his glass. "I would like to make a toast to a new beginning and a great future for us and for Latvia. May we be able to get on with our lives. I raise my glass to our son Arturs, a hero of Latvia, who will now become a *peacetime* army officer!"

The others stood up and yelled. "Uz veselibu! Priekā!"

Heinrich was not finished. "To Adolfs, who will be able to restart his university degree in forestry. And to Karlis, who will be able to finish his schooling and hopefully go to university as well."

Heinrich then put his arms around Wilhelmina. "Finally, to my beloved wife, who has been my rock in these troubled times."

"Uz veselibu! Priekā!" her sons yelled and drank deeply.

Wilhelmina beamed broadly, so relieved and proud of them, and thankful they were lucky and had gotten through the terrible war and were all together again.

Heinrich silenced his sons' exuberance. "On a more serious note … let us pray that we never have to go through such a terrible time again and that there will be peace and prosperity forever!"

Just as he finished a waiter brought out a pot of black coffee, sugar and some traditional Latvian white fruit cake.

Heinrich smiled. "Ah, here is the coffee and cake. How about some rouf? Waiter, please get us five shots of schnapps!"

He poured everyone a small cup of the hot, aromatic, black coffee. When the waiter brought in the liquor, they poured it into their coffees. Wilhelmina, in the meantime, had cut and served the cake. They all sat down and sipped the strong, black, sweet, liquor coffee and ate small portions of the rich cake.

A few weeks later Heinrich and Wilhelmina sat the table in front of the fire. They were alone again, all of their sons away: Arturs to his regiment in faraway Daugavpils, in restive Latgale, near the Lithuanian and Soviet borders; Adolfs in Riga, back at university, continuing his forestry degree; and Karlis at a boarding school in Jelgava. Outside, their yard and fields were thick with snow, the fruit trees in the front yard stark and grey, matching the sky. Heinrich had come to a decision; a decision that was a business gamble, but his instinct told him it was the right one. He looked across the table contemplatively at his wife and sipped a hot cup of tea.

"I'm thinking of concentrating on dairy farming," he said abruptly.

"Why is that, love?" she asked.

He shrugged. "Instinct, I guess. It makes sense. We already have some cows and a good bull that can be the foundation to expand the herd and we have the equipment to milk them. It's just becoming too hard and expensive to crop at the moment. I've heard the dairy in Dobele is expanding its quota."

Wilhelmina thought about it, then said, "Well, we have a bit of money saved and we may be able to pick up some good animals cheap, as it is winter. Also, as a result of that awful war, people need money and may have to sell some of their stock."

Heinrich smiled, appreciating her pragmatism and support. "Alright, let's do it! I'll go into Jelgava as soon as I can and see what I can arrange. It would be a good opportunity to visit Karlis as well."

Heinrich didn't get into Jelgava until early in the spring, when the light was slowly starting to get better, but it was still cold, with a pale blue clear sky. Rugged up in his greatcoat and boots, he rode in on his horse, the same one he used for ploughing and harvest,. There was still snow on the ground and the trees were still stark and leafless, but he knew in a week or so the first leaves and buds would appear. The first signs of spring.

When he reached Jelgava, he decided to go to the school first and visit Karlis, before he went about his business. He rode into the gate of the austere-looking compound and asked a young lad to stable his horse for his short stay. He then went straight to the headmaster's office, saying hello to the pretty young receptionist as he passed.

The headmaster looked up from his desk, surprised, when Heinrich entered. "Ah, Mr Kohler, how are you? I was just going to send you a message. This is quite a coincidence."

The man looked flustered, which caused Heinrich concern. He had never seen the man like this. "Is there a problem? What's Karlis done?"

"Nothing, nothing. Your son is very bright, one of our best students. I'm sure he will have a fine future. Please come with me."

The man hurried out of his office, opening the door for Heinrich, before directing him down a corridor and around the corner. He showed Heinrich into a small austere, brightly lit, white room. Heinrich became immediately alarmed.

"This is our infirmary, Mr Kohler. I'm afraid I have bad news. Your son is very ill. He's over in the bed near the window."

His face turning pale, Heinrich rushed to the bed indicated; found his son lying with his eyes shut. Karlis was a pale yellow colour. A nurse stood beside him taking his pulse. Karlis opened his eyes and smiled wanly at his father.

"How are you, son?"

"I'm feeling a bit better," Karlis answered weakly.

The nurse asked quietly. "Mr Kohler?"

Heinrich nodded.

"Your son is very ill. He has a bad dose of the Spanish influenza. He is quite weak and has a fever and is nauseous. There has also been blood in his urine. I'm sorry, but there is very little we can do for him here. He's a strong lad and should make a full recovery with rest, a clean environment and good water."

Addressing the headmaster, she said. "I suggest that he be sent home, for at least a month."

The man nodded. And Heinrich nodded as well.

"He's quite weak at the moment, but should be able to travel tomorrow. Can you arrange transport, Mr Kohler?"

Heinrich nodded again, numb at this bad news. "I'll arrange something straight away."

"Good, I'll make some notes for his treatment," the nurse said, businesslike.

"You can stay in the guest room for tonight, Mr Kohler," the headmaster added.

"Thank you, thank you. Can I sit here for a while?" Heinrich mumbled.

"Stay as long as you like."

Heinrich arranged for a cart and a driver, and Karlis was carried out of the bed and placed carefully in the back on a mattress and wrapped in a warm blanket. They tried to make him as comfortable as possible.

Before he left, the headmaster said to Heinrich, "Good luck, Mr Kohler. Your son is welcome back as soon as he gets better."

Heinrich made sure they travelled slowly and carefully to minimise his son's discomfort. He walked his horse alongside and chatted about nothing much, until he noticed his son had drifted off to sleep.

When Karlis woke up, the first thing he felt was searing pain in his back. He felt hot and sweaty and desperately needed to piss, but it hurt. He peered upwards, confused; wondered where he was. Everything looked familiar. Then he remembered. He was at home, in his parents' large bed. He noticed his mother sitting beside him.

"You're awake, son!"

"Help me up, mother, I need to piss."

She frowned at his vulgarity but helped him up and looked away while he urinated, grunting with pain, in a porcelain chamber pot then she helped him back into the bed.

"Here, sip this. It's special tea I made. I have used some of the herbs from the garden. Also, drink water. There is some in the jug near the bed. You have to rest."

She helped him drink his tea.

He took a sip and then gagged, almost spitting it out. "What's that? It tastes awful!"

Wilhelmina blushed a bit. "It's a special remedy I learnt off my mother. It's good for you. Drink up."

He did so dutifully, grimacing with pain.

"Good. Make sure you drink water and rest. You are to stay here until you are better. I'll clean out the chamber pot," she fussed, before fluffing up his pillows.

The effort to sit up and drink his tea exhausted him and he fell asleep again. Wilhelmina looked at him sleeping for a while, before slipping quietly out of the room, taking the chamber pot with her. It was stained red.

Karlis was weak and in pain; bedbound for what felt like an eternity. He drifted between being awake, in pain, sweating, shivering and sleeping. When asleep he tossed and turned and dreamed.

His mother sat at his bedside every day, treating him with a variety of home-made remedies, all of them tasting awful. But Karlis was grateful for her attention. Sometimes she would sit and knit in her rocking chair, watching him as he slept. Occasionally, during the evening, Heinrich would come in and sit awkwardly beside him and talk about nothing in particular. He would talk about the farm and the cows he had procured; about adding onto the barn for his expanded herd; about not planting crops this year, but hay for the cattle in the winter.; about getting a new contract for his anticipated milk production in the summer. Karlis listened intermittently, not hearing much, finding it hard to concentrate. He was too wracked with pain and always hungry. It still hurt when he had to piss and he wished the fever would break. But it didn't. He had not eaten any solids for a long time.

Wilhelmina worried about her son. He just did not seem to be getting better, despite her best ministrations. He was listless and his skin wore a pale yellowish sheen. Worse, after more than a week there was still blood in his urine. She did the best she could, making sure he had plenty of clean water and hot tea. She fussed around, keeping the room spotless.

Finally, the fever seemed to break and, much to her delight, his urine colour improved. She knew at last, to her great relief, her son was on the mend. He would survive. And quietly she thanked God.

Indeed, after two weeks being bedbound, Karlis started to improve. He was able to get up and sit in the garden, when it was warm enough. Wilhelmina cautiously started to introduce solids, in the form of chicken soup, into his diet. Gradually the pain faded. As he improved, as if God was watching, spring arrived. The days lengthened; the sky grew bluer. Leaves and flowers slowly appeared on the trees, and grasses in the fields grew. Instead of sleet and snow, it started to rain, though it was still cold enough for frost in the mornings.

Karlis started to eat proper food, as he and Heinrich put it: sauerkraut, bread and eggs. After a month Karlis decided he was well enough to get out and about again.

Heinrich sat him down. "I think you are well enough, thank God, to go back to school. The headmaster kindly has kept you a spot, but you'll be behind. You'll have to work hard, Karlis. I forbid you to touch any alcohol! You are lucky, as you were very sick. Your mother was very worried about you for a while there."

"I feel fine, Dad. Of course, I will do as you say." Karlis grinned cheekily and added under his breath. "For now!"

Karlis returned to the boarding school in Jelgava, determined to finish the education disrupted by war and sickness so he could get into university. He wanted to study mechanical engineering so he could do his bit to help rebuild the nation. There was, however, a major problem he had to confront. He had completed his entire education in Russian. With the victory by the nationalist forces in the War of Independence it was decreed by the new Latvian Government that all education, including university entrance examinations, would be conducted in the Latvian language forthwith. Karlis was literate in his native tongue. He had been taught it by his mother, along with Russian. However, he had to learn and understand all the sophisticated Latvian engineering terminology. This he did by getting a book on mechanical engineering and by dint of hard work and a good engineering dictionary, he mastered the jargon.

Despite all the disruption, Karlis passed his examinations with ease. As one of the top students in the school, he graduated into the university in Riga to study mechanical engineering. Heinrich and Wilhelmina were proud of him, as they were of all their sons. Heinrich was, though, a little sad as he had quietly hoped Karlis would one day take over the farm, but he wanted what was best for his son, and being an engineer was a worthwhile ambition.

Excitement came to Karlis in the summer of 1921, when he made the big move into Riga. He'd always been a bit embarrassed to be so old and still at school, now, finally, he was free to start living his own life. Both Heinrich and Wilhelmina accompanied him to the railway station. He shook his father's hand and hugged his mother, who struggled to hold her tears as her last son left to face the world.

Karlis smiled at her still pretty face. "I'll see you soon, Mum."

The train left and he watched as his parents disappeared into the distance.

Adolfs, who still had a number of years before he completed his degree, met Karlis at the Riga train station; he took him to the small, rundown flat he lived in, not far from the university. It was a typical student haunt he shared with two others – one of them, Aldis, a rather slovenly young man, who 'studied arts' but seemed more involved in student politics – the other, Oto, a mousey, quiet, bespectacled man who was going to be a teacher.

Karlis quickly fell into the lifestyle of a student at university. He enjoyed the engineering lectures and practicals; he was bright, with a strong mathematical and analytical mind. He was interested in building things and was a practical person. He soon established friendships with the people he lived with and other students he studied with.

Soon after settling into life in Riga, Karlis went with Adolfs and his housemates to a rather dingy little cafe not far from where they lived. They sat down on hard wooden chairs at a rickety table near the grubby window and ordered coffee.

Aldis slurped at his coffee and started to regale the others about the recent War of Independence.

"Is this independence the best for the people? Is this dysfunctional constitution what we really need?" he pontificated, not necessarily rhetorically.

The others looked at him astounded. "What, did you hope …

that we would be absorbed into Soviet Russia? Are you a Bolshevik? Or perhaps you wanted us to become part of Germany!"

"I loathe the Germans. They were treacherous scum," Aldis spat out angrily.

The others thumped the table.

"We are with you there," they cried. "But Russian Bolshevism? They're just as bad as the Germans, if not worse!"

"I'm a Latvian socialist; I'm not interested in Russian ideology. I support the rights of the workers and farmers."

"You're mad. So, you do support the great agrarian reform? Land has been distributed to lots of farmers. There are small farms being carved out from the German estates right now and that is the right thing, especially after the Germans betrayed us in the war."

'No, I don't support Kulak farmers. We should aspire to collectivise. That is the only way for truly equitable land distribution."

Both Adolfs and Karlis glowered at him. "Our father, a hard-working Latvian, is one of those so-called Kulak farmers."

"No, no. The existing small landholders should retain their lands for now. I'm talking about resuming the German exploiters' farms."

Oto spoke up for the first time. He had been listening with some interest but, as a city person, he had other issues on his mind.

"Well, Aldis, what's the problem with our constitution? We are able to sit here and talk politics. That's not the case in Soviet Russia from what I've heard."

"That's propaganda and misinformation spread by the imperialists who want to oppress the Russian people," Aldis countered heatedly. "Any of these so-called repressions are a result of the civil war. When that's over, things will get better. As far as our constitution is concerned, it's too easy to form a party. Mark my words; it will be very hard to govern as the main blocks will have to deal with a whole bunch of silly little parties."

"You could at least give the constitution a chance!" Oto said.

Aldis finished his coffee and got up to leave. "How can I? It's an anathema to me. I prefer strong, centralised government that supports worker rights."

"Are you sure that's going to happen in Russia?"

"It will. Wait and see. Wait until the NEP gets going," Aldis said over his shoulder as he opened the door and walked out onto the cobbled street.

Karlis and Adolfs shook their heads. "That's crazy talk! He wants us to get into bed again with the Russians. Independence is the best thing for us. Free of the Russians and the Germans."

Otto nodded quietly in agreement. "I think we should agree to disagree with old Aldis. How about we get something stronger?"

The three of them paid up and followed Aldis out onto the street. But he was nowhere to be seen. So Adolfs led the way around the corner into a narrow, dark alleyway. They trouped into a bar and ordered the cheapest, nastiest vodka in the place. A tall, slim, dark-haired woman with beautiful green eyes served them. Karlis made a mental note to try and get to know her sometime. Strange that she was working in such a dive, he thought as the three of them chugged down their vodkas.

Karlis gasped and his eyes watered. "Urgh, that's awful. Want another one?"

The others laughed. "One more, perhaps."

Karlis called the bar girl over and ordered the drinks.

When she brought them to the table, he stuck out his hand and said boldly, "Karlis!"

She smiled, her pretty face lighting up as she put the shot glasses down.

"Ilze!" she gasped, before hurrying off.

"Ooohhhhhh!" Oto snickered.

"Bottoms up!"

Karlis managed to instill himself into Ilze's life over the next few weeks. He visited her at the bar; often waiting for her outside when she came off shift. Eventually, he asked her out and they went dancing. They danced the night away to a fabulous jazz band and had a great time. They dressed up, as best they could, and joined the crowd. He swung her around as he gained confidence and fell into the rhythm of the music. Ilze looked gorgeous in her low-cut, sequined dress, its tightness accentuating her slim body and showing off her pretty knees and breasts. Karlis found her incredibly alluring but also, somehow, untouchable.

During the weeks that followed, as the leaves coloured and fall arrived in the city, Karlis spent his days studying and attending lectures and practicals, and did well. It was all too easy for him. But he looked forward to the evenings; spent them talking and drinking in cafes and bars with his housemates and other friends, or dancing with Ilze. Sometimes she joined them during their 'discussions' and contributed eloquently. They were all poor, but somehow managed to find the money for it all.

Karlis was not sure how it happened but one day, after a night of dancing with Ilze, he found himself kissing her. She put her arms around him and kissed him back, passionately. He ran his hands through her long, dark hair and put one hand gently under her tight dress cupping a small, pert, firm breast. She thrust her tongue into his mouth.

Realising what was happening, she gently put her hands on his chest and pushed him away. "No! Please no! I'm sorry."

They broke apart from each other that night, but both wanted more. He wanted her slim hips and pert, small breasts. He wanted to feel her body against his and to be able to run his hands through her lovely long dark hair.

But it didn't happen. A few days later, late in the year, Karlis began to feel ill. He became listless and developed a persistent cough. He also tossed and turned during the night and would wake up sweating, despite the fact it was cold outside. Adolfs worried and insisted he spend a few days in bed to get over the fever. But Karlis did not get over it. He grew worse daily. After three days, the cough and sweats still persisted. One day, after a particularly bad fit of coughing, Karlis noticed blood had soaked his handkerchief. He called out to Adolfs, who came to his bedside. Adolfs went white when he saw the bloody cloth.

"I'll get a doctor," he gasped and ran out the door.

The doctor came straight away. He glanced at the young man, noticing how thin and wan he was and gingerly examined the bloody handkerchief.

"It looks like TB. He'll have to be isolated," the doctor said grimly.

Adolfs gasped. "What can we do?" he asked, his voice strained with worry.

"He's very ill," the doctor replied. "There is little we can do. It's best that he goes home and be made comfortable. He can more easily be kept in isolation there and be looked after. I have to stress, keeping your brother in isolation is very important as this is a very contagious disease. I suggest that you be the only one allowed in this room until your brother can be moved."

"I'll call our parents and make the arrangements," Adolfs said grimly.

"Good." The doctor almost ran out the door.

Wilhelmina sat by her son's bed watching his shallow breathing. He was pale like a corpse and she felt distraught knowing how close to death her beloved youngest son was. She gently wiped his sweating face, understood his exhaustion. His blood on the white cloth was a deep red.

She prayed. "Please God, save my son. He is a strong and good lad. Please, please, help him get over this terrible disease."

Outside the room, Heinrich paced and fretted. Wilhelmina would not let him in his son's sick room. He heard his wife praying, and although not an overly religious man, he prayed silently as well. Soon, not able to bear it any more, he went outside into the bleak snow to check the cows in the barn.

Karlis was strong. As if in answer to his mother's prayers, he slowly started to recover. At first, she just heard him moan.

"What is it, son?" she asked gently.

He did not answer, as he was still asleep.

She felt hope and prayed fervently. "Please God, is this a sign? Is he getting better? What shall I do?"

Her son stirred a little. He was still sweating, but, or was it just her imagination, his colour seemed a little better. Suddenly his eyes fluttered open, and he looked up, bewildered, at his mother.

"Mother?" he murmured. Then he coughed that awful wracking cough.

Wilhelmina held a cloth to his mouth. It was clear!

She fell to her knees. "Oh, God. Thank you, thank you."

She then wiped her son's face again. He was very weak and fell asleep again immediately. Suppressing her joy, Wilhelmina ran out to the barn. "Heinrich! He has turned! He will get better now, I'm sure of it."

She then broke down and wept with relief.

Heinrich put his arms around her and hugged her, a wave of relief rolling over him as well that his son was over the worst, and gratitude and love for his kind, caring, and brave wife.

Karlis' recovery was very slow. His mother ministered to him every day; wiping his face, fluffing up his pillows and keeping his room as clean as she could. When he was a little stronger, she administered her awful tasting country remedies, and he gagged and gasped every time he had to drink them. But he forced them down anyway. Eventually he was able to sit up and take some chicken soup. As the spring arrived, Karlis improved and was soon able to walk into the yard and enjoy the sunshine. He was still very weak and could only walk a short distance before collapsing exhausted into a chair.

As summer approached, the light increased and days became warmer. As his strength increased, he was able to walk around the yard and enjoy the green of the fruit trees. He would sit in the yard and watch the small humming birds and bees flutter and buzz around the flowers. Soon, Wilhelmina decided, he would be able to start eating solids. She was so pleased he looked so much better and was thankful that her prayers had been answered. She was sure, like last time, that her home remedies had helped as well.

In early May 1922, Karlis decided he was better. He was strong again and had even started doing a bit of work around the farm. He found he was enjoying the work and the farm life. He'd been ill for around six months, cooped up in the house, and was enjoying the fresh air and exercise. And he was aware that he'd nearly died. His luck had held.

A short time later, when Karlis was completely recovered, Heinrich decided to breach a subject that was close to his heart. He had started to feel his age and wanted to retire to their house in Jelgava. It was now time to talk about it, as for the first time in over a year all his sons were all together. Arturs had arrived from his regiment the previous day and Adolfs had just arrived from Riga.

The family sat around the table laden with plenty of food, most of it from the garden. Spread around the table, so everyone could serve themselves, were sauerkraut, dill pickles, potato salad, black rye bread, hard-boiled eggs and roast chicken. Heinrich and

Wilhelmina had also provided a special treat of some home-made sausages and pīrāgs. When everyone had eaten and now sat around the table sipping sweet black coffee, with a bit of rouf, Heinrich hushed the hubbub of conversation.

"I have something to say … we have a lot to celebrate. Karlis is well again after recovering from an awful disease. We have to discuss the future."

He paused and thought for a moment while everyone sat and quietly sipped their coffee.

Then Heinrich continued. "It is time for me to move on. I'm not young anymore and want to put my feet up for the twilight of my years in Jelgava. We have to decide what to do with the farm. I really want it to stay in the family."

Everyone nodded. Arturs and Adolfs guessed what he was about to stay.

"I would like to pass the farm to Karlis, rather than sell it or break it up. Arturs and Adolfs, as you all have rights to the farm, I proposed that we come to an arrangement so that Karlis can buy your share. First of all, are you willing to take it on, son?" he asked Karlis.

Karlis did not have to think about it long. Over the time of his illness he had decided that farming was something he wanted to do.

"Yes, I would love to take over and continue your vision, Father. But I will only consider it if it is okay with everyone here." He smiled at Wilhelmina. "That includes you, Mum!"

Wilhelmina nodded and smiled back at him. She knew what he was saying.

Arturs said blandly, "I'm an officer in the army. I can't farm."

Adolfs was pensive, but he nodded and said. "I hope to finish my forestry degree. If we can arrange for you, Karlis, to pay for my university, that'll cover my share."

Heinrich nodded. "Good. I'll work this out with Karlis and we'll get a lawyer and put together a document for you all to sign."

He rose and went to a cupboard; found a bottle of schnapps. "Let's drink to that. Uz veselibu!"

Everyone stood up and responded as they raised their glasses. "Priekā!"

Karlis took over the family farm, Plumshē, in the summer of 1922. He was young for such a responsibility but he threw himself into the enterprise with gusto. He decided to continue with his father's idea of concentrating on dairy farming. He marvelled at his father's foresight and felt lucky, for the market for milk soared and prices were forecast to continue rising, as demand for butter in Germany and Britain increased. The grain market, however, had declined. Heinrich had made the change just in time!

The first few years of Karlis' tenure as a farmer were difficult. Despite rising prices for milk, most of his excess income paid his debt to Arturs and paid for Adolfs' education. It was hard work as he had to do everything himself. He just did not have enough money to pay for help. Heinrich and Wilhelmina helped him when they could, despite his protestations. He really wanted his parents to enjoy their retirement, which he thought they heartily deserved. He made a habit of riding into Jelgava every Sunday, when he could, to visit his parents for lunch after church.

The hard graft of the first years was worth it. By 1925 Plumshē had thrived. Karlis had paid all his debts and Adolfs was ensconced in the flourishing Forestry Department. Forestry and farming were crucial to the Latvian economy as demand for timber and farm produce improved in Europe. Arturs' career had stalled somewhat. He was still only a major, but was enjoying life as a soldier. All in all, it was good times for the Kohler family.

Eventually, Karlis was able to employ a lad to help him around the farm, so he started thinking about moving forward with his life. He was still a young man and wanted to have fun and, more importantly, he wanted to find a wife. While he enjoyed the challenge of managing a thriving dairy farm, he felt life was passing him by. It was the roaring twenties, and Karlis hadn't been doing any roaring – it had been all work, work, work. He decided to do something about that.

Karlis first met Maria in Jelgava in the summer of 1925. He was immediately smitten. She was stunning, a beautiful, beguiling young woman with long brown hair and lovely dark eyes. And she was totally taken by this handsome, strong young man. They began to see a lot of each other straight away. Jelgava was not a big town, but it did have a few cafes and a dance hall, which had a fabulous jazz band playing most Sunday evenings.

Karlis asked Maria if she wanted go to a dance with him one Sunday, and much to his delight she agreed. But she told him she would meet him at the dance hall – he was on such a high that he didn't even notice how unusual, even daring, that request was.

That Sunday, after lunch with his parents, Karlis dressed in his tuxedo, a deep black suit he had recently splurged on during a trip to Riga. He looked dashing, but felt a little uncomfortable. When he saw Maria he forgot all his misgivings. She took his breath away; her large, plump, firm breasts and long legs accentuated by her body-hugging dress that was cut above the knees. She was wearing the height of fashion, at least for Jelgava, and wore a small feathered hat, tilted jauntily on her lovely long hair. When they entered the hall, they made quite an impression. The band struck up; Karlis led her onto the dance floor and they joined the other couples. Dancing exuberantly, he took every opportunity to swing her around.

When the band stopped playing and the people shuffled out of the hall, Karlis stood outside with Maria in the warm night air. A full moon shone down on that beautiful, clear night. He was tired, but happy – it had been a great night. As he bent to kiss her hand and say goodnight, he noticed she was pensive and distracted.

He asked her quietly. "What's troubling you, Maria? Didn't you have a good time?"

"No, No. It's been lovely. I love jazz music and dancing …" Her voice faltered.

Suddenly she looked him directly in the eye, her lovely eyes earnest, even affectionate. "It's all been so sudden. This has been our first real date and I feel a strong emotional attachment for you already."

"Is that a problem? I feel the same way! You are a beautiful woman!"

She blushed at how forward and bold he was.

"I have something to tell you …" she faltered again.

"What is it?" he prompted gently.

She grasped her courage in both hands and blurted out urgently. "I'm engaged! My fiancé is a captain in the army. He's away in Riga at the moment!"

Karlis felt suddenly cold; felt momentarily at a loss. Then he exclaimed boldly and wildly: "I don't care! I still want to see you, if you wish."

"I do wish it!" she answered warmly.

If Karlis had any qualms about dating an engaged woman, he didn't let that affect his relationship with her. He spent as much time as he could with her. He took her out to dinner and dancing; enjoying her company so much he started to believe he was falling in love with her. Maybe he naively hoped that somehow, somehow, she might change her mind and marry him.

One Sunday, after dancing the night away, they stood outside the hall in the enveloping darkness of a lovely, warm summer's night. Romance hung in the air. They were hot, tired and deliriously happy. He was not sure how it happened, but he forgot all decorum and kissed her on the lips. At first, she looked shocked, then she collapsed into his arms and kissed him passionately back. He put his arms around her and pressed her body against his and ran his hands through her hair.

It seemed that time had stood still, as if they were the only people on the planet …

Then she gently disentangled herself from his grasp. "I have to go!" She touched his cheek, with loving gentleness and disappeared into the night.

Karlis stood in the darkness for a long time, wondering if he had gone too far. Then he realised he didn't care. Unfortunately, unseen by both of them, a man lurking in the shadows had noticed their passion.

Karlis floated on cloud nine, so infatuated with her he didn't see the storm clouds brewing. And worse still, neither did Maria. It all came to a head with shocking suddenness. Maria's fiancé came to Jelgava from Riga. Somehow, he had heard about her affair with Karlis: perhaps they hadn't been as discrete as they thought.

Karlis was at his parents' house after his normal Sunday lunch with them, his parents both aware that something was up with their son. He seemed dreamily happy.

"He's in love!" Heinrich guessed.

Wilhelmina hoped so – it was time her youngest son settled down and got married.

Suddenly, a loud knock on the door. Without even waiting for them to get up and open it, the door crashed open. A wild-looking, handsome, young man rushed in, dragging Maria unceremoniously with him. Her pretty face was white and her lovely hair dishevelled.

"Is this him?" the man asked, wild-eyed, glaring intensely toward Karlis.

Maria nodded, terrified and mute.

Then the man realised where he was and with incredible will pulled himself together. He spoke with stilted courtesy to

Heinrich. "Sir; are you Heinrich Kohler?"

Heinrich leapt angrily to his feet. "Yes, who are you? How dare you barge into my house like this!"

"I'm really sorry, Mr Kohler, I mean no disrespect, but I have business with your son."

With that, the man strode towards Karlis and, producing a riding glove from his pocket, slapped him across the face, once on each cheek.

"Dawn! In two days, at the river, sir. You may choose the weapons. Please deal with my second!"

Another young man, unnoticed, stood at the door. In that instance, Maria screamed. Heinrich, Wilhelmina and Karlis stood stunned.

Heinrich managed to gasp. "What's this all about?"

The young man calmed down enough to answer. "Your son has been having an affair with my fiancé and I demand satisfaction." He bowed elaborately, and left, dragging Maria with him.

Heinrich glared savagely at his son. Red-faced and apoplectic, he roared, *"Is this the truth?"*

Karlis nodded, ashen-faced, unable to speak.

Wilhelmina went to her husband and, reaching up, put her hands on his shoulders. "Please, husband, calm down. Duelling is illegal. We shall go to the police and see what is to be done."

Heinrich nodded, yet he glowered at his son, still very angry.

"Come!" he barked, as he marched out of the house.

The duel did not occur – the police would not allow it and visited the aggrieved man, who agreed he'd acted rashly. He wisely decided to forgive and forget, with one stipulation: Karlis could never to see Maria again.

"It will be done!" Heinrich growled.

Heartbroken, Karlis returned to Plumshē and threw himself into his work. It was the only way he could think of to get over the heartache. Somewhere, in the back of his mind, he realised how foolish he'd been. But it didn't help. Hard work and the support of his parents did. The farm prospered and Karlis was now a moderately wealthy man.

Heinrich, after a while, came down off his high horse and forgave his son. "Just let that be a lesson for you. You are a man of substance now. Start acting like one!"

He came out to the farm and looked around, once again ran his hands through the deep, rich brown loam and looked over the lush, green pastures. Fat, black and white cows dotted the gentle slope up to a small thicket of trees. It was perfect farmland. He realised how lucky he'd been to get hold of this beautiful farm all those years ago.

"What you've done here, son, is impressive. I'm really pleased that you have taken up on what I started and improved it one hundred percent!"

Karlis nodded. "Come inside, father. Sit down and have tea with me."

The winter of 1926 was one of the coldest on record. In the city of Jelgava, ice and snow lay everywhere.

He walked into his parent's house, worried. Inside was quiet. Arturs, Adolfs and their wives, his mother and a minister huddled in the main room near the fire.

Karlis asked quietly, "How is he?"

Wilhelmina looked up, red eyed; she came over and hugged him. "He's comfortable. The doctors can do nothing for him now. It's only a matter of time."

She suppressed a sob. Karlis admired her for her calmness and strength. "Can I see him?"

She nodded.

He walked quietly into the room and sat at his father's bedside.

Heinrich breathed softly and easily; he looked strangely peaceful. Karlis sat quietly without disturbing his father's serene repose for a long while, then he finally spoke, quietly. "Dad, it's Karlis."

Heinrich's eyes fluttered open. "Karlis?" he whispered.

"Yes, dad."

"I've not long now, son. I've had a good life. Promise me you'll look after your mother and Plumshē."

"Off course I will, Father."

Heinrich smiled, lifted himself up from the bed a little and spoke slightly more loudly. "Get yourself a wife!"

He coughed and fell back into the bed, exhausted from the exertion.

"It's getting dark," he whispered, his eyes still wide open. "Please get your mother and the minister."

Karlis stood. Bending down, he gently kissed his father on the brow before quietly walking out into the main room.

"It's time," was all he said.

VII

The Latvians Part 2 (1927–1939)

The three brothers sat in their mother's parlour in the house in Jelgava. Outside in the dark, with small flurries of snow swirled coldly in a light breeze. A bright fire roared merrily in the fireplace. As they sat by the warmth of the fire, each quietly contemplated the flames, their moods sad and reflective. Wilhelmina, who was tired and distraught after the funeral, had retired to her room.

Arturs stared into the fire.

"I have something to say…" he said, then hesitated, unsure if it was the right time to bring up something he'd been thinking about for a long time.

Adolfs looked up. "What is it, Arturs?"

After a long pause, Arturs decided to let out his thoughts. "I've been thinking about this for a long time, in fact, since the war. I think it's time to change our name."

His brothers looked up, shocked.

Arturs hurried on, somewhat breathlessly. "I've not mentioned this before out of respect for our father …"

"What about our mother? Surely this is not the time to discuss such a thing!" Karlis interrupted.

Arturs answered defensively, "There's really no better time. Please, just listen to what I have to say."

He paused and looked at them. They both stared back, then nodded. "We are Latvian now."

"We have *always* been Latvian!"

Arturs sighed. This was going to be difficult. But he had

expected that. "I mean we are a Latvian nation. Not a part of Russia. Our name is a German name. I really think we should have a more Latvian name."

"Why?" Karlis asked, intrigued by this outlandish proposal.

Arturs hesitated and then blurted out. "I know this is selfish on my part, but having a German name means that I'm being discriminated against. Surely, you are having the same problem as well, Adolfs?"

Adolfs nodded.

Arturs hurried on. "It's holding back my career."

"This is crazy, Arturs …" Karlis said, flustered. "How can that be the case … you are a hero of Latvia, Arturs. Doesn't that mean anything these days? You were one of the first to join the Latvian nationalist forces! There are not many better Latvians than you!"

"The past is not important now! They have forgotten. There is a new breed of radical nationalists in the government and military who only consider name, not deeds! The only thing they all have in common that they despise the Germans and anything German!"

Adolfs nodded. "I've noticed that in the department as well."

Karlis was shocked by these bland statements. But he considered them before replying. "This really is crazy. The Germans are amongst our best trading partners. They buy a lot of our butter … Okay, okay, what do you propose? Going back to Ķenkus?"

He grimaced when he said it.

Both Adolfs and Arturs looked at him with horrified expressions before blurting out. "No! No! The Baron, way back, did us all a big favour when he changed *that* name!"

Arturs paused, then said. "How about Kelers or Keleris? They're good Latvian names."

"Okay, they sound good … but only if mother agrees."

Wilhelmina, with some misgivings, agreed to the proposal, so it was done. The Kohler brothers changed their name by deed poll.

However, in a stuff-up that was almost comical, managed to end up with two different names. Arturs and Karlis took the name Kelers, while Adolfs ended up with the name Keleris! Adolfs, later when he was spruiking his nationalistic credentials, claimed that he had done it deliberately as Kelers *was still too* German. The other two didn't believe him.

The name-changing episode was a distraction as Karlis had other things to worry about. Grim tidings came from overseas: the reverberations from the recent crash on the stock exchange in New York were only just being felt worldwide. He knew in his heart of hearts the good times, the 'roaring twenties', were over. The depression had started to hit Latvia hard. People were being thrown out of work and, for the first time for at least ten years, he could see some people suffering real hardship. The market for Latvian dairy products had collapsed.

Karlis, after much agonising, made the bold decision to go back to cropping, thinking he could diversify more easily. His instinct was correct, as time would prove this decision to be the right one. Luckily, he had kept the farm equipment he needed and also was able to buy more equipment as he sold down his herd. By the spring of 1930 he decided to plant rye, wheat and flax, while keeping a number of cows for his own use. After he had planted, Karlis decided to use what was left of his savings to fertilise his crops. This was a bold and innovative decision. He had little money and it was perhaps unnecessary. The soil at Plumshē was exceptionally good and could produce a good yield without any enhancement. However, Karlis believed he could increase the yield of his crops substantially by investing in the fertiliser. Once again, time would prove him correct, as he not only improved the yield of his crops, but also the quality, meaning he could get a good price even in a depressed market.

While 1930 had been a very hard year for Karlis, his business decisions meant that by the summer of 1931, despite the depression, the farm at Plumshē thrived. Karlis was one of the few farmers in the district who was actually made money in very trying times. He was lucky. The depression did not stop it being a bumper season.

He was able to turn his attention to another matter that worried him: he was lonely. He needed company and, despite serious reservations, decided he was ready to find a wife. While still haunted by his failed relationship with Maria, he had been distraught and resentful when he'd read in the local newspaper that she had dumped her fiancé and married another man — a wealthy high official in the government. Why had she done that? Surely, she had been in love with him? Belatedly, he realised that his feelings for her had not been reciprocated. Depression hung over him for a long while, but he compensated, as before, by throwing himself into his work.

Then things started to change: Karlis, by chance, met a quiet, gentle, young woman called Lydia Bergs. She was petite and pleasant-looking, even plain, with fine brown hair. Karlis sensed she had a kind heart. He found her intriguing. He was sure he knew the name Bergs, but was not sure how, and he resolved to get to know her if he could. Lydia was receptive to his charms, but her grandmother, old Mrs Bergs, the formidable family matriarch, was not.

After the disaster of his relationship with Maria, Karlis decided to be cautious and respectful with Lydia. He even formally approached her grandmother and requested permission to court her. It was the one of the scariest days of his life.

Dressed in his best suit, he rode to Kambaris, the large estate the Bergs family owned, not far from Plumshē. As he rode, he looked over stark brown fields that spread away in the distance.

He noticed a thicket of old gnarly oaks on a small hill, the leaves on the trees the yellows, reds, oranges and browns of the fall. It was a lovely scene and he quickly realised this was potentially very rich land. As he approached the farm, he was overawed by the house. It was a large, stately country home, surrounded by lovely gardens and lawns.

Karlis was so nervous approaching such a place, that he nearly turned the horse around and rode away. Just as he was about to turn away, he noticed Lydia in the garden. She waved and ran up to him.

"You came! I'm so pleased. Come in!" she gasped, directing him into a pleasant room with wide French doors that overlooked the garden.

"Lydia! Leave us, at once! Who are you, young man?"

It was the old lady. Lydia, blushed, but smiled encouragingly, before hurrying away to another room.

"I'll see you soon," she whispered over her shoulder.

"Well, boy, cat got your tongue?" the old lady quipped rudely.

Karlis felt offended by this. A strapping man of twenty-nine years, he resented her tone, but swallowed his pride. He answered respectfully, deciding to get to the point straight away. "My name is Karlis Kelers, ma'am. I wish to ask your permission to court your granddaughter."

She snorted. "Want to court my granddaughter, do you? Why should I let you do that?"

He hoped it was a rhetorical question.

Then, she said abruptly. "Kelers? Kelers? I don't know that name. Where are you from?"

"I own a farm nearby, ma'am; Plumshē."

"Plumshē!" she frowned. "Is Heinrich Kohler your father?"

"Yes, ma'am," he answered.

She grumbled in response. "So, you changed your name then."

He said nothing.

Then, indiscernibly, her attitude changed. "My late son knew your father back in 05 and spoke very highly of him. How is your father?"

"He passed away over four years ago."

"Oh! I'm sorry about that."

The old lady glared at him, before saying tersely. "You may come back."

She waved him away dismissively.

Karlis gathered together his shredded dignity and bowed before leaving the house. As he fled down the path towards the front gate, Lydia breathlessly hurried after him. She had heard it all and had rushed out another door to catch up with him before he left.

"I'm so sorry, Karlis. That was awful!" she gasped as she smiled shyly at him. Then she said, "She liked you!"

Karlis laughed at that. "Can I see you next week?"

"Yes, I'd love that!"

Lydia watched as he untethered his horse and waved as he rode away. He turned and waved back at her, smiling. Lydia was thrilled. He was such a handsome man! She turned and went back inside. Her grandmother was waiting for her.

"So, do you like him?" she asked abruptly.

"Yes, very much."

"Bit low class for you," the old lady grumbled.

"Oh, Grandmother," Lydia sighed. "He's one of the most respected and successful farmers in the district."

Then she added boldly, "Also, Grandmother, we don't live in the old empire anymore."

The old lady said dismissively, "More the worse for it too!"

Karlis rode out to see Lydia as often as he could, while it was still fine. If cold, he would make sure they were rugged up and walked with her around Kambaris. He talked to her, wanting to be as open and honest with her as he could. He even told her about his affair with Maria, which upset her and caused a strain in their relationship. She quickly got over it, appreciating his honesty. He knew then she was the one for him and hoped she felt the same way. He knew there was real strength in their relationship.

One day, late in the winter of 1931, just before Christmas, he felt able to broach a subject that intrigued him. Her father. He was sure now why he knew the name Bergs.

"This is such a lovely farm. How did your family get hold of it?" he asked her one day as they walked in the fresh and picturesque garden, their feet crunching in the icy snow. Icicles hung off the trees around them, making it enchanting, dreamlike.

She clutched his arm and cuddled as close as she could to him in the cold. "My father bought it," she said. "He fell in love with the place a long time ago and decided to buy it. He was never a farmer, but he paid for a good manager and would spend as much time as he could here."

Karlis smiled at her; put his arm tightly around her slim waist, encouraging her to continue. "What did your father do?"

"Oh, he was some high official in the Tsar's government here and did very well," she said proudly, then added coyly, "He was ennobled for his services to the Tsar, you know."

"I didn't know that. Your grandmother mentioned that your father knew mine back in the first revolution in 1905."

"Really? That's nice. Maybe you met him!"

Karlis laughed. "I doubt that very much! What happened to your father?"

Her face fell. "He died in Russia in 1917. He decided to evacuate us there during what they now call The Great War. My mother has never gotten over his death and still misses him, even now. You should have seen the place when we got back here in 1918. It was a mess."

She took his hand and led him back into the house. A servant took their coats as they walked into a study.

"This was my father's room, when he was here. My mother has insisted that we leave it exactly as he had it. I want to show you something."

She went over and rummaged in a drawer in an old oak desk. Inside she found a map and a ring.

Holding them reverently she said quietly, "This is a map of Kambaris and this is my Grandfather's ring."

Karlis gently held the map. It showed the full extent of the farm. It was large: he guessed about four times the size of Plumshē, which was not small. He then admired the ring. It was a small, gold signet ring with a crest on it.

She took his hand and whispered, "This is our family crest. The ring is a family heirloom. My grandfather used it to seal letters and then passed it onto my father. I hope this will be yours one day."

She blushed, realising what she had said.

He, for the first time, took her in his arms, forgetting at that moment all his vows about taking it slowly with her. "Do you mean that?" he said quietly.

She nodded, melting close to him and looking up at his face. He smiled at her, delighted, before kissing her.

Arturs Kelers' heart sang. He had an official letter in his hands from the War Minister, Jānis Balodis, himself. The letter said briefly: *I'm promoting you to Colonel, congratulations. Please report immediately to the War Ministry. Balodis.*

Arturs hurriedly packed and, taking his army vehicle, had himself driven to Riga, where he went into the army store and, using the letter from Jānis Balodis, received his new uniform. He went to his accommodation, put on his new uniform and immediately drove to the War Ministry and was announced.

Jānis Balodis received him in his office. "Ah, Arturs, please come in and sit down. Do you want coffee?”

Arturs was surprised by his informality. “Thank you, sir, coffee would be nice.”

Balodis nodded to an orderly, who hurried away, before quickly returning with a pot of coffee and two cups.

Balodis dismissed him and poured the coffee himself. “We’ve known one another of a long time, Arturs. Before I give you your new orders, I want to talk to you – man to man with someone I can trust.”

Arturs was once again taken aback, but answered, “Yes, of course, sir. I would be glad to help.”

“Good, good,” Balodis said somewhat absent-mindedly.

Then he looked directly into Arturs’ eyes. “I want you to be honest with me. I want you to say things without fear of what I may think. What is your assessment of the situation now?”

Arturs took a deep breath while he gathered his thoughts. “To be brutally honest, sir, in my opinion things are very bad at the moment internationally. Hitler is growing stronger in Germany, while the Soviet Union is also strong. They are a lot stronger now than in 1919. As you are probably aware, sir, Stalin is conducting a purge at the moment. We can only assume it will strengthen his regime, but I urge that we wait and see how it affects the country. My feeling is no good will come of it and it will weaken Soviet society. Despite that, sir, we must have peace. If there is war, Latvia as a nation, is doomed.”

“You think it’s that bad? There are no signs of war at the moment.”

“It’s only a matter of time. Our intelligence says Hitler is rapidly rearming Germany. In my opinion, he *is* preparing for war. It’s only a matter of when and where.”

Balodis looked grim. “I hope that will not happen. But what do you suggest?”

“Well, sir, one thing for sure is that Latvia can’t stand alone against these two giants. We can't rely on British support as we did in 1919. They're too weak, both militarily and politically. So, we have to do something for ourselves."

Arturs paused. Balodis nodded encouragingly.

So Arturs continued, warming to his subject. "We must have a defensive alliance with countries in our region. We must involve Estonia, Lithuania, Finland and even Poland in this alliance. That's the only way we *might* have the strength to influence outcomes and even defend ourselves in the worst-case scenario."

He paused for effect, and then went on. "I'm aware this will be difficult. However, all the regimes in the area, while nationalistic, have similar philosophies and political structures. They also have similar geopolitical problems and issues to deal with. With good will and strong leadership from someone, it can be done. We did, after all, work very well with the Estonians, Lithuanians and Poles back in 1919."

Balodis' face was expressionless as he took this all in. "Thank you, Arturs. I appreciate your candour. Your analysis of the situation is succinct and thoughtful. You have shown me that you are the right man for the job I have in mind."

He sipped his coffee. "I have your orders here. I want you to be our next Military Attaché in Moscow. You will collect your credentials at the Foreign Affairs Ministry but will report directly to me. Your brief will be to report anything of interest regarding the Soviet military and liaise with the Soviet military. *It will not be an intelligence role.* The government is determined to have good relations with Stalin's Russia, difficult as that is. Unfortunately, you will not be able to take your family with you, so I want you to take as much time as you need to get your affairs in order. However, I want you in Moscow by early September this year."

This thrilled Arturs. Though disappointed that he could not take his wife Nelija and their sons with him, he recognised that they may not be safe in Moscow. He didn't think Nelija would raise any objections to this appointment.

So he said decisively, "Thank you, sir. It will be a great honour to serve in such a way!"

Balodis smiled and stood up proffering his hand. "I hoped you would say that."

Things went well for Karlis. He'd taken over the management of Kambaris and had some big ideas about how to improve the property. The depression was over, and Plumshē thrived again. By using modern and innovative farming practices he'd made a good income from Plumshē and was sure he could make a lot more from Kambaris.

He and Lydia decided to get married on 30 August 1936 and excitedly planned the wedding. Karlis received a letter from Arturs and was thrilled about his brother's posting to Moscow; was further thrilled that Arturs would be able to attend his wedding before taking up his new posting.

Karlis and Lydia Kelers' wedding was the largest the district had seen in a long time – it was talked about for years afterwards. Karlis had laid on a generous spread of food and drink. Lydia looked lovely in her mother's wedding dress. Both of Karlis' brothers attended with their families, along with a number of cousins, friends and others. Karlis had even invited all the Kambaris and Plumshē farm workers and the servants not involved in the catering of the celebration. Wilhelmina, liking and approving of Lydia, felt overjoyed her youngest son was finally getting married. Arturs stood resplendent in the dress uniform of a full Colonel and Adolfs wore a sharp black suit. However, the radiant and lively Lydia was the centre of attention – Karlis would have it no other way. It was Lydia's day and he beamed contentedly at all the attention she received. At the end of the day, he carried her over the threshold of the house at Kambaris through a shower of flower petals. They made love, passionately, for the first time that night.

The next day, Karlis walked with his brothers through the fields of Kambaris, their wives happily partaking of tea in the parlour, so the three brothers had some time to themselves. The lush, green crops Karlis had sown were thriving. In the distance, horses pulled the new harvesting machine as the workers rushed to harvest the bumper crop. Karlis bent down and ran the rich brown soil through his fingers.

"I have a lot of plans for this place," he said almost lovingly.

Arturs nodded. "It's a beautiful farm. There's a lot of potential here. Is that little oak forest on the hill in the property?"

Karlis smiled. "Yes. I'm thinking of opening it up for limited hunting. What do you think?"

Adolfs, breathing deeply of the fresh, cool air, nodded. "Good idea."

"See the horses over there?" Karlis pointed out, "I'm planning to harvest using one of those new tractor machines. I'm sure it will add a lot to the efficiency of the harvest. I'm planning to crop wheat, oats, clover and hay. I've read about a new potato seed available in France and am investigating purchasing some. Perhaps, in time, I will farm chickens here as well."

Karlis smiled and put his arm around his oldest brother's shoulders. "Here I am jabbering away about Kambaris when you are off on a big adventure to Moscow! When are you going?"

Arturs smiled. "Next week. Jānis Balodis wants me to settle into Moscow as soon as possible."

Adolfs frowned. "You'll be alright? We keep hearing rumours about a terrible purge there."

"Yes. I'll have diplomatic immunity – even the Soviet government respects that. It'll be one of my duties to monitor and report on the purge. Not something I'm looking forward to, but I'm hoping I will be of real service to the republic there."

"I'm sure you will! I cannot think of a better person to do the job!"

Arturs smiled at that. "Funnily enough; that's what Jānis Balodis said as well!"

The brothers reached the boundary fence of the farm and leaned against it, enjoying each other's company. They didn't know it at the time, but it was to be the last time they would all be together.

Dressed in his best uniform, Arturs Kelers strode across the vast open area of Red Square in the heart of Moscow, carrying a locked briefcase. As he approached the Kremlin, where he was to present his diplomatic credentials, he felt unnerved. The high red wall brooded menacingly in the light misty rain. He walked up to a Soviet soldier at the gate and presented his pass. The soldier glared at it, then picked up a phone. He spoke briefly to someone and then waved him through. Arturs presented himself to a reception room and was politely asked to sit down.

"Minister Molotov will see you as soon as he can, Colonel. You can leave your briefcase here."

Arturs sat and waited, and waited. Three hours later, in what was undoubtedly a diplomatic snub, he was ushered into a large office. A bespectacled man with a lush moustache and thin black hair sat at a large desk. Standing in the shadows near a window, was another man. Noting the hard, craggy face, cold cruel eyes and a small moustache, Arturs guessed this was Genrikh Grigoryevich Yagoda, head of the feared NKVD.

Molotov looked up from his desk. "Well?"

The man at the window surveilled Arturs.

"Colonel Arturs Kelers, the new Military Attaché for Latvia. I'm here to present my credentials, Comrade Minister Molotov."

Molotov imperiously indicated he wanted the papers, yet barely glanced at them before waving Arturs away. Arturs turned and left, feeling decidedly uncomfortable.

Arturs settled into life in Moscow. He had a small office on the second floor of the Embassy overlooking Chaplygina Street in central Moscow, not far away from the so-called garden ring and had been given a comfortable apartment in the embassy grounds to live in. Arturs found the position challenging, the Russian authorities not forthcoming with respect to military affairs. However, he persisted. Ironically, Arturs thought, one of the first despatches he sent to Balodis was:

Yagoda, head of the NKVD has been dismissed and replaced by Nikolai Yehzov. I expect that under this new leader, the NKVD purge of 'Trotskyites' will intensify.

He was later saddened to report that he was correct – he'd noticed a marked increase in disappearances. In one of his despatches, Arturs wrote: *A reign of terror of an unprecedented scale has been launched by the NKVD.*

Having made a few contacts in the Russian military, Arturs became increasingly alarmed as they ceased to be available. He would ring up and ask for Comrade Ivanov, an officer he knew only to be told by a nervous, unknown voice that Ivanov was sick, or he was away, or somebody else was doing his duties. On asking who, Arturs would be given an evasive answer. It became obvious to him that dealing with foreigners was poison for Russian officials as more and more of them disappeared. The terror on the streets was discernible and frightening even for Arturs. NKVD agents seemed to be everywhere. People energetically denounced others, often just because they were jealous, or wanted his wife, or his job, or his apartment. Then people started denouncing the denouncers. The Latvian embassy was not exempt. Their cook and one of their drivers failed to arrive at work on separate occasions. They were never seen again.

Amidst all this activity, Arturs sent regular despatches to Balodis. However, none of it was militarily significant. That all changed in June 1937 when Arturs managed to intercept a communiqué that announced Marshal Tukachevski and a number of other Marshals had been charged with high treason. He then received communiqués announcing their full confessions and executions. He immediately sent a coded despatch marked top secret to Balodis: *Tukachevski and six other Marshals purged. An intense purge of the Soviet High Command and officer corps is commencing. This should significantly reduce the Red Army's ability to fight a major war.*

Not long after the demise of Tukachevski, Arturs, along with many other diplomats, surprisingly received an invitation to a reception. He felt grimly amused by the fearful faces of all the generals and admirals attending. They stood by themselves in the shadows and, whenever he attempted to approach them, they made excuses and sidled away. He noticed they didn't talk to each other either, and assumed it was due to the impossible task of determining who might, or might not, be one of the 'traitors' the Trotskyite wreckers and saboteurs that had allegedly infected the military.

On occasion, Arturs would don civilian clothes and go out into the streets to get a feel for Soviet life, and to meet some of his contacts in person. This was still possible, but elaborate precautions had to be taken to avoid the ever-present NKVD. He would walk past poorly stocked shops and shabbily dressed people who often queued for hours in the snow just to get the bare necessities of life. Arturs would record his observations and forward them to Balodis. In his secret despatches, he urged Balodis to be cautious with Stalin and not position Latvia too closely to the Soviet Union. He also reported his appraisal of the Soviet economy; that it was geared entirely to heavy industry, especially armaments production. The plight of the ordinary people was of no concern to Stalin or his regime.

It depressed Arturs that his warnings fell on deaf ears. He hoped not, because it would be disasterous for Latvia if the government tried to appease Stalin. He was convinced a man like Stalin would only see appeasement as a sign of weakness. Arturs truly believed the only way to stand up to a paranoid megalomaniac like Stalin was to push back. But he sometimes despaired, and eventually realised, the reality of Latvia's weakness.

During all his secret walks, one thing continued to astound him: the bravery and hospitality of the ordinary Russian people. Often, after his business with his informants was completed, he would be invited into their houses. These tiny flats were usually dirty, cluttered and badly constructed. Nevertheless, they offered what they had, usually very little and the food available was poor. However, they always provided some bread, thin watery borsch and vodka, and they would smile and talk a bit too loudly and drink a little too much vodka. Arturs would have to sneak out of their houses and take a circuitous route back to the embassy. With time, this sort of activity became harder and more dangerous, and most doors were closed to him. Arturs found himself spending more time drinking, dining and talking with the foreign diplomatic corps.

On 13 March 1938, Arturs attended one of the strangest events in Stalin's state: the last of the great show trials, held in a grandiose, brightly decorated room in the Kremlin that had revolutionary paintings on the ceiling. With its dark wooden panelling, however, it looked strangely grim and foreboding.

Arturs was not above the irony that one of the 'stars of the show' in the dock with the other 'traitors', was Genrikh Grigoryevich Yagoda, along with the famous revolutionary Nikolai Bukharin. The public prosecutor, Andrey Vyshinski, a neatly dressed man with a trim moustache and a ruddy complexion, read out the indictment, a long list of the crimes committed by the defendants. So ridiculous were they that Arturs almost laughed when he heard them.

When he was finished, Vyshinski asked dramatically, with a leer, knowing the answers. "Do you plead guilty to the crimes you are charged with?"

They each stood up – Yagoda included – and droned, tonelessly, "I'm guilty."

However, much to Vyshinski's consternation, one of them, Krestinski, a pale, seedy little man with steel-rimmed spectacles, in a rare show of courage and bravado, said, "I'm not guilty of the crimes I'm accused of."

Vyshenski vigorously waved a paper in Krestinski's face, and screamed at him. "How do you account for your statements in the preliminary investigation?"

Krestinski's simple, and quietly defiant answer was devastating. "I was forced to make the confession against my will."

Vyshenski paled at this answer. His easy trial seemed to be slipping away from him, with catastrophic consequences for himself. He asked for an adjournment, which was eagerly granted by the judges. At that time, Arturs thought he saw … or was it his imagination … a beady eye peering at them through the eye of a painting on the ceiling. The eye looked different and seemed to move … Was he getting paranoid?

The grim and foreboding outside seemed to reflect the forbidding trial inside. Arturs didn't want to go to his little flat in the embassy. Quietly and contemplatively, he walked through the cold drizzle, accompanied, he was sure, by his almost constantly present NKVD tail; he sat in the pleasant warmth of a little café that he liked, not far from the Kremlin on Arbil Street. He didn't drink tea. As he sat and sipped his vodka, the bottle in front him, he was quietly joined by a young British colleague and friend.

The tall, thin, ruggedly handsome man had penetrating eyes, and sported a dark pencil moustache; he spoke furtively, well aware of the ever-lurking NKVD.

"Well, that was one for the books. Who would ever think that a little weed like Krestinski could actually show some spine?" he drawled in fluent German, but with a posh English accent.

Arturs signalled for a waiter to bring a glass for the man, and when it arrived poured a large shot before saying somewhat cynically. "We'll see what happens tomorrow!"

The man smiled. Taking his glass, he raised it and knocked back the shot in one gulp. "Tomorrow!" he echoed in English.

Arturs smiled, finished his glass, and poured two more shots.

The next morning, Vyshinski once again asked Krestinski, "Do you plead guilty to the crimes you are charged with?"

A pale and drawn Krestinski shakily answered, "I plead guilty."

Vyshinski looked relieved. The situation had been saved.

Arturs' jaw dropped at this sudden admission of guilt, but he knew he shouldn't really be surprised. He muttered to the man sitting next to him. "They must have really gone to work on him!"

He considered the rest of the trial a farce as the defendants tripped over one another in their eagerness to incriminate each other. It was a strange, grim drama of blood and fury. Vyshinski set out to prove the defendants were not political prisoners but common criminals who had inflicted on the Soviet people the most heinous of crimes, his abuse and invective therefore remorseless, implacable and highly imaginative. Vyshinski, dramatically playing to the audience, seemed to enjoy his victim's discomfort and perhaps even started to believe his lies and innuendo, as he worked himself into a crescendo of fury.

Vyshinski's dramatic oratory worked for all the defendants except Bukharin. While Bukharin readily professed his culpability, he boldly stated that he was only guilty of opposing Stalin's policies *because they were wrong,* this statement totally unacceptable to Vyshinski. He tried everything – blustering, threatening, cajoling – to make Bukharin appear a common criminal. Bukharin refused to play the game and adamantly stated he had never worked for a foreign government and had never been involved in a plot to murder Lenin, the most serious indictment he was under. Bukharin was a theorist of revolution, with an impeccable reputation. He was guilty, he admitted, of the other charges. For which, Bukharin declared, he deserved to be shot. However, he claimed stridently, unbowed by Vyshinski's arguments, everything he did was for the good of the Soviet Union. This was not at all what Vyshinski wanted. He had failed to paint Bukharin as a common criminal but he had little choice and moved on.

Not at all surprised by the eventual verdicts – that all the defendants were declared guilty and sentenced to be shot – Arturs puzzled over why Stalin had bothered to have such a farcical trial in the first place. Why not just make them disappear? He couldn't define an answer to his satisfaction. He guessed it was all about the demise of the old guard. Stalin couldn't tolerate anyone with a greater revolutionary pedigree than himself. He, in his great paranoia, had to inflict public humiliation on them.

Arturs joined the throng and left the courtroom. He walked out onto the icy streets of Moscow, wishing he was back home in Riga.

At the same time that Arturs was in grim and depressing Moscow, a nice spring day shone back in Latvia. Kambaris was slowly recovering from the long winter and starting to look lush and green again, rather than stark and grey. Karlis sat in the office with Lydia, going through the books with her. He smiled: he had developed a thriving agribusiness with the two farms, and happily admitted he had been lucky. They'd had a number of bumper harvests and were doing well. Not far away, in the nursery, lay Karlis' pride and joy, a beautiful baby daughter. Life was good.

Karlis had become a very wealthy man. With his innovative agricultural practices, diversification and a bit of luck, the business had made exceptional profits. He was, as he had envisaged years ago, growing wheat, oats and potatoes. He had set up a chicken hatchery and had also put aside a part of the farm for an orchard. While it had put him under considerable financial stress, his new tractor had improved the efficiency of his cropping.

He smiled wider and looked out the window. He could see his workers moving around the big new barn he'd recently built. Nearby, parked in its shed, he saw the big American Studebaker he'd recently purchased. Being a good manager, Karlis looked after his workers. He resisted the urge to import cheap labourers from Lithuania and Poland, preferring to use hard-working, loyal Latvians and pay them well.

Often liking to discuss certain issues with Lydia, as he valued her insights, he now mulled over a number of issues. "This fellow, Schmidt, keeps asking about me allowing him to hunt in our oaks. I'm thinking of letting him …"

Lydia's lips thinned a moment. Then she said, "It wouldn't be good to have someone shooting in the wrong place … on Roberts farm, for example." Then she thought a little more. "Well … the oaks are on the far side of the farm, a long way from the house. It should be okay, as long as he tells us when and where he is going to be. He must not shoot in the direction of the house and farm buildings."

Karlis nodded.

"Good. I'll tell him. There's another thing," he said picking up the accounts, which he showed her. "We have enough cash to buy the watermill in Dobele. It would be a very good way to diversify the business."

"Mmm. The mill is owned by that fellow Adams? I know this is a bit silly, but his father looks a lot like the pictures I've seen of Heinrich."

Karlis laughed. "I'm sure that's just a coincidence and bad photography! I'm not aware of him being some long-lost cousin! What do you think about purchasing the mill?"

She smiled at him. "Are you really sure, love, that you want to take on more? You are very busy with the two farms."

"That's true," he said reflectively.

It *was* true. Karlis had to work hard to manage the two farms. Owning two hundred and fifty hectares made him the biggest and most prosperous farmer in the district. So he decided not to purchase the mill.

In contrast to her husband, Lydia lived a life of leisure and luxury. Karlis made sure she had all she needed. He employed a nanny and wet nurse for their beautiful little baby girl, Inta. Lydia also had a maid, and a housekeeper, cook, kitchenhand and gardener. The servants helped maintain the house and garden in a grand state.

Even though everything was going well for Karlis – he was wealthy; had a loving wife and a beautiful young daughter – he worried. He had been receiving letters from Arturs in Russia and had heard about the purges and the living conditions there. He worried about Hitler's aggression in Austria and Czechoslovakia. He was afraid of war. But, as an optimist, he believed Hitler was only trying to right the wrongs of the Treaty of Versailles and protecting the German people. That, he argued unconvincingly to himself, is what is expected of all rulers. Hitler was just trying to do his job.

Karlis reluctantly supported the authoritarian government that ruled Latvia, thinking that getting rid of the dysfunctional Saeima in 1934 was necessary. He was, however, troubled by the Ullmanis Regime's drift towards Soviet Russia. He could see nothing good coming from that at all. He totally opposed the abhorrent regime that was Stalinism. Sometimes, in despair, he thought it would be better to align with Hitler but knew that was impossible. The government was dominated by men who had a strong distrust of the Germans, a distrust brought on by the betrayal in 1919, so long ago – it was a vexing issue. Karlis knew Latvia was weak, and it stood alone, between two radically different giants and the regime seemed to be doing nothing about it.

Arturs stared with horror at the note in his hands. "Are you sure about this?" he asked the man standing in front of him.

"Yes, sir. It comes from a reliable source in the Commissariat for Foreign Affairs."

"Fuck! Fuck! Fuck them all to hell!" Arturs cursed loudly and leaned his head in his hands on the desk in total despair.

"Fuck!" he said again.

He then got up and paced towards the window, then turned back. The note spelled doom. He knew it was all over: it was only a matter of time before the NKVD came for him. They had been betrayed. He'd heard rumours, which he had duly reported to Balodis, about a German delegation that had flown into Moscow recently. But he'd never expected it to come to this so quickly.

He looked at the man quaking in front of him and spoke more calmly and quietly. "Very good. Please go back to your post and stay calm. You will receive your orders soon."

Arturs rose and walked to a cupboard; pulled out a good bottle of scotch he'd received from a British colleague. He had been saving it. He poured a large shot and gulped it down; feeling the warmth of the raw liquor surge into his stomach. He then sat at his desk and composed an urgent coded missive, marked top secret. It said:

A Nazi–Soviet non-aggression pact, called the Molotov-Ribbentrop pact, was signed in Moscow in the late hours of 23 August 1939. Our source in the Commissariat for Foreign Affairs, who is reliable, suggests there is also a secret protocol that is part of this pact. This protocol divides Romania, Poland, Lithuania, Latvia, Estonia and Finland into German and Soviet 'spheres of influence'. In the north, Finland, Estonia and Latvia are assigned to the Soviet sphere. Poland is to be partitioned in the event of its 'political rearrangement'—the areas east of the Pisa, Narev, Vistula and San rivers going to the Soviet Union while Germany would occupy the west. Lithuania, adjacent to East Prussia, will be in the German sphere of influence. I suggest this pact will result in war against Poland and perhaps even France as Hitler is securing his eastern frontier. I strongly advise that the government prepare for interference to our sovereignty by the Soviet Union and perhaps even an invasion. I am ordering the destruction of all-important documents and the evacuation of all non-essential staff.

Arturs sealed the document and called one of his assistants into the office. "This is to be sent, *very urgently* by our most secure channels, to the Minister of War. Please inform the Ambassador. Also, tell him that I believe we must immediately destroy all compromising correspondence. I respectfully suggest that he immediately organise the evacuation of all non-essential staff. Send in Filips. He can start straight away."

The man nodded and hurried out the door, shutting it behind him.

Arturs sat alone in the office and stared out the window at the grey, wet, bleak Moscow street below. He poured another stiff scotch and sipped it contemplatively. He knew now that he would never see his adored Nelija or his sons again. He would never meet his newest nephew, Karlis junior, who had been born less than a month previously. He felt saddened that he'd never be able to pay his respects at his beloved mother's grave. Wilhelmina had died peacefully in Jelgava hospital at the exact time the little baby boy had been born. Arturs' reverie was disturbed by a soft knock on the door.

"Come in!" he called.

Fillips hurried into the room.

Arturs stood and, putting his bottle of scotch into his desk drawer, walked towards a locked safe hidden behind a wall panel and said, "We'll start here."

VIII

The Dispossessed (1940–1941)

Arturs sat at the desk in his empty office. Everything had been stripped out, except the desk he sat at. Quiet now reigned, the usual bustle of activity in the corridors absent. Outside, it was a grey, rainy Moscow summer day. The day reflected his mood and prospects. He could see the armed NKVD guards loitering on the street nearby, their big black sedan across the road. It was the same outside the embassy's back entrance.

Arturs felt proud of the work he'd done over the last nine months, fruitless as it seemed. He'd been instrumental in secretly helping to safely evacuate all the embassy staff back to Latvia, most likely saving their lives. He'd also destroyed everything compromising and made sure everything of value had been sent back to Riga. The NKVD had discovered his activities and reacted by placing the remaining embassy staff under house arrest. The Ambassador and himself, the only men remaining, calmly waited for the inevitable.

On instinct, Arturs returned to his apartment and carefully showered, shaved and put on his best dress uniform, carefully pinning the cross of his Lāčplēsis Military Order on his chest. He rubbed an imaginary bit of dust off his spotless black leather boots. One last time he looked around the apartment that had been his home for almost four years. It was stark and barren; all of his personal possessions already removed and sent back to his family in Riga. Arturs left the apartment, quietly shutting the door. Back at his office, he opened a drawer and pulled out his bottle of scotch and two glasses. The drawer was empty now. Taking the bottle and glasses he walked out of the office, shut the door and walked down the empty corridor and down the stairs. At the Ambassador's big office, he knocked quietly on the door.

"Enter!" the man inside called.

Arturs entered. The Ambassador was dressed in his best tuxedo, with his sash and ambassadorial regalia carefully draped across his shoulders. He must have had the same thought as Arturs. His room was also empty, except for a sizeable Latvian flag on a flagpole near his desk. It was, in an act of quiet defiance, at half mast.

"Ah, Arturs, come in, come in. Are you expecting someone?"

Arturs admired the man for this bad joke and stoic demeanour. "Yes. The same people as you, I imagine."

Arturs produced his scotch. "Would you like a drink, sir?"

"Yes. Why not!"

Arturs poured two stiff shots and handed a glass to the Ambassador. He raised his glass with morbid irony. "To Latvia!"

The Ambassador laughed bitterly and raised his glass before drinking. Arturs filled their glasses again.

The Ambassador raised his glass again. "May our beloved country rise again!"

Arturs just smiled at that and drank.

At that moment the door crashed open and two NKVD guards, followed by an officer, burst into the room. The officer arrogantly approached the two men. He saw the flag and angrily kicked it over. His men glared at them and fingered their light machine guns.

"You are under arrest as enemies of the Soviet Union. You will come with me," the officer snarled.

The ambassador smiled calmly, ignoring his threatening tone. "Very well, Comrade Captain. We are ready."

He coolly finished his scotch and walked, with unhurried

dignity, towards the door, brushing the guards aside.

Arturs followed. They walked down the stairs, followed by the guards and the red-faced officer, and out the door. Two black sedans, their engines purring, were parked in the front courtyard. Both men stepped in the first vehicle and the door closed behind them. The officer and his men climbed into the other vehicle.

The cars drove out onto the quiet streets. They travelled quickly south towards Lubyanka Square. Any traffic on the road hurried out of the way, everyone recognising the black sedans of the NKVD. The cars rumbled through the main gate of the headquarters of the NKVD and its occupants were hustled out of the car and walked, flanked by their guards, into the building.

They were marched directly into a grim, grey room with a high, barred window that let in little light. A single light globe hung naked from the ceiling.

"Sit here!" the officer said with contempt, and marched out, slamming the door.

Both men tried to make themselves comfortable on the thin, hard wooden bench that lined the wall, and waited.

"Nice room!" Arturs remarked cynically.

The Ambassador laughed grimly. They both knew there were far worse rooms in this terrible building. After a relatively short time the door crashed open and the haughty, nasty officer stalked in.

"Come with me!" he barked.

They followed him out of the room, down the corridor and up a narrow, dark, dank staircase, before being hustled up another rather grand wide curving staircase, with an elegant, impressive balustrade. The officer markedly stiffened and looked increasingly nervous as they walked into the inner sanctum of the feared NKVD.

The officer quietly knocked at a large double oak door.

"Come!"

The officer quietly opened both the doors and indicated them to go in.

The office they entered was large and airy. It had a high roof and high windows. A large chandelier glimmered from the ceiling. A balding, dark haired man with round, steel-rimmed spectacles looked up from a large desk.

Lavrentiy Pavlovich Beria, the new head of the NKVD, looked at the men in his office. He noted their proud, fearless bearing and dress uniforms. He placed the tips of his fingers on a paper lying on his desk and smiled grimly, mirthlessly, at them.

"You are the ex-Latvian Ambassador? And you are Colonel Arturs Kelers, ex-Latvian Military attaché?"

He didn't wait for the answers; he already knew. He noted the Colonel had an enamel cross and ribbon proudly pinned on his chest. Beria recognised the medal.

It irritated him and he thought scathingly, *That man is arrogantly admitting his treachery; this so-called hero of their rebellion against the legitimate Soviet authority in Latvia.*

Beria's stare hardened as he looked at Arturs in his immaculate dress uniform.

He'll die well! he thought, with grudging admiration.

Beria spoke quietly to the two men standing in front of him. "You are bourgeois enemies of the Soviet Union. You are both criminal malefactors and guilty of numerous heinous crimes against the motherland and our glorious leader, Stalin. You have been sentenced to death by firing squad. The sentence will be carried out immediately."

Neither of the men batted an eyelid at the pronouncement, their stony faces even a little contemptuous of the whole process. They were, of course, not guilty of any crimes against anyone. They were guilty of being very much in the wrong place at the wrong time and staying at their posts to the bitter end.

Beria pretended not to notice and raised his voice. "Guards!"

The door opened and the guards marched in. They crashed to attention in front of him, saluting.

Beria stood and haughtily handed the officer the paper – the signed death warrant. "Take these men away! The order is to be carried out immediately!"

He glared at the guards with menacing intent, especially at the officer, who he knew to be a fanatical hothead, and repeated, "Immediately! Do you understand? If they don't get a clean death *you will pay*!"

The officer, standing rigidly to attention, paled noticeably.

The Ambassador bowed at Beria and, turning, walked out the door. At the same time Arturs stood to attention and saluted.

"Thank you, comrade Commissar," he said with a touch of irony, as he turned and proudly marched out the door. The guards and officer marched out behind him.

Beria sat down, and somewhat flustered by their subtle defiance, shuffled the papers on his desk. It was 16 June 1940; the day the Soviet Union finally extinguished Latvian independence.

Karlis drove down the road south of Jelgava. The engine in the big Studebaker growled as he pressed down on the gas and the big car surged forward. On this lovely fine day, small, fluffy white clouds wafted across the blue sky. Karlis wound down the window and enjoyed the breeze in his hair as the car flashed past lush green fields. As he approached a little forested hillock Karlis, acting on some instinct, turned off the main road and parked the car on a side track under a big oak tree within the small grove. He alighted, breathing in deeply the fresh summer air. Suddenly he heard a strange sound and, curious, returned to the main road. Looking back, he noted that the big Studebaker was hidden from view.

The sound came closer, the clanking and grinding becoming

louder as he approached the road. Rising slowly into view, coming up a small slope, the source of the sound revealed itself.

Karlis felt shocked to the core. Rising slowly into view was the massive turret of a tank, with the red star of the Soviet Union painted on it. Its huge cannon seemed to be pointing straight at him. Karlis stepped off the road and hid behind a tree, just in time, as the massive machine ground slowly past him, its tracks churning up dust on the road. It clanked and creaked loudly as the big engine roared, puffs of black smoke pouring from the hidden exhaust. Karlis could see the driver's head and, leaning up casually against his machine gun in the turret, the commander. On top of the huge and intimidating machine sat a squad of Russian soldiers, clutching their rifles. Karlis watched horrified as tank after tank clanked and rumbled past him on the way to Jelgava and then Riga. If the soldiers on the tanks saw him, they paid no attention.

Karlis watched, rooted to the spot in morbid curiosity. Peering to the south, the column of tanks seemed endless.

Recovering from his sudden surge of fear, Karlis crept back to his car. He started it and drove away slowly. When he was sure he was away from the main road and had not been seen by the Russian soldiers, he opened up the throttle and hurtled along, even recklessly at times, down the back roads to Kambaris. Arriving at the house, he braked in a cloud of dust and rushed inside.

Lydia met him in the main room, almost hysterical. "Is it true? Is it true? Has it happened?"

Karlis grabbed her by the shoulders. "What, love?" he asked, trying to be gentle. His voice quivered ever so slightly.

"Have the Russians invaded? I heard on the radio," she quaked, calming down a little.

"Yes. I saw them on the road to Jelgava." Then, unusually for him, he put his arms around her and hugged her tightly. She clung to him.

"What shall we do?" she whispered.

"There's nothing much we can do. I think you should gather together all your jewellery and other valuables and we should hide them somewhere. I know a spot in the barn."

Then he said grimly, "Can you assemble the workers and servants in the back yard in half an hour, love?"

She nodded and smiled weakly.

Brightening, she turned and rushed into the kitchen. Karlis hurried into his office and started sorting out his papers, burning any that may be compromising, in the large open fireplace.

Half an hour passed. Karlis looked at the assembled servants and farm workers; he'd known some of them for years and regarded them as friends. They gathered in a group and looked nervous and shaken.

Karlis spoke quietly, but his resonant voice reached them easily. "I have very bad news. Some of you who have access to a radio may have already heard."

He paused to gather his thoughts and took a deep breath. "We have been invaded by the armies of the Soviet Union. I can only guess they are here to topple our government in some shady deal with the Nazis who, as you may know, are presently invading France and have captured Paris. The fall of the French government is imminent. I believe this is the end of Latvia's independence. Once the invasion is complete, we will become part of the Soviet Union. I think the best thing we can do is carry on as usual until we find out more from the new government when it is formed."

They were quiet as they digested this. A few murmured to themselves, but only the foreman, Robis, spoke up.

"What do you think will happen to us?" he asked.

Karlis answered. "I'm not sure. We'll have to wait and see. Perhaps they will try to collectivise like they did last time? I just hope it will not be war. Perhaps the pact with the Nazis will protect us. But, for now, go back to your homes. You can have the rest of the day off. Please report to work tomorrow as usual."

The workers nodded and, talking quietly amongst themselves, slowly dispersed. Robis looked greedily at the house and barn, taking in the big car in the yard.

"Collectivisation? Perhaps that would not be so bad …?" he murmured.

Karlis went back inside. He found Lydia in the office. She had a small bag and was in the process of locking it in the desk. He slumped in a chair.

"I'll take that out tonight and hide it in the barn. I know a secure place," he said. Then he cried out to her in despair. "I was afraid this would happen. It seems our government just rolled over. They just let the Soviets walk all over us!"

She sat down near him. "They did that to save lives. Our army is too weak. Resisting them would be suicide," she said quietly.

"I know, love. I know. But they should have done something. It seems like such a betrayal! I'm very worried about Arturs. Nelija wrote to me a month ago, saying he had sent all his personal effects and he was on his way back. We have not heard from him since. Maybe he wasn't able to get out."

"Arturs is resourceful, I'm sure he'll be okay," she said unconvincingly.

"I hope you are right," he answered grimly. Then he sighed deeply. "All we can do is wait and see what happens …"

They had to wait for two weeks. Two weeks of living in a sort of stasis; unable to make any crucial decisions. Karlis paid his workers as usual, including their normal bonuses for good work, even though everyone was a bit lackadaisical. The day after supervising the pay run, Karlis sat in his office. Hearing a sound, he stood and went to the window. A black sedan followed by a truck load of Russian soldiers had rolled into the yard.

He walked hurriedly from the room and called to Lydia. "Look after the children, we have visitors."

She nodded and ran to the nursery.

Just as she disappeared, the door crashed open and a group of unkempt-looking soldiers barged in, followed by a Russian NKVD officer. They threateningly pointed their rifles at Karlis. The officer said abruptly and rudely in Russian. "You in charge here?"

Karlis nodded his assent.

"So, you are the bourgeois swine that owns this palace," the man snarled, looking contemptuously around the bright, airy, tastefully furnished room. "Call the workers and assemble in the yard!"

He signalled his soldiers who rudely manhandled Karlis out into the yard.

Karlis called out to Robis who had come forward, looking frightened. "Call all the workers, Robis, we have visitors. Can I offer you a cup of tea, comrade?"

"No! We will not accept your bourgeois hospitality. Call the house workers as well!"

At that moment, Lydia came out of the house with the children. Inta, a toddler, clutched her leg, while she carried Karlis in her arms. The baby started to wail. Lydia quickly hushed him, rocking him gently. Inta's lips started to quiver, but the little girl, bravely, did not cry. Behind Lydia came the servants. The soldiers hustled the workers into a group and frog-marched Karlis to a position in front of them.

The officer harangued the people loudly and aggressively, while his soldiers slouched scowling in a menacing manner. Robis came forward.

"Many of these peasants speak very poor Russian. I can translate for you, comrade," he said fawningly.

The officer glared at him and nodded curtly before continuing. "I represent the Soviet Socialist Republic of Latvia. We are here to liberate all the repressed workers in this bourgeois, fascist state. Workers like you, sturdy peasants. The fate of this bourgeois scum is in your hands …" he said, referring to Karlis.

He glared at the group, most of them pale and shaking. They bunched up; looked around at each other; scanned the intimidating, fidgeting soldiers.

The officer arrogantly and rudely screamed. "Well … what do you want to happen to this oppressive fascist arsehole here?"

The soldiers shoved Karlis forward. He stumbled and almost fell. Lydia gasped.

With great courage the workers, with the strange exception of Robis, spoke up all together in a jumble of Russian and Latvian.

"He's a good man."

"He has treated us well and even looked after our children when they were sick."

"We have always been paid well and usually get a good meal for lunch."

"The boss is a good manager and resisted employing foreigners here. He invited all of us to his wedding."

"I received a bonus, only yesterday, for hard work."

"He is definitely not an oppressive arsehole. He is a good Latvian, who works hard as well."

The officer, mollified by these strident statements of support, glowered at Karlis, disappointment on on his face. "Get in line!" he ordered peevishly. The man wanted blood.

The soldiers shoved Karlis towards his workers.

Then the officer propped his hands on his hips, stood with his legs wide apart, and said in a more measured tone: "We intend to redistribute this land. Everyone will get their own plot. The Executive Committee charged with this great initiative will be here tomorrow. Go home. You do not work for this greedy bourgeois fascist anymore!"

He abruptly turned on his heel and left, waving for his soldiers to follow him. The car and truck roared out of the yard in a cloud of dust. Karlis stumbled inside and collapsed onto a chair looking pale and shaken. Lydia put Karlis Junior down and gently disentangled herself from Inta's iron grip and put her arms around him. He held her quietly.

Only later did Karlis discover how lucky he'd been – how much he owed his life to the loyalty of his workers. He found out from a mutual friend that the mill owner in Dobele, Adams, a nice man he knew quite well, had been sent to Siberia. Karlis had been very lucky that he had listened to Lydia and not bought the mill back in 1938.

The cart pulled by a scrawny horse clip-clopped and creaked down the icy road. It lurched past white fields and stark leafless trees. The grey sky provided dim light. Rugged up in their coats, the family on the cart breathed steam in the cold; they were made even colder by the gusty wind that blew from the north. The cart had stacked on it all their worldly possessions; some large chests full of clothes, crockery and cutlery; Lydia's precious jewellery hidden in their clothes. Piled on top of the chests were a table, six chairs and two small beds for the children. Karlis sat at the front of the cart and drove. Sitting between him and Lydia, who nursed their baby son swaddled in her clothes, was Inta.

As they rolled slowly down the road, Karlis breathed the cold air deeply. He was in a surprisingly good mood, despite the hardship that had so suddenly engulfed his family and thought, with black humour, that less than six months ago he had been a wealthy, successful man with a beautiful house, car and thriving farm. With a wry smile, he looked at the scrawny horse and the creaking cart he was reduced to. Now, he had nothing. But despite that, he was a lucky man. He still had the most precious things in life: he was alive and with his family!

The cart crested a small rise. Below them was the small homestead of their friends, Roberts and Maria Bendze. Karlis slowed the horse as it increased speed down the low hill and walked it into the Bendze's yard. He reigned in and climbed down from the cart, then helped down his daughter and Lydia. Roberts Bendze greeted them at the door.

"Come in. Come in," he said. "You must be cold."

Maria, a strikingly attractive, buxom woman, stood in the main room, smiling a welcome. Karlis shook hands with Roberts warmly and Lydia hugged him briefly before moving into the room and hugging Maria.

"Thank you, Roberts. I'll unpack the cart first, if I may. Do you have somewhere to store our stuff?"

"Yes, yes. You can put it in the alcove, where you are welcome to stay as long as you wish. Come into the warm, Lydia and children," he said, patting Inta's head.

Lydia smiled at him. "Thank you so much, Roberts."

Karlis unloaded the cart, stabled his horse and went inside. A fire roared in the hearth and he warmed his hands against it. Maria had put food on the table – simple fare: soup and dark bread, but it was filling and warm.

Roberts said, "Come and eat, Karlis. We can talk later."

After dinner, when the children had been put to bed, Karlis and Roberts sat at the table and sipped their shots of vodka. A bottle sat on the table before them. Roberts drank and then refilled their glasses.

"Tell us your story, Karlis," he said quietly and curiously, already knowing part of it.

Karlis smiled at his friend. "Where can I start?"

"At the beginning."

"Well … what you see on the cart is all of our belongings. The tractor is now the property of the new collective, as is our barn. There are now seven families living in our house. Our car has been requisitioned for use by the local NKVD and most of the rest of our stuff has been looted by the Russian army …" He paused, sipped his vodka then continued. "About four months ago, the Executive Committee came to Kambaris and conducted an audit. They decided to split the farm into seven small holdings, while Plumshē was split into two and I've been banned from it. Banned from my father's farm …" The last was said bitterly and with despair.

Karlis paused and gulped some more vodka before he spoke again.

"I was allowed to keep thirty hectares on Kambaris and was assigned one room in our house," he smiled mirthlessly and bent closer to Roberts saying quietly and sarcastically. "The authorities even kindly let us keep our table, six chairs and the childrens' beds."

He laughed quietly and bitterly at that and continued. "They had no idea about farming and underestimated how much grain we had stored in the barn. I was able to sell the surplus on the black market and keep food on the table very well for over three months and they were none the wiser. We still have some cash and will pay our way here."

Roberts rose and poked the fire, before adding some more logs and pouring more vodka. "That's not necessary. We have been friends a long time and you have done a lot for my family. Would you like coffee? It looks like the kettle has boiled."

"Yes, that would be lovely."

Roberts poured the coffee and sat down again.

"You have had a bad run," he said reflectively.

Karlis nodded. "That's what you get for being a capitalist swine these days."

He sipped the scalding black liquid and scoffed some of his vodka. "It gets worse, Roberts …"

Karlis ruminated for a while then said sadly. "I always regarded my foreman Robis as a friend and thought I treated him well. But … well it makes his betrayal that much harder to take. He's now the manager of the new collective and was in the forefront of our dispossession. That's not so much of a problem. People have to do what they have to do in these troubled times. What I cannot … cannot forgive is the way he treated Karlis, my baby son."

Karlis was becoming emotional as the vodka started to take hold.

"When the collectivisation happened a few days ago, just before we were forced to leave Kambaris, Karlis had a fever. I asked Robis if we could stay a few more days until our baby got better. Do you know what he said?" His voice rose emotively. "He said: *The son of a bourgeoisie means nothing to me. I don't really care if he lives or dies!* Can you believe that? How can someone be so callous and uncaring? Especially someone I've known for more than ten years. It's a terrible world when that happens."

Roberts had stiffened when Robis was mentioned. Now, he exploded in unrestrained fury, banging his fist on the table.

"That Robis has been a proper cunt," he ground out brutally. "You are far too forgiving. He has been spreading scurrilous lies about people and as a result many fine men, including some friends of mine, have been sent to Siberia!"

Karlis reeled at his fury, but he answered, "You are right, Roberts. I shouldn't complain. I'm here and still with my family … unlike my brother, Arturs, who has disappeared. I have to assume he was sent to Siberia as well."

Roberts, who calmed down from his anger quickly, looked at his friend and thought sadly, *As a highly ranked military officer, he was probably shot.* He, of course, didn't say that.

He finished his coffee, stood up, stretched and said, "I'm off to bed. Goodnight."

"Good night, old friend."

Karlis and his family were only able to stay with the Bendzes for a week. Karlis made himself useful by helping out with the winter farming. Finally, in early March they were forced to move on again. Karlis was in the barn when he heard the crunch of rubber on the gravel drive as a vehicle approached. He walked out curious, as did Roberts. As they emerged, a dark sedan slowly drove in, wheels spinning slightly over the icy drive, and stopped. The occupants, local Latvian communists, alighted and approached Roberts. He greeted them politely.

They rudely asked, "What's he doing here, Bendze?"

Roberts answered. "That's Karlis Kelers, an old friend of mine. He's helping me out on the farm for the moment."

Their leader responded, "I know who he is!" Then he said sinisterly, "You are protecting a bourgeois capitalist pig; an undoubted enemy of our glorious leader Stalin. If he doesn't leave immediately, you'll be thrown out of here as a capitalist lover."

Before Roberts could answer, Karlis spoke.

"We are just leaving, comrade. In fact, as soon as my wife finishes packing. We just stopped at our old friend's house as a guest on the way to Riga. You are right, of course, comrade. I'm a changed man. I've a job as a worker in a factory now," he said, pretending to be proud of this great achievement, while grimacing behind his hand to Roberts.

The men glowered at Karlis and Roberts and their leader said, "Good, comrade. That's very pleasing." He added with quiet menace. "If you are still here in two days, Bendze will suffer!"

Then they climbed back into their car and drove away.

Karlis looked at his friend. "We'll be on our way tomorrow."

Roberts nodded, sad and angry at how awful these so-called Latvian communists were.

Roberts Bendze drove Karlis, Lydia and the children to the train station in Dobele. Karlis had decided to leave the horse, cart and his remaining furniture with him, vowing to come back and pick it up one day. When they climbed onto the train and moved on again, to an uncertain future in Riga, Roberts drove home, fearful of his own future.

Karlis was amazed at how much Riga had changed in the nine months since the communist takeover. The once vibrant, lively, clean city, full of cafes and bars, the Paris of the Baltic, was now drab and grim. Rubbish littered the streets and the once beautiful parks and gardens were unkempt and unused. It was as if the people had forgotten how to relax and have a good time. Scruffy Russian soldiers in ill-fitting uniforms and carrying dirty rifles loitered menacingly on every street corner. Large propaganda posters extolling the virtues of Stalin's communism were hung everywhere, along with huge pictures of Stalin benignly looking down on them all. People hurried to where they had to go without looking up or talking to anyone. Any symbols of the independent Latvian Republic had been destroyed, and the atmosphere felt oppressive. For the first time since the Great War there were food queues, as the people struggled to get the basics they needed to exist. Karlis couldn't believe it. It was worse than during the depression. He quickly decided that he didn't want to stay in Riga, reasoning it would be safer in the countryside.

At that time, Karlis and his family stayed with his cousin, Feldmanis. Karlis worked at the Red Star factory as a worker. Both Adolfs and Feldmanis were doing alright under the new regime, a forestry official and a factory manager being deemed acceptable occupations. Karlis knew that Adolfs' wife Maria had a thirty-hectare farm called Liekraĝis, which she had been allowed to keep. He approached his brother and urged him to let him manage the farm for them. Adolfs was agreeable so the Kelers family moved once again, to Liekraĝis.

Maria's farm was in the Džūkste area just west of Riga. Karlis was pleased with it. While the old wooden buildings on the property were rundown, it had a large orchard and the soil was good. He found he could get hold of fertiliser easily and cheaply, so he worked hard to sow a good crop of wheat. Perhaps things were starting to look up for the family again.

The farm provided them with plenty of eggs, and fresh vegetables from the garden and fruit from the orchard. The crop looked good. He loved the fresh air and for the first time he felt that his children, Inta, four, and Karlis, two, were safe.

Karlis missed the good life of a wealthy man in Kambaris, but was pragmatic enough to know that, in order to survive this new regime, he had to adapt and keep a low profile. He was aware of how difficult it was for Lydia who, for the first time, had to live without servants to cook, clean, garden, help her dress and look after the children. She had to do all that herself now.

Karlis, for the first time in nearly a year, started to feel optimistic. While he was a staunch and secret opponent of Stalinism – as you had to be if you wished to live – his family could now live relatively well if he managed to stay out of trouble. That, perhaps naïve, optimism didn't last long as war shattered the fragile peace and plunged the family into turmoil again. The Nazis shredded the disgraceful Molotov-Ribbentrop pact and invaded the Soviet Union.

Karlis woke with start to the sound of loud banging on the window. His first panicked thought was, *Fuck! Fucking hell. It's the NKVD! We're doomed!*

It was certainly their modus operandi to come in the dark of night. But, perhaps not banging on the window … kicking down the front door was more their style!

Then he heard the urgent whispers through the window. "Karlis, Karlis, please wake up!"

He rose and went to the window. Lydia started awake with a quiet whimper of fear.

"What is it? What brings you here at this time in the morning?" he asked in an agitated voice.

"You must get out! Take your family and hide. The NKVD are rounding up people in the district!" the unknown man at the window said desperately. Then he quietly disappeared into the night before Karlis could say anything else.

Karlis reacted straight away. "Get dressed and go and wake the kids," he said to a now wide-awake Lydia.

She nodded and hurried into the next room where the children slept. Karlis quickly dressed, grabbed an old canvas knapsack and rushed to the kitchen. He filled it with blankets, water, some food and basic utensils. He grabbed a couple of torches and a portable radio. When Lydia rushed into the room clutching their children, he picked up Inta, hoisted the knapsack onto his shoulders and hurried out the door, closing it behind him. He led the family into his lush and beautiful wheat crop and made a spot for them in the middle of the field to hide.

"Stay here and try to get some sleep, I'm sure it is just an over-reaction. I'll go and find out what is going on."

Karlis quietly walked away from his family, noting where they were and keeping low. Not daring to use a torch, he used the moonlight to guide him. He carefully made his way through the darkness to the boundary fence of Liekraĝis, close to where he knew the neighbour's house was. When he reached there, he lay flat on his stomach and squirming forward, peered through the tall, lush wheat.

The scene in front of him was surreal and frightening. In the glare of the lights of two black sedans, he could see a woman crying as she clung to her small children. A group of Russian soldiers were holding a man, bleeding profusely from a gaping wound in his head, at gunpoint as they brutally hustled him into a car. The children screamed and the woman sobbed. A Russian soldier slapped her hard on the face.

He screamed at her in Russian. "Stop that fucking awful noise, you bitch!"

The woman staggered from the blow and tried to stop crying. The children, clinging desperately to her legs, cried even louder until they too were all bundled unceremoniously into different vehicles. The cars disappeared into the night.

Karlis, shocked by what he'd just seen, lay on the cold ground in the darkness for what seemed an eternity, as if he was paralysed with fear. He thought with complete despair, *Could that have been my family? Maybe we got out just in time. Do we owe our lives to that brave benefactor?*

Any optimism he'd felt about the future crumbled. He pulled himself together and crept back to his family and found the children wrapped in blankets, asleep. Lydia was awake, watching over them.

He whispered to her in a frightened voice. "They have taken the neighbours! What's going on?"

She pointed at the radio and said in a hushed, anxious voice. "I was listening to the radio. Between all the patriotic Soviet propaganda and martial music there was some news. The Nazis recently invaded the Soviet Union. Apparently, they are being defeated on all fronts. I don't believe that. The Germans are on their way here now! I'm guessing the Russians are rounding up 'collaborators'."

"Shit!" he whispered agitatedly.

"They were good people and definitely not pro-German! I think the Russians are panicking and anyone is fair game. We had better be careful. I think we should stay here for now."

She nodded in agreement, trying to be brave.

"We should try to get some sleep."

Neither Karlis nor Lydia slept at all that night. Next morning at dawn he decided to move his family to a less exposed place in the nearby forest. They slunk quietly into the bush, carefully covering their tracks as best they could. He set up a small shelter and crept back to the farm by a circuitous route, carefully scouting the place out before going in. Everything looked okay. It seemed that nobody had been there. Heartened a little, he quietly eased open the front door and stole into the kitchen, and quickly stuffed some more water, food, a kettle and tea into his knapsack and quietly left. Back at their temporary camp under the trees, he lit a small fire and boiled tea.

"I have to find out what is going on. Are you able to stay here?"

She nodded. "We'll be alright. It'll be like a camping adventure for the children. Please take care and come back."

He smiled and hugged her and the children and quietly moved away. Karlis decided to go and visit a local police officer, who he knew was an ardent Latvian nationalist. The man must have had the gift of the gab, for he'd somehow survived the change of regime. Karlis went through the fields and forests, staying away from the main roads and any habitations until he reached the policeman's house. The man was still at home and let Karlis in; he was agitated, dirty and unkempt and wearing civilian clothes. Karlis was breathless and dirty, his clothes ripped. The policeman looked at him sympathetically. He had just got back from hiding in the forest himself.

"What's going on? Do you know anything?" Karlis pleaded.

The man said quietly, tensely, "You should stay with your family in the forest for the time being. The Germans are advancing everywhere and the Russian soldiers have lost discipline in their panic. They are very dangerous at the moment. I was at the railway station just today and saw Russian soldiers forcing people into cattle wagons. They were separating out the men from women and adults from children," he shuddered. "It was a terrible sight."

Grateful for the information, Karlis produced a small bottle of schnapps from his pocket. He gulped some of the fiery liquid down, straight from the bottle, and handed it to the policeman who drank. Karlis left the man with the bottle and carefully walked back the way he had come. The family slept another two nights in the woods.

On the morning of their third day in hiding, they woke early, the sunlight streaming through the trees. Birds chirped gaily in the lovely morning, and a slight and gentle, warm rain fell.

Then the peace of the morning was shattered by a strange thump, thump, thump in the distance. With a sense of extreme foreboding, Karlis guessed what it was – the sound of tank fire in the distance. When the wind blew in the right direction the terrifying sound was so magnified in Karlis' heightened senses that he thought the fighting was right upon them. He shuddered inwardly, his nerves frayed. His mind momentarily numbed with fear.

Lydia and the children looked petrified. Though he tried to remain calm, he felt desperate. He made a decision. He would take his family back to Liekraĝis and hide in the house cellar. He hoped the Russian soldiers would be too preoccupied by the advancing Germans, who were very close now, to trouble his family. But what of the Germans? He would worry about that later, if they overran the area. His thoughts raced. With a supreme effort of will, he calmed down and tried to think carefully and logically.

Karlis packed everything up and drew his family together then started the relatively short walk back to the farm. For some reason, perhaps because they were quite laden down and the children very tired, he decided to take the most direct route down the main road.

His eyes widened when his tired and dirty family shuffled out of the fields and onto the road into a stream of frantic civilians, desperate to get away from the fighting. The family joined the throng and were swept towards Riga which, luckily, was in the direction of the farm. He struggled to keep his footing in the crowd and clung desperately to his daughter's hand. Lydia carried their baby son, and seemed calm.

Suddenly, a terrible shrieking sound reached them and the people on the road scattered. Karlis, reacting instinctively, shoved

Lydia and the children unceremoniously into a ditch and covered them with his body. A loud explosion rent the air, and a bomb landed near where they cowered, showering them with dirt and small rocks. A German Stuka screamed overhead, the white of its belly and the ominous black crosses on its wings seeming very close as it pulled out of its steep dive. Inta started to scream in fear, and a shocked Lydia tried to calm her. Their little son remained calm – he didn't understand what was happening. The family cowered in the ditch as another Stuka dived, the terrible shrieking shattering the air. Then it roared overhead, followed by another and another. Karlis soon lost count. Bombs thumped onto the road in front of them, with loud percussive bangs that left them temporarily deaf. Then the aircraft were gone.

Karlis and his family stayed in their ditch for half an hour, as did most of the other people on the road, then they ventured out again.

"Why are they bombing us? Why are the Nazis bombing civilians?" Lydia wailed.

Karlis, just shook his head, numb with fear.

"Maybe they mistook us for the retreating Russian Army," he said shakily, not at all convinced by this explanation.

Bomb craters were everywhere. The road was in ruins and smoking carts and other vehicles were scattered along it. Karlis and Lydia hurried down the road, covering their children's eyes as they passed the bodies of those unfortunates who hadn't got off the road fast enough. The casualties had suffered blast injuries and were bloody beyond recognition. Body parts scattered along the blood-soaked road. The gruesome sight left Karlis numb with horror. Lydia, pale and shaking, stepped over the pools of blood. All the while the ominous thump, thump, thump echoed in the distance. Inta's cries slowed to a whimper.

Thump! Thump! Thump! It seemed to come ever closer. Karlis's skin turned icy.

As he carried his sobbing daughter down the road, all he could think was, *What have I done? How did I put my family in danger? What have I done? What shall I do now?*

The exercise of the strenuous walk and the eerie quiet calmed his shattered nerves. He knew he had to stay strong. He was so glad; glad beyond belief, when they finally arrived safely back at Liekraĝis.

<h1 style="text-align:center">IX</h1>

The Indifferent Farmer (1941–1944)

On that beautiful summer's day, Karlis rode quietly and nervously down the forest tracks, trying to stay out of sight. Occasionally, if the wind blew in the right direction, he could hear the sounds of war. He could hear the distant sounds of tank fire and aircraft high overhead as the Russian army desperately tried to stop the advancing Nazis, with little success. He guessed it was only a matter of time before they would all be living under German rule again. He wasn't sure where the 'front' was, but guessed they were on the German side now. He worried about what that would entail, but didn't think it could be any worse for his family.

He approached the house at Kambaris nervously, checked for any activity before he moved towards his old house. He was struck by how quiet and derelict the place looked. Satisfied with the quiet, he entered the yard. What he saw nearly broke his heart: the garden was unkempt; some of his fences derelict; and the crop was poor. At least, he reflected ruefully, the house and barn looked okay.

As he approached, he shouted. "Hello! Hello! Is anyone here?"

No answer came. There seemed to be no-one around. As he walked up to the veranda, he heard somebody shuffling out the back door. Looking around he saw a man. Robis. He looked awful. His eyes were bloodshot and he was unshaven and dirty. It looked as though he had slept in his clothes. He stared back at Karlis.

"What are you doing here?" he asked in a slurred, resigned voice.

"I just came to see how everything is. Where is everyone?"

"They've all gone. The cowards have run from the Germans," Robis answered listlessly.

Karlis looked unsympathetic. "I would run if I were you as well. If the Nazis catch such a good Stalinist as you, they will probably shoot you," he said cynically and cruelly.

Robis paled and wailed. "Where can I go? Do you expect me to go into exile in Russia?"

"For people like you, yes. If you don't, there's a good chance Latvian partisans will get you instead. You didn't exactly endear yourself to your neighbours. Anyway, I'm just going in to have a look inside."

Dimly aware how heartless and cruel he acted towards this man, a fellow Latvian, a man who, while scarcely deserving any sympathy, had once been a friend, Karlis appreciated that Robis stayed silent. He watched as the man sank to the ground with a look of abject despair. Karlis ignored him and timorously walked into his house, which was in a sad state of disrepair. Dust and cobwebs lay everywhere. In the kitchen, scraps of food and dirty dishes had piled up. In other rooms the furniture looked broken and worthless. He went into the barn. No grain or hay was left and he wondered where all his cattle were. Most of his chickens were missing. His fruit trees were healthy but in real need of some care. Karlis sat in the large double doorway of the barn and despaired.

"How could they let the place go to pot so quickly?" he groaned.

He decided what to do. When he could, he'd bring Lydia and the children back here, clean the place up and start to farm again.

"At least the buildings are in a reasonable state and a lot of my farm equipment is still here," he murmured.

He returned to the house, yelling, "Hey, Robis! Where's my tractor?"

The man didn't answer. He'd fallen asleep. Karlis realised

Robis's drunken state. He left him on the ground to sleep off his despondency. It was the last time he saw him. He later heard, as he had predicted that Robis was caught and shot by the Nazis. He severely regretted his uncaring, hostile and hypocritical attitude towards the man.

Karlis decided to stay at Bendze's house until he could bring his family back to Kambaris. He hoped Lydia would be alright with the children at Adolfs' house in Riga.

Roberts Bendze greeted Karlis warmly. He was back on his farm again, after spending some time hiding in the woods with his family. But he worried. Even though the Soviet soldiers were in retreat, there were still many marauding bands stranded behind the lines. They were heavily armed and dangerous in their desperation. He'd heard a number of people had been shot out of hand and women were raped by these desperate, undisciplined men. They also had the habit of looting, carrying off anything of valuable.

He took Karlis aside. "We should try to get some weapons to defend ourselves against these Russian soldiers. I know a man called Nestors who has a truck. We're going to try to get into Jelgava and get hold of some rifles there. Will you come with us?"

Though reluctant to go on this adventure at first, Karlis eventually relented and went along.

Nestors' decrepit old truck was a 1929 Model A Ford with a rusted out body and holes in the floor and doors. They rattled down the forest tracks in this old machine and made good time, when Karlis noticed the same policeman he'd spoken to a number of weeks earlier. The man frantically waved them down. The truck shuddered and groaned to a halt. The man ran up, puffing hard.

"There's a group of Russian soldiers ahead of you on this track. Please turn back now," he gasped. "I only just managed to get away from them. They are frightened and shooting at shadows!"

Nestors' eyes lit up with wild imagination. He produced a grenade from his pocket. "We can rush down this track and use this on them! They won't know what hit them!"

The others eyes widened as they looked at him.

Karlis blurted out. "No! No! That's much too risky. I know another route."

Nestors reluctantly agreed and turned the truck around.

"Thank you. Thank you for the warning," Karlis yelled as they drove away.

The policeman smiled, nodded and waved as they rattled down the road in the opposite direction. Karlis directed them down the side tracks he knew and they drove into Jelgava without any more problems. They managed to gather ten old rifles that were still functional and had been abandoned by the retreating Russian soldiers, and handed them to other farmers in the district.

They didn't need the weapons though, as the Soviet army finally collapsed and was quickly driven out of Latvia. The marauding Russian soldiers were ruthlessly hunted down by the Germans. Not many were imprisoned.

Karlis spent the fall of 1941 working hard to put the Kambaris house and farm in order so he could safely bring his family home. But first, he had to gain approval from the new German regime for this enterprise. Surprisingly, the German officials he spoke to were polite and supported his intentions. They did warn however that the government auditors would inspect the property soon, to do an inventory, as soon as the new government was established. That was enough for Karlis, and he threw himself into the work. He had to find where his tractor had gone and make arrangements to get it back. It was on a neighbouring farm that had been a part of the old collective, and wasn't surprised to find it had been damaged, but he managed to get it going and drove it back to Kambaris. He then reassembled some of his cattle herd, which had been distributed to the collective's employees for their small personal plots. He found many of them running wild as the whole collective regime had collapsed into disarray. By the first snows of winter, he had arranged for Lydia and his children to return home. It had been very hard work. He now had to do everything himself due to a shortage of workers. But as he stood in his house and surveyed what he'd achieved he felt a great sense of accomplishment.

The Nazi auditors finally arrive at Kambaris in early November 1941. They were dressed in neat, grey civil uniforms, with peaked army style caps and arrived in a small, grey German army staff car. They were unarmed and came without the intimidatory presence of soldiers. Karlis had prepared and had already decided to do as much as he could to keep his family safe, while at the same time, do as little as possible to support the new regime. He knew it was going to be a delicate and dangerous balancing act. He had managed to fix up the tractor, but deliberately left it in an apparent state of disrepair.

The auditors were efficient and polite. They looked in the house, barn and other buildings, noting everything in them.

Their leader observed. "This is a nice house and a very large impressive barn. Where is all the rest of your farm equipment and furniture?"

Karlis answered honestly. "Most of it was stolen by the communist peasants in the failed so-called collective. The rest was looted by Russian soldiers. What you see is all I have … all I have been able to get back together."

The German wandered over and looked at the tractor.

He noticed its state of disrepair. "What's the problem here?"

This time Karlis answered half truthfully. "It was stolen and used by a neighbouring collective. I found it the other day and managed to drive it back. But it has been damaged by the collective. Unfortunately, in getting it back, another part broke," he said, indicating a bit of the tractor lying on the ground. "The machine is unusable. I have to get parts, which is difficult in this damn war."

The German nodded and took a note, before looking closely at the 'broken part'. Karlis held his breath, but the German didn't seem to notice his subterfuge.

Karlis continued with a hint of sarcasm. "The peasants of the collective were better with the old ways. They didn't have a clue about modern equipment. My horse plough is still in good condition and I have managed to get hold of some horses. I will be able to put in a crop this year, but it's going to be difficult as there is no labour available."

The German nodded again. "Do what you can for labour. That's your responsibility. What sort of yield can you get here? It looks like good soil."

Karlis lied, giving the man yields for wheat and oats that were half he had managed to get previously.

The man wrote down the figures and said sternly. "We'll expect that amount of grain for the German army. If you fail to meet your quota, you won't be just getting a visit from us."

He left the threat hanging in the air, before continuing in a more conciliatory tone. "However, if you do meet your quota and pay your taxes on time, there should be no problems."

Putting his file under his arm, he called over his colleagues and left the farm. Karlis heaved a huge sigh of relief. He'd pulled off his deception. Now he had to get on with it and produce some grain. He decided to sell any surplus on the black market.

Karlis now needed labourers so he took his horse and cart into Dobele to the local labour office. He had no luck. There was nobody available. While in a quandary of what to do next, he by chance ran into a local town councillor he knew. The man told him about some Jews who were locked up in the local prison. The German regime was new, but already Karlis had heard rumours of atrocities inflicted on the population as the Germans rounded up communists, Jews, gypsies and other 'undesirables'. If he employed some Jewish workers he might save them from the Nazis. Karlis rode down the road to the small, grey, stone prison built in the Tsarist era. It was forbidding and grim and Karlis nervously entered the building.

The Latvian officer at the desk looked up as he entered. "What do you want?" he asked abruptly.

"I need workers. I've heard you have some Jews that are able to work."

"Yes … I'll have to ask the Commandant."

"Ask him. I don't have much time."

"Okay. Come this way."

Karlis followed him into the commandant's office; the man, a large, red-faced Latvian, looked harassed and stressed. He ran his hands though his cropped, dark hair and asked tersely, "You want some Jewish workers?"

"Yes. I need workers urgently. I have a crop to plant and harvest and a farm to run. I have to keep the German's happy. They don't like delays and expect wheat for the army. If I can't deliver, I'll end up being one of your 'clients'."

The man nodded – he was under the same sort of pressure.

He waved Karlis away. "Okay. Go and choose your workers and I'll organise the release forms. It'll be good to clear some of the cells. They're overcrowded."

Karlis entered the cell block and gagged; he almost reeled out of the place, appalled by the conditions. The cells stunk of faeces and the walls were stained and damp. There were no beds or tables. Prisoners slept on dirty straw mattresses on the floor. Many families crammed into the cells had no privacy. A bucket in the corner served as the latrine. It was full and reeked. The prisoners themselves were dirty and emancipated. Karlis grimly steeled and forced himself to walk into the cell, shocked that his fellow

Latvians could be so callous towards other people.

"I need workers. Are there any volunteers?" he called out loudly.

Everyone put their hand up.

They all surged towards him. "Me! Me! Please take us!"

Saddened by their plight, Karlis felt appalled. "I can only take two families …"

He recognised people he'd done business with previously. "Adamson, Klempneru, your wives and you," he pointed to a large, strong young man.

Their faces lit up.

"Thank you. Thank you. We'll work hard. We won't cause any trouble for you," they babbled with relief.

The other people in the cell looked distressed.

Karlis gazed at them all, and sadly murmured, "I'm so sorry. I can't take you all."

Karlis took the five people he had selected and their children out to the cart. As they loaded their meagre possessions and themselves onto it, he told them. "You'll have to work hard. I'll try to pay you a fair wage and will provide accommodation on the farm. We'll have to work together to get the crop sown and harvested quickly."

As he climbed up onto the laden cart, he thought ruefully. "I wish I still had my car!"

He didn't and there was nothing he could do about it so, sighing, he took the reins and drove out of the town, past the white fields and stark trees of the countryside. The people clinging precariously to the sides of the cart were chilled to the core by a cold icy wind. But they didn't care. There was an almost joyous atmosphere in the cart, the people so pleased to be out of that appalling gaol.

Back at the farm Karlis placed the two women and one girl, Anna, in the house and garden with Lydia. The three men and three boys helped him on the farm.

Karlis and his new workers worked hard. They used the old methods, using horses to plough the soil and sow wheat and oats in the spring of 1942. Karlis' precious tractor was still 'broken down'. They were probably the worst crops he'd ever planted; despite the fact it looked likely to be a reasonable season. His farming methods were deliberately lax and inefficient. He didn't bother to spend money on fertiliser or decent seed and left more fields fallow than he usually did. He was indifferent about the expected low yields and for the first time in his life didn't actually want any good yields. It went against his whole farming philosophy, but from the little he'd seen of this new regime he didn't want to support it at all. He just wanted to fulfil his quota and keep the German occupiers happy and away from his family, farm and workers. He didn't succeed.

Karlis sat in the Bendze's front room sipping a hot cup of tea. Roberts Bendze sat with him quietly. Maria bustled about the room, smiling occasionally at Karlis, pleased to have him back.

"How are things at Kambaris?" Roberts asked eventually.

Karlis shrugged. "Oh, I got some Jewish workers. I rescued them from the prison in Dobele."

He shuddered at the thought. "Such terrible conditions … Well, we put in wheat and oats. It looks good on the surface, but it's a terrible crop. I've sown just enough for my quota, which is really low. I'm glad the auditors who showed up, while efficient, knew very little about yields, cropping and soil in the area."

Roberts frowned. "You're taking a risk."

Karlis shrugged again. "As long as I meet their quota that's all I'm worried about. If there is any surplus, I'll hide it and sell it on the black market!"

Roberts frowned again, sipped his tea and nodded, he was deliberately being very lax and inefficient as well. "It's a delicate balancing act."

At that moment the phone rang. Roberts answered it.

He looked agitated and spoke down the line. "Lydia, please calm down. I'll get him to come back straight away!"

In response to Karlis' questioning look, he said grimly. "Something is up at Kambaris. You had better go home at once."

Karlis was out the door before the words were out of his mouth, leaving his half-finished tea on the table. Roberts sighed, sat down and finished his tea.

Karlis rode back to Kambaris as fast as the old nag he was riding could gallop. As he galloped into his yard, he noticed that his house and yard were surrounded by grim-faced SS soldiers, their vehicles parked outside the front door. His heart lurched into his mouth. He leapt off his horse and ran into his house, brushing aside a soldier who tried to stop him. He found Lydia and his children ashen-faced. Cowering behind them were his Jewish workers. A stern-looking SS captain, in a smart grey uniform with black lapels with the dreaded silver SS insignia shining in the light, stood in front of them, hands on hips. He had an iron cross pinned on his chest and wore a grey and black peaked hat.

Karlis rushed into the room and blurted out in fluent German. "What's going on?"

The captain turned his cold, cruel, grey eyes on him, sending a chill through his spine.

"You are harbouring Jews!" he snapped.

He lifted his hand and the cowering people were grabbed and unceremoniously hustled outside. Karlis followed them.

"Hauptmann! Hauptmann! These are my workers! I need them to harvest my crop!" he cried urgently, pointing wildly over the nearby fence at a field of small green shoots that were just starting to force their way through the soil. "How can I meet my army grain quota without them?"

The captain looked at him coldly. "That's not my concern. These Jewish scum are to be removed. They are enemies of the Fuhrer! Are there any more of these vermin here?"

Karlis shook visibly, but seeing only eight people in custody said bravely, "No! No! That's all."

The captain barked at his soldiers. "Let's go. Load up."

The men, women and boys were shoved brutally onto the back of a truck and the soldiers scrambled into the back of others.

At that moment, Anna, who had been with Lydia and the children, broke away and ran towards the truck screaming. "Mama! Mama!"

One of the soldiers grabbed her, flaying and kicking, and shoved into the truck. The captain, on seeing the little girl, turned around to Karlis and, pulling out his pistol, pointed it at his head. Lydia stifled a scream and the children sobbed. Karlis reeled, frantic.

The captain sneered, enjoying his victim's extreme discomfort and palpable fear and snarled, "I should shoot you here where you stand, Jew lover! The penalty for hiding Jews is death!"

He slammed the barrel of his pistol into Karlis' face and turning, stalked away. Getting into his staff car he drove out of the yard, followed by his soldiers.

Shaken by the savage blow, Karlis almost fell; he grabbed a nearby chair, blood pouring from a gash in his cheek. Lydia sobbed with fear and horror and ran up to him. Karlis Junior bellowed with fear and shock and Inta sobbed, heart-broken … almost catatonic with shock and horror. She'd been very good friends with Anna. Lydia tried to stop the flow of blood with a handkerchief.

Karlis sat abruptly in the chair he'd been clinging to. "Jesus Christ!" he gasped, ashen-faced.

It had been another close call. His luck had held again, but only just.

"Lydia, love, look after the children. I'll be alright. It looks worse than it is."

He gently took the bloody handkerchief from her and dabbed his face. He'd been lucky, no serious damage done to anything except his pride.

Karlis now had a major problem. He had a crop germinating, soon to be harvested, an army grain quota to meet and no workers. He resolved to go into Dobele and find either his Jewish workers or some other workers. He drove his cart into the town and went straight to the prison. There was a new commandant.

Karlis asked, "Where's the previous commandant?"

The new man looked scared and spoke in a hushed, strained voice. "He was taken away, soon after they took away the rest of our Jewish prisoners. Apparently, he treated the Jews too leniently."

"Oh!" was all Karlis could say, remembering the shocking conditions in the prison when he'd been there a few months ago.

He hurried from the prison and found the town councillor he'd spoken to previously. "The Germans took my Jews. Is it possible for them to be sent back? I really need my workers."

The man was astounded at Karlis' naivety.

"Nobody knows where they've been taken." He then looked furtively over his shoulder and leaned closer to Karlis before whispering, "I've heard a rumour they've been taken to a camp near Riga, for their own protection."

Karlis was saddened and troubled by this ominous news.

The councillor said loudly in a businesslike fashion, "There is a certificate hiring system now. You can only employ certified workers. I can show you what to do."

Karlis listened carefully then thanked the man and left. He followed the councillor's instructions and hired a number of certified workers and their families. They were Latvians he knew and trusted, and they had worked on farms before.

Karlis alighted from the train in Riga and, grabbing his light bag, hurried out of the station. Once outside, he flagged a taxi. As they drove down the streets to his brother Adolf's house, he was amazed at the city's transformation. Despite the war, it was vibrant, with cafes and bars operating at full swing. German soldiers on leave partied hard with the local women. German efficiency had cleaned up the streets and the parks and gardens were vivid, green and beautiful, the flower beds well-tended. Young couples walked hand in hand under trees and past ponds. Commerce seemed revived as well. Businesses appeared to be thriving.

However, he sensed a certain desperation about the city, almost as if the locals had remembered how to party and were doing it with gay abandon, partying as though the world was ending – which perhaps it was. He had heard whispers about the Nazi's defeat outside Moscow. Other things, however, were very much the same.

Despite the forced gaiety, the atmosphere was still oppressive. The scruffy Russian soldiers on every street corner had been replaced by smart German soldiers. The NKVD lurking in the shadows and cruising the streets in their black sedans had been replaced by the Gestapo doing the same thing. The Stalinist symbols had been replaced by huge swastikas.

Adolfs answered the door when Karlis knocked. He opened it wide and ushered his brother in.

Maria, his wife, bustled out of the kitchen. "Karlis! Come in. I've just put on an early lunch. Poor fare I'm afraid. It's getting harder, you know. The war …"

"Thanks Maria. I'll love whatever you have. I cannot stay though. I really should get back to the farm this evening."

Adolfs asked. "How are Lydia and the children?"

"They're all well. Karlis is getting to be a big lad now!"

Maria smiled and clucked a bit. "I'm sure he is! Come and sit down. Eat!"

Karlis sat. They had managed to put on a reasonable spread of chicken, bread, salad and eggs, despite the war. After dinner, Maria served cake and coffee. It was all very pleasant. Karlis had come to Riga to visit them, but also on business.

He thought about how to broach the subject, knowing that Adolfs could be prickly about certain things. He decided to get to the subject straight away. "Adolfs, I need workers for the farm. The Germans came the other day and took away the Jewish families I had hired. They, as far as I am aware, have been sent to a camp near here. I was thinking, perhaps, to certify my nephews who are old enough to be conscripted, your son, Vitolds and Arturs' son, Uldis as farm workers. They can then work with me and be safe."

Adolfs contemplated the proposal before saying. "Thanks for the offer, Karlis; they have already decided to enlist. They want to do their patriotic duty and defend our country against the Stalinists. I support their decision."

Karlis gasped, uncertain if he had heard correctly. "Adolfs! That's a death sentence. They'll be sent to the Eastern Front!"

"It's their duty," Adolfs repeated stubbornly. "We have to defend ourselves against this Stalinist scourge. You know it was a lot worse under the Soviets! You were dispossessed and don't forget that Arturs disappeared; most likely sent to Siberia!"

"That's true, but Adolfs!" Karlis pleaded. "Surely you've heard of the Nazi defeat outside Moscow! The war will go on a lot longer now that the Siberian troops have been thrown into battle. There'll be a lot more casualties!"

"I think you're wrong. That, if it is true, was only a temporary setback. The Germans will defeat the Russians, and soon."

Karlis began to wonder about his brother's sanity. "You don't really believe that, do you? Even if you call it a temporary setback, there will be serious fighting before the Russians are defeated. They'll just keep retreating, if they have to. Look at history. Bonaparte, probably the greatest general of modern times, was ultimately defeated. Please reconsider. It's not too late. Farm workers are regarded as essential for the war effort and will be safe."

Adolfs glared at his brother. "They are doing their patriotic duty," he repeated again. "The Germans are the only ones who can save us. They are the only ones who can preserve Latvia."

Karlis' anger exploded. "Adolfs, don't be a stubborn fool! How can you support this terrible regime? Didn't you listen to a word I've said? My Jewish workers were taken away to some camp and have not been heard of since! There have been rumours of gypsies disappearing as well. What happens if the Nazis decide they want to set up a German state here, as was tried in 1919, and Latvians start disappearing?"

Adolfs stood up and slammed his fist on the table. "That has not happened and will not happen! That's all just supposition! You have no evidence at all for such an outrageous statement."

Maria intervened. "Shhhh, please don't shout, both of you. You both don't know who may be listening and we all still have to be careful these days. You'll just have to agree to disagree."

She put her hand gently on Karlis' shoulder and said quietly, "Thank you for the kind offer. The boys are grown men now and have to make their own decisions."

She looked worried and distressed.

Karlis softened and said to her quietly, with real despair. "I've tried to warn him. I'll not take responsibility for my nephews' deaths, if it happens. That'll be on Adolfs' head and Adolfs' head alone!"

He hugged her.

"Thank you for the lovely lunch, Maria," he said quietly with genuine affection and sadness. "I should go."

Karlis walked out of the house without another word, nor a backwards glance at his brother.

Maria rushed after him and urgently whispered, "Please forgive him, Karlis. Adolfs is a stubborn man and a strong Latvian nationalist. He just wants the old republic back. Please take Arturs' youngest son, Ivars. He's a good worker and a strong lad. He'll be of age soon."

Karlis smiled at her and briefly hugged her again. "I will. I'll sort it out as soon as I get back to Kambaris."

He flagged down a taxi and left, waving back at her standing forlornly on the street.

Karlis caught the first train back to Dobele. While sitting in the carriage, watching the fields and forests of the Latvian landscape flash by, he came to a decision. He would talk it over with Lydia, but he had decided that things were only going to get worse. He didn't like the appalling Nazi regime and didn't trust them to do the right thing by Latvia. On the other hand, if the country were reconquered by the Soviet Union, it spelled certain doom for him. Even as a reluctant and indifferent farmer, who was virtually sabotaging his own business, he would still be regarded as a Nazi collaborator by the Soviets and more than likely shipped off to Siberia … if he was lucky.

He decided, with incredible reluctance they had to leave. The realisation that there was no future for him in his own country, caught as it was between these two competing giants, saddened him greatly. The question was where to go and when? He thought deeply about that. There seemed to be two options: try to get to Germany or try to get to the Scandinavian countries. As for when … he would wait and see. Maybe Adolfs was right? Maybe things would improve?

When Karlis arrived at Dobele he had the time and it was a beautiful summer's day so he decided to walk back to the farm. It was a long walk, but he needed to exercise, relax and think about things.

He walked out of the town into the countryside, down the main road, past the lush green fields. It was quiet, with few vehicles on the road. For a while he forgot all about the war and his other worries as he ambled over the low hills. He noticed the crops were sparse this year. The yields would not be good. Maybe there were more indifferent farmers in this district? People, like himself, subtly resisting the Nazi regime.

As he walked, he thought sadly, *This is really good land – the breadbasket of Europe. With good management you can grow almost anything here … well not tropical crops … but almost anything else.*

He stooped and picked up a handful of soil. Deep, brown, rich loam. "Perfect," he thought, crumbling the soil in his hand.

He walked past a small thicket of forest and over a small creek. "It's a beautiful forest. There's much potential here."

He stopped and patted a huge, old, gnarly oak tree. A small bird flitted past him and insects buzzed around. He bent and picked up a flower and held it to his nose, taking in the scent. He crossed a rustic wooden bridge over a small, bubbling creek. Scrambling down the embankment, he drank the cool, clear water.

"There's plenty of water … perhaps it's possible to irrigate? Shame it's so cold sometimes …"

He knew he was getting sentimental. He couldn't help it. Despite his new-found resolution, the stark truth hit him hard. *He did not want to leave!*

Karlis walked into the house at Kambaris late. Lydia had become worried about him and looked up relieved when he walked in. He sat at the table in the kitchen.

She bustled over. "Do you want tea, love?"

"Yes, thank you … … Lydia?"

She brought over a steaming cup of hot tea and put it on the table in front of him. "Yes, dear, what is it?"

"I think we have to make preparations to leave here … at least until this war is over. We must be ready to leave in a hurry. I think we should wait and see what happens, but should be prepared anyway."

He expected her to argue. She didn't. She just nodded and said quietly, "You're right … Where shall we go … if it comes to that?"

"I think, maybe, Germany. I really think the Nazis will ultimately lose this war."

She looked doubtful.

"I know. I can't explain it, but that's what my gut tells me. If we manage to get to Germany, we may be able to come back here after the war or, as a worst-case scenario, be able to emigrate … to maybe Australia or Canada."

She sat down opposite him and whispered plaintively, "I don't want to leave."

"Neither do I. We may have no choice. But let's not worry about that for now. I'm sure we'll still have a couple of years …" He looked glum.

She smiled at him and tried to speak cheerfully, to perk him up a bit. "I'm sure we will. Is there something else?"

"I had an argument with Adolfs. I wanted to certify our oldest nephews as farm workers so they wouldn't be conscripted. He says they have enlisted and was adamant that it remains that way."

"Oh," she said. "That foolish, stubborn man. If they end up fighting the Russians …"

She couldn't say the rest.

He smiled grimly and standing up, walked around the table and put his hands over her shoulders and onto her breasts as she sat there. "I know …"

Karlis found out later, much to his incredible anguish, that both his nephews, Uldis and Vitolds, who had enlisted in the German army, died fighting the Russians on the Eastern Front. He never forgave his brother Adolfs for that.

X

The Lucky Man (1944)

The awful noise continued in the distance. Karlis heard the dreadful sound with an ironic and fearful sense of déjà vu. It seemed louder when the wind blew from the east. *Thump, thump, thump.* The terrible sound continued day and night. *Thump, thump, thump.* It not only continued all the time but seemed to be getting louder and closer. Occasionally, if he bothered to look, the distant drone of high-flying aircraft could be heard as Russian bombers pounded Liepaja. The sound of war drew uncomfortably close as the Heeresgruppe Kurland desperately tried to slow the remorseless advance of the Soviet army. They failed and were forced to retreat to better defensive positions and let the Russian army reconquer Riga in October 1944. Karlis' brother Adolfs and his family escaped to Sweden on a small fishing boat in a hazardous voyage, with only days to spare.

If Karlis had any doubts that it was finally time to leave Kambaris, those doubts were shattered when German soldiers started to arrive in force. A colonel of the Wehrmacht arrived at the door in a large, grey staff car. He was a tall, handsome man with blond hair and steely blue eyes; he wore stained and crumpled khaki and green patched combat fatigues and a meshed steel helmet. Field glasses hung around his kneck and a MP 40 maschinenpistole slung on his shoulder. The man had the tired, strained look of someone who'd seen a lot of action but still exuded a steely determination. His staff car was followed by truck after truck of equipment and weaponry. His soldiers were tired, their uniforms stained and dirty, but they still maintained rigid, even harsh, discipline. They poured out of their trucks and started to spread out. Approximately one kilometre from the house was the small rise, with the small oak thicket on the left.

The colonel was brusque and to the point. "I'm requisitioning this house and barn for the use of the German Army. We're setting up defensive positions here. I strenuously advise you to leave at once. Do you understand? At once!"

He barked the last words urgently. Karlis opened his mouth to say something, but the man glared at him, daring him to say anything. Karlis held his tongue.

A young officer ran up, saluting the colonel breathlessly. "Herr Oberst, the artillery has been positioned on the extreme left of the line hidden behind that thicket over there."

He pointed at the thicket. The colonel lifted his field glasses and peered in that direction.

He pointed with his gloved finger at a crumpled map in his hand. "Good. I want a double line of trenches dug here and here. Make sure everything is well camouflaged. We will keep our tank squadron in reserve, hidden in the barn, to support the part of the line under the most pressure. I want anti-aircraft batteries set up here, here and here. And anti-tank batteries dug in at regular intervals down the line."

The other officer saluted sharply and hurried away.

The colonel turned to Karlis, who had watched all this in fascination, rooted to his spot, and said harshly, with withering impatience. "Are you still here? I want you out of here in one hour. If I have anything to do with it, there is going to be one mother of a battle here."

He then turned on his heel and marched towards the house as two more officers rushed up, clamouring for his attention.

Karlis stood mortified.

As he rushed back into the house he thought, *Fuck, I've left it too*

He called, "Lydia, children, get packed at once! Ivars, come and help me hitch up the tractor and trailer. We have to leave now!"

They had made their preparations for a quick departure. Everything of value was hurriedly packed onto the trailer, including Lydia's jewellery, which was carefully hidden. The tractor miraculously started straight away, the 'broken' part amazingly repaired. He had kept it in good condition; kept it fuelled up and ready. Drums of diesel were strapped on the trailer as well.

"We'll go and pick up Bendze!"

The tractor lurched forward, as Lydia and the children precariously clung onto the trailer. It roared, belching black smoke as it churned forward, easily towing the big, heavily laden trailer. As they chugged away from Kambaris, Karlis looked over his shoulder as the house gradually faded into the distance. He felt incredible sadness as he knew this was the last time he would ever see his beloved house and farm. An hour later, they arrived at the Bendze's house. They were ready and quickly loaded up as well.

The tractor towed the crowded, highly packed trailer down the road to Saldus, the closest railhead still controlled by the Heeresgruppe Kurland. Roberts Bendze perched perilously on the top of the load while the rest of their families either sat tentatively on the trailer's railing or walked. It was going to be a long slow trip.

Karlis eased the laden tractor and trailer onto the main road crowded with refugees streaming away from the fighting. People carried all kinds of paraphernalia; travelled in all sorts of vehicles – horses and carts, trucks, a few cars, and the tractor. Most people shuffled along dismally, carrying everything they owned in battered suitcases or sacks tied on their backs. The completely chaotic scene was made worse by the heavy German military traffic going in the opposite direction. Children cried, but the men and women walked grimly and silently, not looking at anyone, everyone's nerves completely frayed.

Pervading the whole scene was the threat of war. The ever-increasing thump, thump, thump as the Soviet artillery and tanks drew closer. Most people panicked and scattered when they heard the drone of aircraft. Thankfully the Soviet bombers were not interested in the fleeing refugees, their main targets the Saldus railhead and Liepaja. Occasionally lonely and completely outnumbered German Focke-Wulf fighters would streak overhead. The road was heavily cratered and littered with upturned carts, broken cars, and dead and injured horses. Karlis carefully drove the tractor, avoiding people, cars, craters and horse carcasses. He kept his nerve and continued driving, regardless of the threat from aircraft.

He wondered how long the Germans would be able to hold Kambaris against the remorseless advance of the Soviet army; knew in his heart of hearts that his house, barn and farm would be destroyed in the upcoming battle. He almost sobbed at the thought. Grimly, with determination, he kept strong. He had to be strong as everyone was relying on him to get through this terrible ordeal they found themselves in. It was his fault though.

As he drove, despite the brave face he put on, his mind screamed, *I've left it too late. I've put my family in danger again! Why didn't we leave earlier?*

After a long and fraught journey, they rolled into Saldus. The wrecked town was in chaos, desperate refugees everywhere; bomb craters and smashed houses on most streets. The tough German military police barely controlled the desperate crowds. Around the train station was even worse: people milled everywhere as they frantically tried to board the next train to the coast. Those with no money or valuables to bribe the Germans missed out. Karlis paid heavy bribes using some of Lydia's jewellery and managed to get himself, his family, the Bendze family, all their possessions and the tractor on a train. It was a delicate operation heaving the tractor up onto a flat carriage using a crane. The tractor swayed precariously. Karlis thought, for an eternal minute, that the chains holding it might break. But they didn't. He was lucky. When the tractor was finally loaded, the rail workers quickly chained it down, barely finishing before the train lurched forward in a huge cloud of steam, black smoke and screeching wheels.

As the train gathered speed and rattled out of the station into the sunset air raid sirens sounded and anti-aircraft batteries nearby opened fire. The German machine gunners on sandbagged flat carriages nervously cocked their weapons and pointed them skywards. The few remaining German fighters, scrambling to intercept the Soviet bombers, flashed overhead, engines screaming as they strove to rapidly gain altitude. The train escaped unscathed into the darkness.

Karlis fell asleep to the motion and sound of the wheels as the crowded, heavily laden train thundered through the night. He woke and checked that everything and everyone was all right. Lydia and the children slept uncomfortably on the hard bench seats yet they looked so peaceful. He bent over and gently brushed his son's hair off his face. Stretching, he stepped over the bodies of people asleep on the floor and their possessions. Leaning out the window, he breathed deeply of the cold air as the train flashed past shadowy trees. He saw a cigarette glow from one of the German machine gunners as they silently and vigilantly peered into the darkness.

Suddenly, he saw a flash.

He flung himself down onto the floor of the carriage and screamed. "Get down! Get down!"

All hell broke loose. Machine gun bullets hummed toward the train from somewhere in the forest. The arc of the tracers flew everywhere in a colourful, but terrifying display. He cowered on the floor of the carriage, striving to put his body between the bullets and his family. Both his children woke with a start and cried out in fear. Lydia, pale-faced and terrified, tried to hush them, unsuccessfully.

The German machine gunners opened up in the direction of the partisan's fire in a loud, awful rat-a-tat-tat, the tracers from their bullets streaking towards their unseen assailants. Bullets pinged and sung as they soared towards the train as it charged through the night, the dark trees flashing eerily past them. A window shattered in their carriage, showering people with glass. Then, almost as soon as it started, the firing ceased as the train roared out of the forest into open farmland. Karlis crawled to his feet and urgently checked that everyone was alright. They were all shaken but okay.

They arrived in Liepaja without any more problems. It was still dark when the train finally steamed into the train station. Karlis managed to find accommodation for his and the Bendze families and proceeded to organise the unloading of his tractor. This was done under spotlights, with none of the drama that happened on loading. Karlis hid it near their accommodation. When he climbed into bed late, he quickly fell into an exhausted sleep.

Karlis' sleep was interrupted. Near sunrise, the wail of air raid sirens woke everyone. The crash of the anti-aircraft batteries and the silhouetted Soviet aircraft in the searchlights were eerie and frightening. Everyone ran to find shelter in a basement and waited until the all-clear was sounded. Bombs landed nearby, one very close as it shook the ground causing small bits of rock and dust to fall off the ceiling of the basement. The children cried out in fear and some of the adults prayed to God and Jesus. Others stared at the ceiling fearfully. What seemed an eternity passed before the all-clear sounded.

Karlis heaved the basement door open and carefully climbed up the stairs; picked his way out of the damaged house. Part of one of the walls had collapsed and all the windows had been shattered in the blast.

He had to immediately arrange for passage on the next ship.

Collecting all of Lydia's jewellery, he put it in his coat pocket and walked out onto the street in the morning light, and was shocked by what he saw. The city was wrecked, bomb-blasted buildings everywhere. As he walked down towards the port where he hoped to find a shipping office, Karlis picked his way through the rubble and around bomb craters. He walked past a brick wall stark in an otherwise smouldering pile of rubble. Dead horses lay in the street, the smell of them overpowering.

The shipping office had been bombed, but he managed to find someone in a more or less intact part of the building. He picked his way through the dust and rubble of what must have been another very near miss and approached the man behind a shrapnel-scarred counter.

"I really need to get passage on a ship to Germany. I'll pay, I have money," Karlis said to the man politely, but urgently.

The man, eyes wide open and jaw twitching, giggled and said, "You want to get on a ship! You want to get on ship!" He started to laugh hysterically.

"All the ships are gone. All are gone! All are sunk!" he managed to gasp between bouts of loud, insane laughter.

Karlis thanked the man and left, realising the man's state of shock.

He strode down to the wharf, casually walked past the German soldiers guarding the entrance. They lounged in their guard house, smoking. One of them stood up. "Your papers!"

Karlis handed them over. The soldier glanced at them in a cursory fashion and waved him through. The wharf was wrecked, with part of it splintered from a bomb hit. There were bombed-out buildings and a crane leaning precariously creaked in the light breeze. German soldiers manned concrete bunkers at either end of the wharf and concrete-enforced anti-aircraft emplacements.

One ship was tied up at the wharf. Somehow it had survived the recent air raid unscathed. Men frantically loaded the vessel manually and with the one operating crane. Karlis stood at the gangplank and yelled up at a person he thought may be an officer. As he stood there, he cringed as he heard the roar of aircraft flying overhead. Everyone else ignored them. He looked up. Two lonely Focke-Wulfs, wing tip to wing tip, exhausts burning white hot as they screamed low overhead, struggling to gain altitude in a hurry. Karlis knew he had to get passage now or miss out. Maybe the bombers were on the way.

He yelled again, urgently. "Sir, sir, I need passage. I can pay!"

The man didn't hear him because of the frenetic pace and noise of the sailors and port workers around him and the screaming engines of the fighter aircraft. He disappeared into a cabin.

Karlis began to despair. This seemed to be the last ship. He couldn't see any others. He swung around and collided with a man who hurried towards the gangplank.

The man looked startled and then a gradual smile of recognition spread over his worn, weatherbeaten face. "Karlis! Karlis Kelers. Is that you?"

Karlis recognised him. It was the man he had let hunt a number of times in the small oak thicket on Kambaris.

"Schmidt! What are you doing here? It's such luck to see you! It's been a while!"

The two men shook hands.

"It has! Those were good days on Kambaris! Are you trying to get passage?"

"Yes! For my family and the Bendze family. Do you remember Roberts Bendze?"

"Yes. A good man. I might be able to help. I have a labour contract with a major landowner in Germany. He would be interested in employing experienced farmers like you and Bendze. The man also needs a tractor. Is that magnificent machine you used to have at Kambaris still going?"

"It certainly is. In fact, I have it here."

"Excellent! We have to hurry. The ship's leaving as soon as it's loaded and is likely to be the last to leave this port. It is just getting too dangerous. Come on up and I'll talk to the Kapitän."

Schmidt hurried up the gangplank and Karlis followed him. They found the Captain supervising the crane loading something in a sealed box into the hold. He was red-faced, craggy, and elderly and sported deep white hair and a small, trim white beard. He wore an ill-fitting suit and a grease-stained leather cap with a small peak.

"Kapitän. This is a friend of mine, Karlis Kelers."

The Captain held out a gnarled hand and shook Karlis' hand with a strong grip.

"He needs passage for … how many people did you say, Karlis?"

"Ten people, our luggage and a tractor. I can pay."

"Very well, come into my office," the Captain answered.

He turned and bellowed at the man operating the crane as the box started to sway precariously. "Jesus fucking Christ; be careful there! Slow down, you fucking idiot. Do you want to blow us all up?"

The Captain then opened a rusty, grey painted steel door with a round porthole in it and let them into a small bare room. It contained a metal desk and chair and that was all. The Captain didn't sit down. He fidgeted, his body language indicating he was a busy, stressed man.

He said impatiently, "We are almost fully loaded. I can make arrangement for passage for you and your family as long as you are down here in one hour sharp."

He didn't mince words. "It'll cost you 10,000 Reichsmarks for the people and their processions, plus 1,000 for the tractor. Payment in cash or kind. Take it or leave it!"

It was outright extortion.

Karlis didn't hesitate. "I'll take it!"

He delved into his coat pockets and pulled out a small satchel with some of Lydia's jewellery in it. "I have only this jewellery. Is that acceptable?"

The Captain took the jewellery and examined at it carefully, holding it up to the sun that shone through the porthole and weighing it up in his hands.

He mused. "Mmm, are these diamonds? That looks like a nice emerald necklace. This seems to be good quality stuff. Worth good money. My wife will like it a lot … okay, you have a deal. Be here in one hour. We leave as soon as you are on board."

Karlis shook the man's hand. "Thank you so much. You are a lifesaver! You'll get the jewellery when we are all safely on board."

The Captain nodded his agreement and opened the steel door; he walked out onto the deck and repeated, tersely, as his mind was back on the boxes the crane was loading. "Be here in one hour!"

He turned and roared at the crane operator. "Fucking hell, man, do you have a death wish or what?"

Karlis and Schmidt hurried down the gangplank and onto the busy wharf. Schmidt held out his hand and they shook hands warmly.

"I've some other business to do. I'll see you in an hour."

"Okay. I'll be here."

Karlis hurried off at almost a run.

Karlis and Lydia leaned against the railing of the ship; watched as the gangplank was hauled in and stowed away. Steam started pouring from the ship's funnels, and a small tug gently pulled them away from the wharf. Karlis looked towards the front deck of the ship where his tractor had been secured with heavy chains. When he had supervised the loading of it, he had noticed, for the first time, a number of bullet holes in the vehicle. Thankfully they had missed anything of importance.

Karlis had secured two small cabins on the deck for his and Bendze's families. The ship shuddered as it gently moved away from the port and cast off the tug, its own engine now moving it forward. Karlis put his arm around Lydia as they watched the port town of Liepaja slowly disappear. They both stared at it intently, realising this view of the wrecked town may be the last time they would ever see Latvia. It was a sad and poignant moment.

He clung tightly to her. "We've been lucky. I was told that this is the last ship to leave Liepaja. I'm so sorry I had to use up so much of your jewellery."

She looked at him sadly. The jewellery was of no concern. They were all together and, so far, safe.

"Do you think we will ever see Latvia again?" she sighed.

"Perhaps not," he answered sadly.

Neither of them could help it as tears well ed in their eyes as the town faded in the distance. Schmidt silently came and stood near them and stared out at the fading land. There was nothing to say.

As the ship slowly moved out of the harbour, they noticed the masts of others vessels protruding from the water – so many of them. It was so sad to think these ships represented the graves of so many desperate people trying to flee war. The Captain, standing on the wings of his bridge, personally and with great skill conned the vessel past these watery graves. After an intense and nerve-racking hour, they were finally free of the port and out in the open sea. Karlis sighed and breathed in deeply the cold salty air and stared at the iron grey waters of the Baltic Sea. The ship rocked gently as it moved away from the shore.

The ship moved slowly though the gentle sea on that cold but fine day. High grey clouds dominated the sky. The Captain, other officers and lookouts stared intently at the horizon, the radar-less ship relying solely on visual observation. Hence, all remained very nervous. Not only did they have to worry about Soviet aircraft, the threats of submarines, surface vessels and the hidden menace of mines kept everyone on edge.

And Karlis discovered something that made him even more nervous. As the ship moved slowly and steadily through the slight swell, he wandered alone around the decks, stepping at times over soldiers who were bedded down there. On speaking to some of them, all of whom were either injured or not quite of sound mind, he learnt that the ship was heavily laden with ammunition. That explained the Captain's stress levels when the ship was being loaded. He decided not to tell Lydia or the children.

Despite not being a very religious man, he prayed for fog or anything to keep Soviet aircraft or submarines or surface vessels away. And he was not the only one praying. Karlis found the crew's antics grimly amusing – thought them the most religious crew on earth – for when they were not on duty, and perhaps even when they were, they spent an inordinate amount of time also praying. He would have laughed, but for the fact they were sitting on a powder keg. He did though, cynically, wonder if the loudly cussing and profane Captain was a big prayer. Despite these worries he managed to sleep well that night, as did everyone in his party. The nervous tension of the last few days had caught up with them all.

Without any help from God the ship survived the first day and an uneventful, fogless night. The Captain kept radio silence and kept the ship in complete darkness. Any brief sliver of light emanating from a window unleashed his extreme wrath at the unfortunate culprit. By dawn, the ship motored down the Polish coast near the Helska Peninsular, west of the German-held port of Gdansk. The crew, though still vigilant, started to relax slightly. The passengers gained confidence as the relentless tension of the previous day and night slowly eased. People started to smile and laugh again, and athe decks rang with the laughter and scamper of children. The atmosphere seemed almost festive.

Then one of the lookouts screamed, "Achtung! Achtung! Flugzeug! Flugzeug!" and frantically pointed into the rising sun.

People rushed to the side and stared to the east. Two twin engine Russian aircraft rapidly approached at sea level. The Captain immediately ordered the ship to turn and run south-west towards the coast, and sent out a frantic mayday call on the radio.

Karlis grabbed some life jackets and yelled, "Karlis, Inta, come here now!"

The children rushed up and he almost threw the life jackets at them as he hustled then into the cabin.

"Put these on and get down! On the floor!"

He put his arms around them and Lydia, and not too gently pushed them down. With an extreme sense of déjà vu, he covered them with his body. They hit the deck just in time as the Soviet bombers screamed over them, dropping their bombs.

The bombers turned for another run on the ship then suddenly banked and streaked east, their engines howling as they hurtled back to their base. Those who watched knew the reason for their hurry as two ME109s roared over the ship, their exhausts white hot, the pilots pushing their planes to the limit in pursuit the fleeing bombers.

When people on the ship looked around, the destruction was obvious. Three bombs had straddled the ship and exploded nearby, damaging the deck and hull plating, and showering the deck with water. Another bomb hit the ship but failed to explode before sliding off the deck and into the sea. Another had landed near the stern of the ship, exploding and causing a yawning hole in the stern.

The crew, led by the first mate, frantically rushed to shut the bulkheads and man the pumps. The Captain desperately steamed the ship straight at a sandbank he knew existed in the area. The ship was sinking, but they made it. The ship shuddered to a halt on the sandbank, throwing anyone who was not hanging on, onto the deck. It settled bow first on the bank and stayed afloat as the stern bulkheads and pumps held the water level. The Captain sent an urgent call to Gdansk for help. He ordered the crew to throw some things overboard to lighten the stern. He then ordered that the rudder and steering gear be checked. By some miracle they were damaged but still intact. Another miracle was that flooding had stopped a fire that had briefly flared when the bomb first hit. Strangely, while the crew's prayers had not been answered, God had looked after them: the ammunition-laden ship had miraculously survived.

Karlis, shaken, emerged from the cabin. The ship looked in a sorry state as the crew worked to keep it afloat. The Captain had not given the order to abandon ship, so perhaps things were not as bad as they looked. He carefully walked forward, noting the bent plating on the deck and hull from the near misses. Once again, they had been so lucky!

He made his way to his tractor chained on the forward deck. Some shrapnel had hit it, but while battered, it was still intact. He examined it closely and found the engine and fuel tank were still operational. He patted the engine casing, almost affectionately and walked back to the cabin. The relatively able-bodied soldiers on deck were conscripted to help the crew keep the ship afloat. The others lay in the shade and kept out of the way, as did the refugees.

Due to the incredible efforts of the crew and the exhausted officers, the ship remained afloat on its sandbank until a recovery tug, escorted by a small gunboat, arrived. The crew had stabilised the stern enough to secure a hawser between it and the tug. The powerful tug, water churning from its propellers, black smoke pouring from its stubby funnel, gently pulled the ship off the bank. After a short but fraught and dangerous journey, the battered ship eased its way into Gdansk, where it was secured to the wharf. The ship creaked and groaned, almost as though it felt the same extreme relief the crew and passengers felt, as the engines quietly shuddered to a halt.

The passengers disembarked, relieved to be on dry land after the travails of the journey. However, they were now left in limbo. They were required to stay within the port confines, but were provided with a disused warehouse. The ship was assessed and as the Soviet army was reported to be just out of Warsaw, not far to the south-east, it was decided to patch it up and try to get to Kiel as soon as possible. The necessary repairs would take a week, so the refugees just had to knuckle down in the cold, airy warehouse and wait. Someone provided them with mattresses to sleep on, and a soup kitchen was set up by locals just inside the port's entrance.

The battered ship eased out of the harbour at Gdansk early in the morning on a cold but fine day. A slight breeze pushed a gentle swell as the ship, laden with even more refugees – this time Germans fleeing from the Soviet armies in Poland – attempted the still hazardous journey to Kiel. They were escorted part of the way by the same gunboat that had taken part in their rescue. At least its sleek presence off their starboard side provided them some psychological relief. Most passengers remained nervous, but slowly relax a little, so that once more the people started to chat to one another and the children began to laugh and smile.

Karlis leaned up against the railing and breathed in the fresh sea air, finally feeling they were safe; at least as safe as they could be in this accursed war. Kiel, their destination, was a large port in the north-western part of Germany. He hoped they would be far enough away from the remorseless advancing Soviet armies; worried about allied bombers but decided not to mention those worries to his family. He looked out at the grey calm seas of the Baltic and just wanted to get off this ship. He wandered to the stern, past the still-gaping hole in the deck and watched the white-water churning from the propellers. He found the view, along with the cold air and breeze, refreshing. It cleared his head and calmed his nerves.

Lydia joined him and they stood side by side silently watching the wake of the battered ship. Karlis put his arm around her waist.

They were both feeling melancholy, and he wondered what the future held.

"Do you think we will ever get back home?" he asked her quietly.

She shrugged, not really knowing what to say. She thought sadly and perceptively, *I don't think there will be anything to go back to …* but she didn't say that out loud.

She cuddled up closer to him in the cold breeze and stared out at the water. "I hope so. I really hope so," she said quietly.

He smiled down at her. "Whatever happens to us, I'm a lucky man."

XI

The Refugee (1945–1949)

The battered ship slowly entered Kiel harbour. Two tugs, their powerful engines churning up the water, pushed the ship forward. The passengers crowding the railing peered at the city in the distance. What they saw, even for people who had come through so much hardship and war, shocked them. The city of Kiel, being a major port and naval base, had been bombed to oblivion by allied bombers. The city had been completely destroyed. Bombed shells of buildings stood everywhere. To the passengers gaping in utter astonishment, the town centre and area around the harbour looked totally obliterated. They wondered how anyone could live in such a place. But, a few hardy souls, tiny in the distance, were visible picking their way through the wreckage.

As the ship moved quietly to its wharf, they passed two huge German warships that had been destroyed in their docks, one of them looking sunk, the only thing keeping it afloat were the ropes tying it to the wharf. The other had been destroyed in dry dock, its huge guns skewed at weird angles. Large steel gantry cranes leaned precariously, a mass of crumpled and bent steel. Amazingly, they had not collapsed completely. With a tired shudder the ship bumped gently against the wharf and the sailors and wharf workers hurriedly secured the lines. The ship seemed to sigh and settle low in the water.

As soon as the gangplank swung into place the passengers disembarked in an unruly mob, some of them so pleased to be on solid ground and relative safety they kissed the ground or sank to their knees and prayed. All the non-Germans, on grasping their meagre possessions, were herded into a building for processing. Karlis made sure all his and Bendze's possessions were taken off the ship in an orderly fashion and not lost in the rush to disembark.

Schmidt hurried up to them. "Quickly, Quickly! This way. We have to get a move on!"

He hustled both families to the front of the line. Karlis heartily agreed. The sooner they left Kiel, the better.

Schmidt spoke breathlessly as he hurried them along. "My patron has a large agricultural business in the town of Schleswig to the north of here, halfway to the Danish border. You'll be safe there. It's a small town and has not been that affected by the war."

When they reached the customs and immigration officials, Schmidt showed his papers and spoke rapidly in German to the man.

Both Karlis and Lydia, who spoke German fluently, heard him say. "These people…" he indicated Karlis and Roberts with his thumb, "… have been hired to work as agricultural experts at Schleswig. As such, they'll be essential for the war effort. They need their papers and travel passes as soon as possible."

The official wouldn't be harassed by Schmidt's bluster and continued to work in a slow methodical way.

Two hours later, they were outside. They had their papers and were to be sent to a refugee camp that had been set up in an old lunatic asylum in Schleswig town. Schmidt found a truck and they loaded up all their processions and drove to the train station … what was left of it.

Karlis made sure his family and the Bendzes were on what he thought was the right train. He had to stay in Kiel to get his tractor off the ship.

He briefly hugged Lydia and his children and said to Roberts Bendze. "Please look after Lydia and the kids. I'll catch up with you in Schleswig in a few days."

Karlis watched as the train moved out of the bomb-damaged station, slowly gathering speed. He waved until they were out of sight around a bend. Lydia and the children hung out of windows and waved for as long as they could see the forlorn-looking figure on the battered platform. For the first time, Karlis felt his family were finally safe – it was a great relief.

With Schmidt he drove back to the port, past the smashed buildings, down potholed, bomb-cratered roads strewn with rubble and glass. Once again, he felt great admiration at the fortitude of the people in this city.

They found the wharf a hive of activity as the crew and wharf workers frantically unloaded the ship, imperative that its precious cargo be unloaded before the next bombing raid. Karlis said goodbye to Schmidt who had other business to attend and went and found the Captain.

The man was impatient.

"I've been looking for you. We have to get your tractor off as soon as possible. The ship is going into dry dock. We're going to try to fix her," he said with some pride.

"I agree. We have to get it off before the next air raid. Is all the ammunition off yet?"

The Captain knew that his secret could not be kept. "Yes. We got it off straight away. The last crate is coming off at the moment. I want to get your tractor off now. I've heard this is the British air raid zone. The air raids usually come at night, so we have to get everything off by then!"

"Good! Can I go on board?"

"Yes. Come with me!"

Karlis followed the Captain and supervised the crew as they unchained the tractor from the deck and hitched up chains under the front and rear wheels. A gantry crane, lifting the machine carefully, swung it over the side and lowered it onto the wharf. It was done.

Karlis walked down the gangplank and inspected his machine. Though battered with bullet holes and shrapnel scars, it seemed to be intact. And it still had fuel in it. He found the crankshaft and cranked her over a number of times, until the crank kicked back in his hands. It was hard work. Then he clambered up onto the hard metal seat and with considerable trepidation tried to start the engine. The engine coughed and spluttered a number of times, pouring black smoke out of the exhaust then, with a roar, it started. Karlis almost gave a whoop of joy.

He leapt out of the driver's seat and asked the Captain, who stood near one of the port officials, "Where can I put her?"

Then the air raid sirens wailed.

"Shit! I thought you said they only came at night!" Karlis said anxiously.

The port official answered coolly. "They usually do. Quickly get that thing under cover in that concrete shed. The air raid shelter is over there."

Karlis hurriedly scrambled back into his seat and as fast as the lumbering tractor could go, drove it towards a concrete reinforced shed. While he was driving, the anti-aircraft guns opened up ineffectively as a couple of twin-engine Mosquito bombers screamed low overhead. They appeared to stand on their wings as they banked tightly to the left, their engines howling as the pilots pushed them to the limit. They were so close Karlis felt the shock wave and could see the pale heat from their exhausts, and the pilots' heads in their leather helmets. The sleek and powerful machines levelled out and streaking low over the murky waters of the harbour dropped their bombs on the other side before powering skywards in an ear-shattering climb and disappearing as rapidly as they'd come. Karlis had never seen anything move so quickly. They were gone before what was left of the German air force even scrambled. Shaking, he nevertheless kept his nerve and manoeuvered the tractor into the shelter.

After parking up, Karlis found the Captain and the port official again – they'd not even made it to the air raid shelter.

"What the hell was that?" he asked in a jittery voice.

"Oh. The British sometimes raid with those damn Mosquitos. Especially the U-boat pens over there." The official waved his hand in the general direction of a series of long concrete structures.

"They come out of nowhere and then disappear, rarely doing much damage, but they keep the navy boys in a state! Boy, are they fast though …" he said quietly, almost with admiration. Things like that weren't said, especially if there was the chance of prying ears of the Gestapo being around.

"Very scary …"

"Yes."

Karlis witnessed a 'real' air raid that night. He'd been directed by Schmidt to a 'reputable' person and sold one of Lydia's necklaces on the black market for some Reischmarks. It was the only one he had, as the little remaining jewellery she had was with the family, and he desperately hoped he had enough money. He found temporary accommodation in a dilapidated, but largely intact hotel near the port. It was a cheap hotel in an area that had suffered heavily from the incessant air raids. The paint was peeling, the steps up to the front door were almost unusable, and most of the windows were boarded up, making the tattered decor look even worse. But it had clean sheets and relatively clean bathrooms. The water and electricity, perhaps to be expected, at best, were sporadic. Best of all, as far as Karlis was concerned, this dump sat across the road from an air raid shelter.

He had just dozed off when the air raid sirens started wailing. Cursing, he woke with a start and, yanking on his shoes and coat, ran out of the hotel. Out in the dark and eerie street, the searchlights swung beams across the sky and loud crashes of anti-aircraft gunfire made it apoplectic. To make it worse, snow had started to fall and the cold felt bitter. Shadowy figures hurried towards the air raid shelter.

An air raid warden rushed up to him, urgently shouted at him, "This way! This way! Quickly!" as he directed him towards a dark, dank buried concrete room dimly lit by bare light bulbs and torches.

As Karlis ran across the road, the terrible drone of hundreds of heavy bombers grew louder and the anti-aircraft gunfire reached a deafening crescendo. He rushed into the shelter, followed by the warden, just as the first bombs fell with a terrifying whistle.

One of the worst nights of Karlis' life, this bombing raid made the Russian efforts he'd already been through seem tame and pathetic. The explosions of the bombs seemed to last forever. The near misses shook the whole shelter, causing bits of concrete to rain down from the roof onto the occupants.

Once again, Karlis felt astounded by the stoicism of the other people in the shelter. They all seemed blasé about it all – some curled up in a corner and slept; others played cards or read books in the dim light; still others ate and drank away their limited rations. Someone had a gramophone which scratchily played slow music. And when the bombs fell close, the needle would jump and make an awful screeching sound. Despite this, one couple, apparently in love, danced close.

So nervous, Karlis couldn't do any of that. He paced up and down in the limited space, his nerves jumping at every near miss. Eventually, someone yelled at him to sit down. After what seemed a nerve-shattering eternity, the all-clear finally sounded. Karlis, in a daze, scooted across the road to his hotel, to his room, which had somehow survived the terrifying bombardment, and there he collapsed into an exhausted sleep.

He spent the rest of the next day organising, with the help of well-directed bribes, for his tractor and himself to be put on a train to Schleswig. While at the port, he noticed, to his considerable alarm, the ship had gone. Its spot on the wharf sat empty!

He asked the first person he found,. "Where's the ship? The *Stormanis*!"

"Over there," the man pointed down towards the other end of the wharf.

Karlis walked the short distance and looked up at the battered ship in dry dock. It was a miracle ship! It had survived the recent tempest! What he saw made it all the more apparent how lucky they'd been to make it here at all. The ship was a wreck. The bomb damage to the rusty hull plating was worse than he had imagined. Where the near misses had occurred, all was buckled and bent. A gaping hole revealed where the bomb had hit. The temporary repairs hurriedly completed in Gdansk had sprung apart soon after the ship docked. He was amazed that they had even managed to get it into dry dock.

Karlis felt glad this was a quiet day; he didn't think his shattered nerves could take another bombing raid. When everything was organised, with his tractor to be loaded early the next morning at the port, he, for the first time in years 'settled his nerves' by getting a little drunk on good German beer in a small bar down the street from the hotel.

The place was shabby and dark, with scuffed up tables and torn upholstery on its chairs. A battered, dusty, raised stage area, and dance floor that had once jumped with good bands and people dancing, was sad in its dereliction. The place would have been quite swank in times past, a reflection of the times in this battered city. It was, however, still a place of good cheer, full of desperate people attempting to have a good time in a grim and depressing environment. Perhaps some were trying to relive the bar's glory days, long gone. The woman serving at the bar was an attractive, buxom, blonde in her early forties; she wore a patched, threadbare dress, and quite happily to talked the handsome stranger with an unusual accent.

She poured a glass of beer for Karlis, and on receiving the money asked perceptively, "You've just come in from the east?"

"Yes," he smiled, somewhat grimly.

"What's it like?" she asked quietly.

He looked around and answered furtively, "Terrible. We had to abandon our home. It's probably been destroyed now. We were very lucky to get out alive. There is so much suffering; so many displaced people; so many wrecked lives. The Russians are at Warsaw and advancing relentlessly. I think it's terrible everywhere now."

She smiled sadly and said in a mere breath, "I've heard the allies are approaching the Rhine as well. Germany is doomed."

Karlis' answered with just a slight nod. She quietly poured him another drink before moving down the bar to serve another customer. All the while a gramophone played scratchily, old swing songs from a forgotten era. Karlis had an uninterrupted sleep that night, a small mercy.

When Karlis rose the next morning, the first thing he noticed was his hangover. The second thing he noticed was the lack of hot water, and the room was cold. He fetched a bucket of water from somewhere and washed his face before venturing out into a dark, icy, extremely cold morning. Fine sleet fell and landed in his eyes, ears, nose and down his coat. He felt cold and damp. While supervising loading his tractor onto a flat car, he stamped his feet and blew into his hands to keep warm. The tractor, thankfully, loaded quickly and efficiently. When the train eventually steamed out of the shattered city and into the flat, white countryside he felt further relieved, and so very glad to be leaving the grim, depressingly dangerous city and to be rejoining his family in what he hoped and prayed was a small country town largely unaffected by the war.

As the train steamed rapidly through the quaint countryside of northern Germany, Karlis tried to relax and reflect on the future. He hoped the camp they were staying at was alright. He didn't expect comfort, but he hoped – desperately hoped – for peace and safety. He wondered about food, about work, about his children's education, about access to medicine. He wondered how this war-ravaged country would support refugees when it was obvious the economy here was in a state of terminal collapse. It was all so uncertain. He had now, with deep sadness and despair, accepted they had little hope of getting back to Latvia any time soon. But, if they couldn't for some reason, where would they go? Stay here in Germany? He just didn't know and that depressed and frightened him. With these thoughts he drifted into a light sleep to the sound and motion of the train.

The trip to Schleswig didn't take long. As the train steamed into the pretty little town, Karlis' heart lifted on seeing little war damage. It looked a peaceful place on a deep blue fjord that joined the Baltic Sea. It had a number of lovely blue lakes and was dominated by its cathedral, with its tall slim spire, and its castle, Schloss Gottorf, the former residence of the Dukes of Schleswig. The castle sat on an island overlooking Burgsee Lake. Though in a state of disrepair it was a magnificent building, three storeys high, with a central tower, a large attic taking up the whole roof, and surrounded by large grounds.

Once he and his tractor were off the train, he received directions and drove the tractor up to Displaced Persons Camp Number One – an old lunatic asylum at the edge of the town. Here, in this rather grand, two-storeyed building in large grounds, Karlis found Lydia and the children, and the Bendze family. He felt so relieved to be back with his family, he hugged them all profusely.

The Kelers family settled down into life in the camp. Each family had a room, and the children had plenty of space to run around in the large gardens. Karlis and Bendze worked on a farm for a small wage, as had been arranged with Schmidt. To supplement his income, Karlis also worked in the Agricultural College, teaching students how to drive and maintain tractors.

Life was hard in the camp, especially for Lydia — she was not used to being so poor. She was not used to having to cook, clean and mend clothes herself. And she was not very good at it. The children ran around in tattered clothes and very often their food was overcooked or undercooked. But she did the best she could.

And she didn't complain. Safety and peace were important, and even more important, her family were all together. Lydia felt incredibly blessed by that. She'd heard many stories, even amongst the refugees in the camp, about families being torn asunder.

One man, Vladimir Klavins, a person they became friendly with, was one such case. In the chaos of the last days in Latvia, he'd become separated from his wife and daughter. Lydia and Karlis welcomed this kindly, caring man into their family and he became a kind of adopted uncle for their children.

Everything essential for life, including education for the children, was provided. A number of Latvian teachers in the camp taught in Latvian. The food, especially during the war, was poor and scarce. Often, if they looked closely at their food, they would find 'protein supplements' in the form of various weevils, worms and bugs. Meat was never available and the bread, when they could get it, was made from imported corn. It was heavy and tasteless and Lydia nicknamed it the 'yellow peril'.

Sometimes Karlis wondered how his brother Adolfs was and tried to correspond with him. He never heard anything back, and Karlis grew resentful. From what he'd heard, life was good in Sweden. The refugees there had plenty of food and received regular parcels of clothes and shoes from churches and other aid agencies. These were things the refugees in Germany could only dream about. In Germany, there was simply not enough of anything to go around. Karlis resented his brother's selfishness and lack of correspondence. He had hoped, in vain, that Adolfs might consider sending some secondhand clothes for his children, who ran around in tattered, threadbare clothes and worn out shoes.

The local Germans treated them all very well. Sometimes in lieu of wages they would be given cabbages, potatoes and apples. Karlis had relative freedom in the town and local area, as the elderly, lazy, camp guards turned a blind eye to people coming and going. He could therefore supplement the family food rations on the weekends by catching eels and picking berries in the woods surrounding the town.

He cobbled together an eel trap using wood, wire and old fencing mesh. It was a rudimentary item, with bits of wire and wood hanging off it, but it worked. He would set his baited trap in one of the myriad of small streams in the area. Roaming the woods and creeks in search of these delicacies reminded him of his time in Russia. He found it quite pleasant and relaxing. Once he had caught the eels, they were salted, smoked or prepared as a jellied food. He found them not to his taste, having a slimy texture, a lot of very fine bones and thick skin, but the others, especially Inta, liked them very much.

In early May 1945, Karlis sensed something was up. Rumours flew around the town about the rapid Soviet advance and that the Soviet Union was going to try to conquer all of northern Germany and even advance into Denmark. Everyone, even the local Germans, felt anxious. They all knew the end of Nazi Germany would be soon. Then rumours spread of Hitler's death and that it was all over: it was just a matter of which allied army conquered their area. For a few days, Karlis found himself in a state of nervous indecision. *What to do? What if the Russians get here before the Americans? Will we have to move again?* There were whispers amongst the refugees about hardships, looting and executions behind the Soviet lines. It was a very worrying time.

With great relief on 5 May 1945, he noticed the Nazi flag being lowered over the castle. He asked an elderly German soldier he saw on the street, "Sir, sir, what's going on? Is the war over?"

The man looked tired, depressed, and answered grumpily, "No, the war is not over yet! It will be soon though. The British have taken Kiel. They say only five hundred soldiers took the city … just five hundred!" His voice trailed off in despair, even shame.

Then he said, "The Führer is dead. Großadmiral Dönitz has taken over and ordered us to surrender. The British will be here soon …"

Karlis almost leapt in the air. He grabbed the man's hand and shook it vigorously before almost dancing down the street. The *British are coming! We're safe!* The man stared at him dumbfound and just shook his head.

On 8 May 1945, now known as VE day, a celebration occurred at Displaced Persons Camp Number One in Schleswig. People gathered in the dining hall and brought all they could. They pooled their food and drink and sat down and had a festive meal. An old gramophone played records in the hall, and people danced, cheered, smiled and chatted. People grinned, some of whom Karlis had never seen smile before, and joy and happiness flowed all around. The children, sensing the adults' relief, ran around exuberantly. Karlis, usually quite strict with his children, smiled benignly as they raced around the hall with their friends. It was such a great day – a joyous day! – and the people relaxed and enjoyed the moment.

After the excitement of the war ending, the Kelers family settled down to the grind of life in a displaced persons' camp. Not much changed for them even though the camp administration changed and the German soldiers in the castle were demobilised and replaced by British soldiers. A British army major took over as commandant and the food improved a little, though meat was still scarce. Other than that, life continued as before.

Soon all the refugees in Displaced Persons Camp Number One, in the old lunatic asylum, moved into the Schleswig Castle. The Kelers family received a room on the third floor at the front of the amazing building. They could see the waters of Burgsee Lake over what would once have been a very nice garden. The back of the castle looked out over a large park on its island. Their room had high ceilings and ceiling-high windows, which made the room light and airy in the summer time. Unfortunately, the castle was in a state of disrepair. The once magnificent gardens, especially those behind the large and impressive building, were unkempt and overgrown. During the winter it was dark, drafty and cold in the rooms, though still a fantastic place for the children to run around and play.

During the first months after the end of the war, the camp swirled with rumours and whispers amongst the people. The children were terrified by a story whispered by the lads in the camp that, because of the shortage of meat, the larger houses in Schleswig had grills installed in the pavement in front of them. The grills had trapdoors fitted to catch children and turn them into sausages. Though Karlis Junior and Inta were traumatised by this silly tale, Karlis and Lydia were amused by it.

Karlis joked with the children, trying hard to keep a straight face. "That's just a silly story … besides, nobody would want to eat skinny little children like you … they would only go for the nice fat people!"

Of far more concern was another nasty rumour that all the Latvian refugees were to be sent back to the Soviet Union. This caused great concern for Karlis and Lydia, as there were terrible whispers about the hardship and treatment of refugees in the Soviet zone, behind what was already being called the Iron Curtain. There were also tales of rape, torture, looting and random shootings by Soviet soldiers. The notorious NKVD was still out in force. People deemed enemies of the Soviet Union just disappeared. Then Karlis heard a rumour that repatriated Russian prisoners of war, heroic men and women, who had suffered horrendously at the hands of the Nazis, were being sent to Siberia. He knew if his family were sent back to Latvia, they would end up on a one-way trip to Siberia; if they were lucky.

The following week, Karlis, with all his worries, visited the camp commandant. He went down the stairs to the ground floor, below the tower and near the grand front entrance of the castle where the commandant had his office. Nervously, he knocked on the door.

"Come in!" the man inside called in slightly accented German.

Karlis gingerly opened the large door and walked in.

The commandant was a small, elderly man, with spectacles, wearing a slightly crumpled British army officer's uniform. He had a harassed look and his desk was piled up with papers. A number of black phones sat on his desk and overflowing filing cabinets filled the room. The man looked up at Karlis over his glasses.

"What can I do for you?" He raised his eyebrows quizzically.

"Karlis Kelers, sir, room 3.12."

"Ah, yes, Kelers … is there a problem?"

"No sir. Everything is fine. I want to ask you though, about these rumours we keep hearing in the camp that we are to be deported back to Latvia." Speaking rapidly, Karlis hurried on. "We cannot go back at the moment, sir. Don't get me wrong, I really do want to go back home. It's just not safe now … we keep hearing more and more whispers and rumours about atrocities being committed in the Soviet zone … I'm sure if we were sent back, we would get a one-way trip to a labour camp in Siberia!"

Karlis stopped, breathless and a little embarrassed.

The man had listened patiently to this diatribe.

He answered quietly. "Don't worry. You'll not be sent back by our government, until it is safe … if at all. Please be patient. The authorities are slowly trying to resettle all you people. You'll most likely be sent to either Canada or Australia, but it will take time."

Karlis sighed deeply, and a smile spread on his face. "Thank you, sir, thank you very much!"

The Commandant shuffled his papers. "Is there anything else?"

"No, sir."

As Karlis left, one of the phones rang shrilly. The commandant wearily lifted the receiver.

Karlis leant against the railing as the ship slowly moved into the deep blue, perfectly flat waters of the Gulf of Naples and the Mediterranean Sea. He stared at the looming mass of Mount Vesuvius, the top of the massive cone shrouded in clouds. In the distance the beautiful city of Naples slowly faded into the haze and the horizon.

They were finally on their way: to a new start, in a new country. Karlis reflected on this as the ship slid through the water in the lovely warmth of the Mediterranean. He was still sad that they were not able to go home, not able to return to Kambaris and Latvia. It had been a long five years in the displaced persons' camp but finally, in the year of our lord 1949, they had been accepted as refugees in Australia. The ship was starting a voyage to an unknown dot on the map called Fremantle, on the vast and underpopulated west coast of the island continent.

Karlis breathed deeply of the warm air; he was not overly worried about the future and looked forward optimistically to life in Australia. While he was certain there would be challenges in their new country, not least being the language, he knew that workers were required there. His family would be alright. He was not afraid of hard work and was certain he would get a job easily, even if it was only as a farm labourer. He had read about the vast wheat and sheep farms in Australia. While he was disappointed that his brother Adolfs would not be coming with them, he had belatedly heard from him that he and his family had been accepted by Canada and were on their way to Toronto.

As the ship churned through a gentle swell, a thin white wake trailing behind it, he thought about the language and culture of the new country. While he was fluent in German, Russia and Latvian and had learnt a smattering of French, he didn't know one word of English. He was trying to learn the language but finding it difficult. At forty-seven, it was challenging, but he was certain his children would have no such problem.

He didn't worry about the unknown culture of the people in the new country either, there would be plenty of other Latvian refugees there. The ship was full of them, including his friends Bendze and Klavins, which he was pleased about. They were all going to Fremantle.

As the vast bulk of Mount Vesuvius faded into the horizon, Karlis took another deep breath, savoured the sweet warm air. He turned and clambered down the steep stairs into the heart of the ship to the large, austere compartment they shared with five other families. Here, Lydia and the children had settled in for the long voyage to a different, strange land and a new life; a life free of war and suffering, in a land of plenty.

XII

The Little Boy (1969)

On a typically hot summer's day with not a cloud in the deep blue sky, a gentle but hot breeze blew in from the east. The harsh Australian sun beat down on their heads, causing shadows from the trees in the large back yard to appear weak, as if to conspire with that large ball of fire over their heads. If they looked closely enough, they could see the heat shimmering in the hot, dry air.

The old man opened the creaking wood and wire gate of the chook pen.

"Come on, come on. Don't let the chickens out!" he said to the little boy in accented, but easily understood, English.

The little boy scurried through the gate a little apprehensively. The old man followed him, shutting the gate behind him. The little boy feared the big birds in the yard in front of him. They were fenced off from the chickens, in another yard, but he was still bore the irrational fear of a small boy. The turkeys gobbled and flapped around, preening themselves as they attempted to counter the oppressive heat. The little boy stayed away.

The old man smiled to himself; he bent down and with practiced ease caught one of the chickens. The bird squawked and flapped about a bit, before settling in his strong arms.

"Here," he said. "Take it. Careful now."

The little boy, eyes agog, took the chicken in his arms. It was a large bird, but appeared larger by the smallness of the boy. The little boy clutched the bird tightly in his skinny little arms. At first the bird was quiet, but it soon tired and with a squawk and flap of its wings scrambled out of his clutches.

The old man laughed quietly.

Then he noticed the little boy's lower lip start to quiver and said kindly, "You're a big boy now. No crying! Here, hold this."

He handed a plastic ice cream container to the boy.

The little boy, distracted, forgot that he was about to cry and asked in his piping voice, "What for, Tete?"

The old man smiled. "I'll show you!"

He bent down and, rummaging in the chook hutches, produced an egg, which he put in the container. "Careful, careful. Don't break them."

The little boy gingerly held onto the container while the old man collected the rest of the eggs. Some of them were big, pale brown, duck eggs. A large white duck splashed about in the half forty-four-gallon drum that was its pond. Quacking and shaking itself vigorously, it splashed the old man and little boy with muddy water. The little boy squealed with delight and almost dropped the eggs, the old man grabbing the container just in time.

He smiled down at the boy. "Come on. We should take these to your Meme!"

Carefully carrying the eggs, he opened the gate and let the little boy through, before closing it behind him.

The old man and the little boy walked out of the chook pen down a narrow dirt path through the fruit trees and past the vegetable patch. They walked past a small rusty shed, down a small stone wall onto a small, though lush and green lawn, down another low wall and onto the back veranda of the small, old and slightly dilapidated house.

The old man opened the back door. The little boy rushed inside.

"Meme, Meme, look what we have!" he said excitedly.

Meme looked at him kindly. "What have we here?" Her accent was thick, the little boy always finding it hard to understand.

"Eggs. Look eggs! We found lots of eggs!"

She smiled and took the container from the old man.

The old man smiled fondly at her. "The cabbages are ready to pick now. I'll be able to make some sauerkraut tomorrow."

She smiled back and answered him in Latvian, "Good, that'll be nice. I've made some pîrâgi. We'll have lunch soon. Can you go out the back and get some pickles?"

The old man took the little boy by the hand and went outside again.

"Where are we going, Tete?"

"To the shed. The pickles are in there. You can come in with me as long as you don't touch anything."

The little boy nodded. He wouldn't touch anything. He loved the shed and was a little in awe of it. There was so much interesting and dangerous stuff in there: a dusty, high wooden work bench, rusty old tools and spider webs. The old man opened the shed door and went inside. They were both soon sweating in the heat. He found what he was looking for: a large, dusty jar of his home-made pickled cucumbers; grown in his garden.

He took it down from the shelf, cleaned it with a rag and gently handed the jar to the little boy. "You can carry this. Don't drop it!"

The little boy proudly carried the jar inside and handed it to Meme who took it from him.

Just then the front door crashed open and, in a gust of heat and sound, a tall, slim, young man and his pretty, petite, young, dark-haired wife came in, carrying their beautiful little two-year-old daughter.

The old man looked up at them as they noisily trooped into the room. "You're just in time for lunch."

Meme bustled in and put on the tacky, plain, red-laminated and metal table a large bowl of egg and potato salad. She also put down a bowl of onion, tomato and dill salad next to the bowl of pickles already there. All the ingredients in the salads were freshly picked from the garden. She went back into the kitchen and fetched the fresh pîrâgi, some dark rye bread, butter and a cold roast chicken, which she also put on the table. Lunch was served.

Karlis looked warmly at his wife, son, daughter-in-law and grandchildren and thought. "Life is good!"

List of the Main Characters

The Baron	Fictional, high-ranking German-Baltic Nobleman
Amelia	The Baroness
Anna	serving maid; Yuris' fictional lover
Yuris Ķenkus/Kohler	serf coachman; forebear of the Kelers family
Emmanuel von Stanecke	Governor General of the Baltic Provinces (1816–1824)
Count Pavel Andreyevich Shuvalov	Russian courtier and large landowner in Latvia
Countess	Catherine Shuvalov
The Tsar	Alexander I; Emperor of Russia (1801–1825)
Heinrich Kohler	My paternal great grandfather
Wilhelmina Kohler	My paternal great grandmother
Janis	Friend and cousin of Heinrich. Killed in the disturbances of 1905/1906
Ferdinand Bergs	My paternal great grandfather. High Tsarist official in the Baltic States
Pyotr Stolypin	Prime Minister of Russia (1906–1911)
Karlis Kohler/Kelers	my paternal grandfather; Heinrich's son
Arturs Kohler/Kelers	My paternal granduncle; Heinrich's son
Adolfs Kohler/Keleris	My paternal granduncle; Heinrich's son
Jenkis	Friend of Heinrichs who looked after his sons in Riga, circa 1914. Karlis' godparents, looked after Karlis in Yuryev (now Tartu) in Estonia, circa 1915 – 1917 and 1918.
Lomanis	Friend of the family who looked after Karlis in Russia, circa 1917
Jancka and Nikoaijs	Lomanis' sons; friends of Karlis

Lebegiv	Friend of Karlis
Colonel Oskars Kalpaks	Latvian military officer
General Rüdiger von der Goltz	German officer commanding the Freikorps in Latvia
Major Alfred Fletcher	Commander of the Baltische Landeswehr
Rear Admiral Walter Cowan	Commander of the British naval squadron in the Baltic
Colonel Jānis Balodis	Latvian military officer; later War Minister
Jorģis Zemitāns	Latvian military officer
General Põdder	Commander of the Estonian Third Division
Aldis, Oto and Ilze	Fictional university friends of Karlis
Maria	Friend of Karlis; his first true love
Lydia Kelers nee Bergs	My paternal grandmother
Karlis Kelers (Junior)	My father
Inta Albany nee Kelers	My paternal aunt
Robis	Karlis' foreman
Roberts and Maria Bendze	Friends and neighbours of Karlis
Maria	Adolfs' wife
Schmidt	Karlis' fictional benefactor

Author's Note

Between two Giants: My Grandfather's story, is fiction. It is fiction based on the known facts of my grandfather's life and that of his family.

I have written what I imagined could have happened, around the known facts. As such, some of the chapters in the book are more fiction than fact.

The first chapter is a prologue about the family story of one of our forebears being a serf coachman, who was emancipated by a German Baltic nobleman. That is all I know. So, I wove the story around the legend and included some historic facts, including the serfs being emancipated in the Baltic provinces during the reign of Alexander I between 1816–1819.

The second chapter weaves around all I know about the events of the 1905 revolution in Russia, with respect to my great grandfather Heinrich Kohler and his family (including my grandfather, Karlis Kelers, who was born in 1902); that one of Heinrich's friends, the local school teacher, died during those troubled times in the empire. I tried to imagine how the revolution and its aftermath may have impacted Heinrich and his family. I am also uncertain how the family managed to acquire the farm at Plumshē. It may have been as a result of Heinrich taking advantage of Stolypin's agrarian reforms, or him receiving the land in the 1920 land distribution after Latvian independence.

For the rest of the story, I am on slightly safer ground. This part reflects Karlis' memories, as written down by my mother and aunt, and spoken about by my father. For example, Karlis and his brothers were separated from their family during the Great War,

Arturs (Karlis' brother) did participate in the Latvian war of Independence and was the Latvian military attaché in Moscow prior to disappearing in 1940. Karlis did get the Spanish influenza followed by tuberculosis (etc.). Once again, I have woven my story around the memories of Karlis but have had to fill in the details from my imagination.

My grandfather's life, and many others like his, during the terrible times of the first half of the twentieth century, are well worth remembering. I hope you enjoyed his story.

About the Author

Kurt is a geologist by profession. As such, he has travelled and worked extensively throughout Western Australia, as well as in the Republic of Guinea and the Democratic Republic of Congo (DRC), in Africa. An enthusiastic writer, he has written extensively about his travels in Africa, Israel, Eastern Europe, China and Taiwan.

These travels included a number of visits to Latvia, where he developed and interest in his grandfather's story, after visiting the family's former farms there.

Kurt is married to a Congolese woman and has a child with her. He currently lives in Perth, WA, and his wife and child live in Lubumbashi, DRC.